T-MINUS

SHANNON
GREENLAND

Entangled Publishing, LLC
2614 South Timberline Road
Suite 105
Fort Collins, CO 80525
rights@entangledpublishing.com

Entangled Teen is an imprint of Entangled Publishing, LLC.

Visit our website at www.entangledpublishing.com.

Edited by Candace Havens
Cover design by Bree Archer
Cover image by PeteSherrard/GettyImages
Interior design by Heather Howland

Print ISBN 978-1-64063-664-4
Ebook ISBN 978-1-64063-665-1

Manufactured in the United States of America

First Edition August 2019

10 9 8 7 6 5 4 3 2 1

an imprint of Entangled Publishing LLC

THE PRESIDENT'S COUNTRY HOME

Northern Virginia
Saturday, 1:00 a.m.

La-la-la-la-la-la-la.

With a moan, I roll over.

La-la-la-la-la-la-la.

Groggily, I open my eyes.

La-la-la-la-la-la-la.

My hand flies out to the nightstand, batting at my phone. Erik, my goofball brother, must have programmed it with a new ringtone. I would never pick a *la-la* tone.

Through the darkness of my bedroom, I squint at the display. *Dad?* I look at the time. 1:00 a.m. Why is he calling me from downstairs?

"Dad?" I croak and then clear my throat. "Why are you calling me from downstairs?"

"Sophie," Dad rushes, and his voice shoots the sleepiness right out of me.

I sit up in bed. "What is it?"

"I need—" His voice catches, and with it, my heart lurches.

"What's going on? Are you okay? Where's Mom?"

"Please tell me you know where your brother is."

Bang. Bang. Bang.

"Sophie, wake up," Frank calls from the hallway.

"You need to come downstairs," Dad orders. "Now."

Bang. Bang. Bang. "I'm coming in."

My door opens, and Frank, my Secret Service agent, steps inside. He takes one look at me sitting in the bed with the phone clenched in my hand, and his expression turns calm. He does that in order to keep me just as calm.

My dad clicks off, and I still can't move. *What's going on?*

Frank efficiently glides around the room, turning on a light before grabbing jeans, a white hoodie, and my running shoes. He lays them on the bed, gently takes the phone from my hand, and quietly puts it aside. Numbly, I stare at the clothes he's laid out. *Why am I getting dressed?*

Frank crouches down beside my bed, and I turn my head and look into his kind blue eyes. He's been with me and my family forever, even worked for my mom back when she was governor.

He doesn't have any children. *If I had a daughter I'd want her to be just like you.* He told me that once, and I remember thinking I would do anything to make him proud.

"You need to get up and get dressed," he says softly.

My throat rolls with a swallow. Something is really wrong.

He stands. "Two minutes."

Erik… I close my eyes. I have to focus. Why does Dad want to know where my brother is? My God, did he sneak out again? I'm going to kill him.

"Sophie." Frank firms his tone. "I need a verbal response."

My eyes open, and my brain shifts and moves with the facts. Dad just called me. He needs me downstairs. They can't find my brother. And—my lungs contract for a breath. "Where's Mom?"

"She's safe," he assures me. "For now."

Oh, Jesus. What does that mean?

"Two minutes," he reminds me and then leaves my room.

I slide off the bed, and with trembling hands I take the clothes he laid out, tugging them on over my tank top and boxers.

On my nightstand lies the vintage American flag necklace that my grandmother gave me and that I only take off when I sleep or shower. I clasp it on, grab my iPhone, and meet Frank out in the hall. As we head downstairs, I bring up the tracker on my brother's phone, but it registers that he's here. Meaning his phone is here, not him.

Downstairs, our living room is packed with agents, my parents, and other people I don't know. This is definitely not just about Erik.

Dad sees me, and his jaw hardens as he comes straight toward me. "Did you know your brother left?"

Icy alarm skips down my spine, and I run a worried look around everyone in the room. "What's going on?"

Dad's light brown eyes narrow in on me. "Did you?" he sternly repeats.

My head jerks with a shake, and panic clenches through me. "No, I promise. Please just tell me what's going on."

His firm jaw does not soften as he puts a warm and

heavy hand on my shoulder. This isn't him. He's never scared and is the most levelheaded person I know. Even more so than my mom, the president. But looking at his strained expression, it's not good.

He takes a breath, staring deeply into my eyes. "There's a domestic terrorist group that's put a hit out on your mother."

"What?" I gasp.

Dad's arm slides around my shoulders as he pulls me over into the corner so we can talk privately. "Protocol dictates they separate all of us in these situations. We'll each be taken to a secure location until the threat is eliminated."

"No." I shake my head. "I don't want to be separated." The sound of everything going on in the room buzzes in my head, and my father's expression softens a little.

"It's going to be okay. Go with Frank. He'll keep you safe."

My fingers dig into my dad's sturdy forearm. I'm aware of protocol, but this is the first time in the three years Mom has been president that we've ever followed it. Which means they think the threat is serious. Very serious. "But what about you and Mom? What about Erik?"

Dad's momentary soft expression turns hard again. Brave, like he's trying to demonstrate how he wants me to be, because if he's scared, it'll frighten me more. But he doesn't answer my question because the room is breaking up now, and we're about to be separated.

He pulls me in for a hug, and I grip him hard as I lay my head on his chest. He shifts a little, lowering his mouth to my ear. "Do not trust anyone. Your mother thinks this is coming from someone on the inside."

My breath hitches. "What?"

Mom moves away from the people she is talking to and across the room to where we stand.

Earlier in the evening we argued over the nose piercing that I want. It didn't go well.

Yesterday we argued over my desire for independence. I swear I wasn't complaining. I have an amazing life, but every once in a while, it would be great to have a little free time.

The day before that my parents were so crazy about my college choices. We've been disagreeing a lot lately on pretty much everything. I'm just as annoyed with them as they are with me.

Now, though, the whole thing seems so trivial.

Taking me from Dad's embrace, she wraps me up in slender arms. For someone so tiny, she has the sturdiest hugs. I close my eyes and inhale her familiar coconut scent. I've always loved that she doesn't wear perfume and smells like the homemade soap we make together.

These days our soap making is the only time we *don't* argue. It's an unspoken truce that gives us a chance to be together without all the crazy in the rest of our lives.

"Dad told me," I whisper, and she doesn't respond, just kisses me firmly on the cheek before stepping away.

She looks me in the eyes, smiling a little. It's a forced one, meant to give me assurance. It doesn't, though. It only ramps up my nerves.

Agents step in then, and we're ushered off in separate directions.

'm now in the back of a Town Car with Frank driving. We left our country home in Northern Virginia in separate cars, each going to a different secure location.

With my forehead pressed to the chilled glass, I stare out at the darkness zooming by. Karen, another Secret Service agent, occupies the passenger seat. I don't like her. Never have. She rarely says a word to me, which is why I find it so strange that she mumbled *Happy birthday* to me as I was climbing in the car. Maybe it was her odd attempt at making me feel better. I don't know.

Yeah, happy seventeenth to me. One thing's for sure— this will be a birthday I'll never forget.

Mom waves a hand in the air. "Absolutely not. When you turn eighteen you can pierce whatever you want. But as long as I have a say in things, then no. No tattoos. No piercings. No."

With a sigh, I look to Dad. But he simply shakes his head.

My eyes refocus, going from the scenery outside to my reflection, specifically my nose. Later today, I'm scheduled to give a speech with William, the vice president, and then I was going to do my own nose. I bought the jewelry, the needle, and the piercing clamp. I watched videos.

But where yesterday my act of defiance was the most important part of today, followed by the nighttime zip-lining I was going to do with my friends, now the whole thing is ridiculous.

Lifting my head up off the glass, I take the red ponytail holder off my wrist and tie my dark curly hair into a quick bun. Then I grab my phone and dial Erik's number. It's in his bedroom and not with him, but I still want to leave a message.

It rings twice, a digital voice picks up for the mailbox, and I say, "I hope to God you're safe. Of all the nights for you to sneak out, this was not the one. You have got to call me. Please get this message. I only have one big brother, and even though he makes me nuts, I love him. Please call me."

I tell myself he's safe and that he's just ignorant to what's going on right now, but my brain naturally veers off with the what-ifs, the biggest one of all being—what if whoever has threatened Mom has taken him?

Though Mom and I have been bumping heads lately, of the two of us, Erik's always been the "challenging" one, as my parents say. My God, he picked the wrong night to pull one of his stunts.

Frank exits 495 heading into D.C., and I bring up the tracker on my brother's phone to see it still sitting in his room. I just wanted to double-check.

I'm sure his service detail has already called all of his friends, but still I dial his girlfriend, Britta. It goes straight to voicemail, and I leave a quick, "When you get this, can you please call me?"

Next, I dial his best friend, Max Grayson. He picks up on the third ring with a groggy, "What now?"

My caller ID comes through as UNKNOWN, but all of our friends know that means us on our secure line. "This is Sophie. Have you seen my brother?"

He lets out a yawn. "Yeah, about an hour ago. We all had some beers over at the river. I already told his hound dogs that."

I roll my eyes. It really bugs me when he calls our detail "hound dogs." "By 'we all' you mean…?"

"Danforth, Erik, me, and Britta." He yawns again. "Now can I go back to sleep?"

I try not to get irritated because he doesn't know the extent of what's going on. He probably thinks it's funny that everyone is out looking for my brother.

"Any idea where the three of them took off to?" I ask.

"I don't know. A party, I think. I'll call if I hear anything." Then, without saying bye, he just clicks off.

I don't waste a second dialing Danforth's number. But like Britta's, it goes to voicemail. "If you know where my brother is, please call and tell me. It's important."

I click off and sit for a second, trying to think of who else my brother might be with. Really, though, those are the three people he hangs out with.

Frank's deep voice cuts through the quiet car. "We'll find him. Don't you worry."

I take in his square jaw and his bald head. In the rearview mirror, he gives a reassuring smile. In return I nod, though my stomach tightens with the strain. If my brother is still with his girlfriend and Danforth, then they're probably somewhere just drinking beer and not in immediate danger.

At least, this is what I tell myself.

Do not trust anyone. Dad's words come back to me, and with them, my eyebrows pinch together as I look back out the window. What does that even mean? Frank, too? But I've always trusted him. Always.

SAFE HOUSE

Washington, D.C.
Saturday, 2:30 a.m.

F rank pulls up to a garage off Connecticut Avenue and keys in a code. The door opens, and he pulls us down into the underground parking area. Behind me, metal clanks on metal as the door goes back down, and the sound vibrates through my skull.

Do not trust anyone. Those words have been on repeat in my mind for the past several minutes, and with each repeat, more and more uneasiness curls through me. I wish I knew who Dad meant when he said that. I'm not sure even he knew.

There are several cars already here, and I recognize them as undercover vehicles, just like the one we're in.

There's a woman walking toward us, and from her functional dark suit, I peg her as secret service. Before Frank has had a chance to cut the engine, or Karen has had the opportunity to open her door, the lady has mine open and is grabbing me.

"Taffy Pop's here," the secret service lady says into a

phone as she takes my arm and pulls me out. Taffy Pop, my code name.

Mom has a thing for old-fashioned candy. So, when it came time to name us, we each took on a themed name. Erik is Bit-O-Honey. Dad got Rock Candy. Mom, Cinnamon Drop. And then me, Taffy Pop.

I tug free from the lady's hold. It's the new ones who tend to handle me too much. "I can walk on my own," I tell her, and she gives a respectful nod.

A camera mounted near the ceiling whirs. Behind me, Frank and Karen exchange muted words. I strain to hear but can't make anything out.

We cross the garage, and as we reach the door that leads into the building, it swings open, and a man, I'd say in his early twenties, is led out. I don't recognize him. But from the bloody nose and swollen eye, someone has definitely roughed him up.

"An asset," the secret service lady tells me, and I take a step back to give everyone room.

The asset lifts his head, and his light eyes lock with mine for an unnerving second. Something, though I'm not quite sure what, flicks across his expression. Like he recognizes me, but not the type of recognition others usually have. His comes across as if he knows something.

Something the rest of us don't.

He sneers. "Your mother will get what she deserves."

"Come on," an agent snaps, yanking the man away.

I stand, not breathing, as he's roughly led across the underground lot. My family gets threats all the time, but I'm not impervious to them. They don't just bounce off my skin like they seem to for Erik or Mom. That knot in the pit of my stomach tightens, as I understand things are about to get real.

I've had this feeling before.

Outside the car, someone yells, "Your mother should be ashamed of how she handled Cuba!"

Inside the car, I tense. "They don't know what they're talking about. Because of Mom those kids got the aid they needed."

Erik shakes his head. "Ignore it, Soph. They see what they want to see. You know that."

"Our mother is amazing. How easy people forget the equality she champions, the treaties she has signed, not to mention the recent prisoner release she negotiated."

My brother chuckles.

"What?"

"Nothing, it's just that I love how you defend her even though you two seem to be arguing over everything these days."

I sit back, wanting to glare at the protestors outside the car but keeping my expression calm. "Just because she didn't like my eye makeup doesn't mean I'm going to give up on her," I grumble.

Yes, Dad and I are different. We're always affected by the haters. I wish I weren't, but I am.

My eyes stay on the man until he's shoved into the back of the car. The windows are dark, and I have no clue if he's looking at me. I hope he is, though. I narrow my eyes, giving into a glare I've been told time and again not to. But I want him to see how wrong he is about my mother.

Chaos has officially broken out in the multi-room condominium that doubles as a safe house. One agent is on the phone. Another one is on a laptop. Two more are arguing. It takes everything in me not to interject my own questions and opinions, but I stay quiet and do my best to listen to all the fragmented conversations.

"We don't know demands…"

"…a bomb goes off."

"We should try partial negotiation…"

"…Director Prax said to keep it confined."

No one knows what to do. And a bomb? What bomb are they talking about? Plus, what about that asset? Where were they taking him? Shouldn't they be interrogating him more?

Someone touches my arm. "You need anything?" Frank asks.

"No." My frustration mounts with the voices in the room. "No one seems to know what's going on. And I just heard someone say, 'partial negotiation'? You know as well as I do, we don't negotiate, and that's just going to piss them off."

The whole room falls silent, and I look around to see what's going on.

"The asset is dead," an agent reports. "His transport was attacked, and his two escorts were killed as well."

It's like a vacuum sucks the air out of the living room before pushing it back in, and voices once again fill the space, crowding to be heard.

Your mother will get what she deserves. Maybe the asset got what he deserved. But the two agents? I didn't know either one of them, and my heart aches for them and their families. They lost their lives protecting my mom.

Protecting me.

It takes a second for that monumental information to sink in. *There is only one way to deal with a terrorist, and that is to either capture or to kill him. They don't just go away, they never give up, and where there is one, there are others.* Mom said that when she was running for office.

The question is, how many others are out there, trying to kill my family?

E veryone talks over one another, speculating on next steps. I keep hearing Prax's name. He's the Director of the CIA, but he's an arrogant asshole. If he's the one running this show, this is going to get screwed up. He only has one agenda, and that is to do whatever makes him look great. He's going to try to "save the day" and do a partial negotiation, and it's going to blow up in his face.

The same woman who tugged me out of the car enters the living room. With an iPad gripped in her hand and a determined look on her flushed face, she crosses the room toward me and Frank.

"What is it?" he asks.

She hands the iPad over to him.

"A list of extremists who have recently been making some noise on our channels." She turns to address the other agents in the room. "Check your IMs. The director wants all eyes on the list."

As Frank runs his finger over the screen, I ask the agent lady, "The asset that's now dead, did he give any indication of demands other than the president's life?"

She glances down at me, like she can't believe I'm talking. I try not to get offended. There are only so many things they are allowed to loop me in on. "This is my family we're talking about," I implore.

She takes in a deep breath, like she's praying for infinite patience. "Why don't you try to take a nap or something?"

I shoot straight to my feet. "I'm sorry, what did you just say to me?"

Frank intercepts, giving my arm a little tug. "Let's go."

He leads me from the living room and out into the hall. I pull free from his grasp. "I hate when people placate me."

"I know. She's new. Just ignore her. I'll tell you whatever I can, when I can. Trust that."

With a sigh, I nod.

From down the hall a bedroom door opens and out steps a man with a Doberman. With the dog on his left, they approach, and I flatten my body against the wall to give the dog wide space.

Erik has a German shepherd named W.D. after his favorite show, *The Walking Dead*. W.D. bit me so hard it left a huge black, blue, and yellow bruise on my arm. My parents wanted to get rid of the dog after the biting episode, and so did my brother.

But he loves that dog, and so I went to bat for it, insisting the encounter was more my fault than anything. To be fair, I did get in its face, and anyone who owns a dog knows that's not a smart idea.

Yes, I went to bat for W.D., and our parents hesitantly agreed to let Erik keep it, but I certainly feel no love when it comes to that dog.

Or any dog, for that matter.

After the Doberman passes, a tall and lanky man emerges from the same room. It's Norman, the CIA's top analyst. The last time I saw him, just last week, he sported a bushy blond beard. Now he's clean-shaven.

He nods to me. "How you holding up?"

"I'm okay." I fiddle with my necklace. "Worried."

"I know. We're going to figure this out."

"What's going on?" Frank asks him. "Why aren't you at Langley?"

"When Prax called me in, this was the closest place to set up." He blows out a quick breath. "Man, we are picking up a lot of traffic."

"From?" Frank asks.

"Everywhere. The threat may have come from a domestic source, but the buzz is international."

"What are you hearing?" Norman won't placate me like the new agent did.

"That's just it," he says. "It's all encrypted. At minimum, we'll get a source, but when I say it's encrypted, I mean it's locked down tight."

Frank's phone rings. "Yes? Shit. Okay, thanks."

"What's going on?" Norman asks him.

But he doesn't answer and instead turns to me. "I have to go out. You'll be safe here."

I nod, but my mind is already reeling about that encrypted data Norman just mentioned and the list Frank was looking at. Even though Norman's good about telling me what he can, I also know there's only so much he's allowed to share.

Which is why I need my good friend, Jackson.

Jackson's constantly changing his number, and I never keep up, and so I begin dialing the first one...

I've been in the teen program at the CIA since I was fourteen. Initially, it wasn't something I wanted to do, but my dad insisted, and so I enrolled. By the end of the first week, I was hooked. The TIA, Teen Intelligence Agency, is open to the children of agency workers. Dad used to work there, and that's how I got in. Funny enough, Mom being president had nothing to do with it.

My friend doesn't pick up. I dial the next number...

I like the TIA for two main reasons. I get a chance to study and train with some of the coolest people, like Norman. And it's where I met Jackson, Callie, and Zeke, my three closest friends.

Zeke—his name alone tumbles my heart, and the first time we trained together comes back to me...

On his stomach, Zeke lays down beside me and moves in. "Okay, now sight down the length of the rifle, blow gently out, and tap the trigger."

Instead, I close my eyes and swallow. Oh goodness, he smells good—fresh like soap and laundry detergent.

"Something wrong?" he asks.

I peel my eyelids open and I stare at the life-size target some twenty-five yards away, and the clown painted on it. A lot of people think clowns are creepy. My friend, Callie, sure does. But I've never had a problem with them.

"Something wrong?" he asks again.

"No." Yes, God yes. He's too close. I can't think when he's this close.

"It's just a paint ball," he teases.

I cut him a look, and my gaze takes on a life of its own as it travels from his dark hair, down to his deep green eyes, across his perfect cheeks, and on to his strong and beautiful lips. Those lips twitch with amusement, and though my skin is light brown, it's probably showing every bit of the flush creeping through me.

I'm only fourteen, but somehow, I know this boy is going to be the love of my life. Even if it is only one-sided.

Jackson doesn't pick up, and so I dial the next number…

Yes, Zeke and me—the thing that will never happen. I'm destined to forever have a crush on a boy who will only ever be my friend. He's so far out of my romantic reach, it's ridiculous. He's two years older, and though he's never said it, I'm pretty sure he's always looked at me like a younger sister.

At first glance, people tend to see this focused and handsome guy. I know I did. But there's so much more to him.

Like the way he's always calm in the most stressful situations. The sharp intellect and wit that even the sourest of people respond to. His loyalty to friends. The willingness to help anyone, anytime. And the fierce determination that makes him go above and beyond in all situations.

I sigh. Yep, the love of my life.

I try the next number for Jackson, and he finally picks up. "I knew you'd call me," he says as a greeting.

"All your numbers irritate me."

"I know, but you're the only one who seems to have an issue with it." The humor he carries in his voice makes my lips twitch.

I say, "I take it you know what's going on?"

"I do." I hear him shift and then click keys.

"Where are you?" I ask.

"My cave."

By cave he means his basement.

"Where are you?" he counters.

I look up and down the hall that now sits empty. "Safe house."

He says, "There is a freak-ton of traffic on the waves right now."

"I've heard. There's some encrypted data floating around—"

"Boom!" Some more clicking. "Encrypted, my ass. I got it." He shifts again. "Okay, so there's definitely been a hit placed on your mom. Huh"— he clicks some more— "and it appears as if these terrorists plan on bombing random places until your mother is delivered to them."

"What?" My body slumps back against the hallway wall. "What the hell is going on? Bombing random places? As in, here in D.C.?"

"Yes, from what I can tell," he mumbles, and his voice trails off as the clicking gets faster.

My phone buzzes with a text. "Hang on," I tell him. PRIVATE comes across the screen, and I swipe my finger to read the message:

ERIK HERE. OUT PARTYING. COVER FOR
ME IF ANYONE NOTICES.

My heart leaps with relief, and I forward the message to Frank, but clearly my brother has no clue what's going on.

I type back.

YOU HAVE GOT TO CALL ME ASAP!
EVERYTHING IS NOT GOOD HERE. I
REPEAT, NOT GOOD.

I wait, staring at my phone, waiting for him to call me. A second goes by, followed by another, and still he doesn't call me. What the hell?

"I have to go," I tell Jackson, and then I dial the number that my brother just texted me from. It rings once and goes straight to a generic voicemail. "God! You just texted me from this number. Where are you? Call me!"

I jab my finger down on my phone to end the call, and another one comes in. It's Britta, Erik's girlfriend. Oh, thank God. "Britta?" I answer. "Please tell me you know where my brother is."

"Sophie," she pants. "Someone's following me."

The fear in her voice constricts my chest. "What are you talking about? Where are you?"

Her voice shakes as she whispers, "I'm at our spot… hiding."

My fingers squeeze into the sides of my phone. "Call nine-one-one."

"No," she whispers. "Please don't. Your brother told me not to call anyone but you."

My brother? But I just got a text from him. "Wh-what is going on? Who are you hiding from? Who's chasing you? Where's Erik?"

She draws in a raspy breath. "Oh God, I'm so scared. Please," she pleads, "please just come."

But before I can ask anything else, the line goes dead.

BRITTA'S HOME

Washington, D.C.
Saturday, 3:15 a.m.

My heart cramps as I stare mindlessly at the phone. My brother just texted me that he's partying, and then his girlfriend tells me that she's being followed. He told her not to call anyone but me.

Dad tells me not to trust anyone.

Mom says there might be an inside person.

My hands shake and I force myself to take a deep breath.

With a swallow I study the shadows flicking through the laser course, my gun armed and ready. I saw my TIA opponent run right, but the play of shadows tells me he went left. Maybe I'm wrong and I didn't really see him do that.

"Trust your gut," Frank whispers from behind me. "Where did you see him go?"

"Right."

"Then which way should you go?"

I step right and spy my opponent hiding behind a brick

wall. I aim and fire, making contact.

"Good thing you didn't go left," Frank says, nodding my TIA opponent to exit the laser tag course. "Remember, always trust your gut."

I don't know what the hell is going on, but Frank is right. I need to trust my gut, and it's telling me to get out of here and go to Britta.

I'm in the hall of the multi-room condominium that is doubling as a safe house. Other than the living area, I haven't been in the other rooms. I spot a camera mounted at the end of the hall above the private elevator where we came in. There's a bathroom off to the left with its door propped open.

Every muscle in my body coils tight.

I backtrack down the hall toward the elevator, surreptitiously eyeing the camera and its rotational path. I count six seconds between sweeps, and my plan falls into place.

I step into the bathroom, and my heart almost beats right out of my chest. One. Two. Three. I count the six and go right back out, glancing up to the camera as it moves away from me.

With a shaky finger, I press the down button on the elevator, and it opens. I step inside, the doors close, and my nervous breath flitters in the air as I study the buttons for a second.

We came in on G, the garage level, and that's likely where I'll run into Frank coming back, or where I'll run into someone else. I press B for basement, and the elevator starts its descent.

This is the first time I have ever broken protocol and

gone somewhere without notifying Frank. I don't know how my brother does it when he slips through the secret passages back at home. I'm still in the elevator, and I swear I'm about to have a heart attack.

The door opens, and with a deep breath, I step out into another underground garage, just like the one we parked in. A few dumpsters dot the right-hand side, and a couple of cars, the left. Other than that, a wide cement space spans the area between me and the giant open door that leads straight out to an alley.

Behind me the elevator door closes. If I want back in, it's too late now because I don't know the combination to the keypad mounted beside the door.

Above me and to the left, a camera whirs, trained right on me. If security didn't know I left, they do now. I am officially in so much trouble.

I take off running, and blood pounds in my ears as I weave left around a black BMW, dart to the right around a red Mustang, and sprint out into the night. I head straight across the street and up an alley.

I race right past a car window, and my hoodie flashes white in the surrounding darkness. Oh crap, I wasn't thinking about my clothes.

Ripping the hoodie off, I sling it to the side and keep running. My fingers automatically go to the American flag necklace hanging around my neck, making sure it's still in place.

As I emerge from the alley, my breath hitches when someone looms in front of me, but it's just a drunk person passed out against the wall, his shadows morphed by a nearby street lamp.

I skirt around him, and a quick peek over my shoulder shows I'm not being followed. I scan up and down the dark street, getting my bearings. Red-light cameras. Shit. I need an off-street alternate route, and the only one is Rock Creek Park.

My pulse spikes all over the place.

Our TIA tactical instructor breathes deep, and then blows it out forcefully. "That will level your blood pressure quicker than patient breaths."

He does it again—deep breath, then blows it out fast. "Remember that—because your first instinct will be to inhale and exhale slow. It's what stress wants you to do, but not an effective way to deal. This way, you calm yourself quickly."

I do that now—deep breath in, then blow out forcefully through my mouth. It calms me a little.

Headlights pierce the night, and I squint against their sudden brightness. They get brighter, and brighter, and it seems like they're coming right toward me.

I don't wait to find out as I dash across the street and disappear into Rock Creek Park. I start down the uneven path, and the darkness of the early morning hours moves in on me, becoming pitch black.

My toe snags on a root. I catch myself and keep running as I pull my iPhone out of my back pocket.

GPS tracker. Shit, I forgot about that, too. I chuck my phone as hard I can behind me and keep going.

Britta. My chest tightens. Please be okay.

The first time we met was right here in Rock Creek Park.

"Keep up, you twerp," Erik jokes, picking up pace and showing off.

I pick up pace, too.

"Stay where I can see you," Frank warns.

My brother leaps across a muddy patch, cuts right through a clump of trees. When I dart after him, I nearly run smack into him.

A girl with messy blond hair sits with her back to a boulder, holding her ankle. She glances up at us and her eyes widen. "You're Erik and Sophie Washington."

Smiling, my brother wipes the sweat off his face as he squats down in front of her. "Yep, that's us. What's your name?"

"Britta."

Panting, I kneel down in the leaves next to her. I note the bloody scrape trailing the entire shin of her right leg, and I cringe. "What happened?"

She makes a face. "I'm stupid is what. I was running, cuing up my next song, not looking where I was going, and I tripped." She nods to her ankle. "I sprained it pretty bad."

"Are you alone?" Frank asks, and she nods. "Can you walk?"

"I can try…"

Frank ended up carrying her all the way out of the park, and the whole time, she and Erik just chatted away. They were so cute together, him laughing and her giggling.

Six months later, they officially became a couple, and they've been inseparable ever since. This fall they'll be freshmen at Hopkins and have already been talking about getting a place together.

I try not to be jealous of them, but I am. A happy jealous. I'm going to be a senior and have barely been on a date. I wish I could have what they have with Zeke, but that would mean I'd have to tell him how I feel, and that takes a level of courage I'm not ready to display. I don't want to risk our amazing friendship by opening my soul.

I keep following the trail, heading toward the creek. It will fork soon, but I need to go straight, which means no more trail. And there it is, up ahead, the fork. I take the bridge over the creek, then leave the trail and cut through the woods. Her house isn't far now.

Something smacks me across the face, and I cringe at the exact second my right toe catches on a root, and I go flying forward. Flailing my arms, I try to keep upright, but my left foot hits the ground, and with a grunt, I stumble and roll.

It knocks the air out of me, and wincing, I grab my knee. A wave of pain goes through my lower leg, and I ride it out. I cannot get injured right now. Gently, I extend and contract my leg, and the fabric of my jeans scrapes across raw skin on my knee. Other than that, I'm okay.

Somewhere over to the left, an animal scurries, and the sound of it propels me back to my feet. I give my knee a quick test, and then I take off running again.

Finally, I emerge into a residential neighborhood of small freestanding houses, most with brown yards from the recent drought. I walk, trying to catch my breath and figure out where I am. I'm still blocks away from Britta's home.

I spy a kid's bike lying in a yard and race over. It's three something in the morning, and no one is even watching, but still I tell the house, "I'm just going to borrow this. I'll bring it back."

At five foot five, I'm not a tall girl. I'm average, but

my knees nearly hit my chin as I pedal away. I go as fast as I can through the neighborhood, cut across someone's front yard, and come out on a road.

I stay to the side, pumping my legs faster. Faster. Faster.

Panting, I zip through a stop sign, and then another.

I reach Britta's home, and I drop the bike. I stop to catch my breath, looking up at the three-story brick townhouse. Her parents are gone for their anniversary, her little sister is at summer camp, and Britta told me she was so looking forward to having the house to herself.

Someone's following me.

Her words race through my mind, and I take a step back into the cover of shadows. I stare hard at her house, my eyes starting at the roof and trailing down each floor. I study each window, looking for any sign of movement. But other than a soft yellow glow from interior lights, nothing seems off.

There's a small, square front yard and two narrow strips of grass down both sides. She said she was hiding in "our" place. Meaning her and Erik's place, which is the fort in the backyard. With her little sister and her parents always around in the house, the fort was the only place she and my brother could have alone time.

I take one more look up and down the empty street, and then I step from the shadows and cross over to her yard. Both sides of her house are well lit by exterior lights. A bead of sweat trails my cheek, and I wipe it away as I creep down the left side.

Their flowerbed catches my eye, and I grab a large rock. A weapon. That I might use this to hit someone pitches new nerves through me.

"Be aware of your surroundings," our TIA combat instructor says. "No matter where you are in the world, a weapon is not far."

We're standing outside, and she turns and points to a flower pot. "Break that into shards." She points a stick. "Ready to go." She nods to a yard light. "Pull that from the ground and you'll find a nice sharp edge."

Sure, I've practiced all kinds of things in the TIA — martial arts, various weapons, self-defense, driving, lying, espionage, language — but in real life?

No, never.

I've never hurt anyone. I've never used a weapon with purpose. I've never put my learned skills into real-life practice. I knew I would someday, but not right now at seventeen years old.

My pulse hits a fast cadence as I step along the narrow side yard. On my right towers the house, and on my left, a six-foot-tall tongue-and-groove fence. If I have to, I can go up and over that.

I come to the end of the strip, and the fingers of my right hand tighten around the rock. Through the dimness of the backyard, I spot the fort in the rear corner. From here it appears dark and empty.

The backyard looks exactly like it did last week when Britta's parents had my whole family over for a barbecue. Which was odd, given the number of Secret Service agents who attended, and how the whole street was basically shut down for the two hours.

Yet another thing Mom and I argued over.

Our car pulls up outside, and I look out the window to where Britta and her family stand in their front yard

waiting on us. Secret service line the street. One house over,
a curtain moves as someone peeks out.

I sigh. "This is so embarrassing. 'Look everyone, it's
the First Family. Don't mind us. Go about your business.
Oh, that's right, you can't. We shut down your street.'"

Mom smiles at the agent approaching her door. "Oh,
stop griping and come on. It'll be fun."

Did the neighbors mind? I would.

But that's Mom and Dad for you. They're adamant
we have as much "normal" family time as possible, even
if it means shutting down an entire neighborhood.

Of course, a meet-and-greet with the neighbors
afterward helped to smooth things over, but still. It
would've been easier to have Britta's family come to us.

I inspect the yard—the deck, the play set, the
surrounding fence, the bordering bushes, and even the
furniture, before looking again at the fort. Nothing seems
off. Could they have a different "our" place now? One I'm
not thinking of? I don't know. Nothing is coming to mind.

With my senses on full alert, I cross the backyard,
heading toward the fort. I want to call out, but I don't.
If she's in there and looking out, she sees me coming.
Which means—my steps falter—if someone else is in
there looking out, they can see me coming, too.

I wish I had pepper spray or a Taser or, better yet, one
of those rubber-bullet guns we use in TIA tactical classes.
I hold the rock firmly and keep moving toward the fort.

I might be insane for doing this. But Erik told her
to call me and not anybody else. My brother might be a
goofball and a prankster, but he would never cry wolf. If
he told her to contact me, then there is a vital reason why.

I come to the bottom rung of the ladder that leads up to the fort. Only five rungs. "Britta?" I whisper, my heart pounding clear down in my toes.

But silence greets me. *Oh God, Sophie. I'm so scared.*

Her whispered words come back to me, and my throat goes tight and dry. With one last glance over my shoulder to her empty yard, I grab onto the ladder and climb.

If someone was in there, they would have already come out, or I would have heard them, or seen them through the small windows. These are all the things I tell myself as I reach the last rung, the rock out and ready to bash a head if need be.

But the fort is empty, and relief hollows out my stomach as I slide up and in. Though, if it's empty, then that means Britta was calling me from someplace else. I scoot all the way back against the wall, taking a second to breathe and get my nerves under control.

I close my eyes. Think, Sophie, think. Where would she be? I wait for it to come to me, but nothing does.

Unless she was here, and she had to run. My eyes fly open, and they land on the tiny hidden door built into the wall of the fort. It's where they leave each other messages and love notes. It's corny, but way beyond adorable.

Scooting across the wooden floor, I press my fingers into the spot on the wall where the tiny door sits, and it pops open. I stick my fingers in, fumbling around, and my breath hitches when I pull out a flash drive.

She left this. Or my brother did. Either way, I'm taking it, because my gut says this isn't some love note between the two of them. This is somehow connected to whatever is going on.

Why they have this, I have no clue, but I'm going to find out what's on it. I slip it into my front pocket, climb down the ladder, and I'm off again. I'm going to Jackson's, but blood seems to stop flowing when the next thought slams into me.

What if the terrorist has Erik, and that text he sent me back at the safe house was fake?

That's a very real possibility. Max said Erik was with Britta and Danforth. Someone from the extremist group could have been chasing them, and they split up or got separated. She came here. But that still doesn't explain why they have this drive.

Which brings me back to finding out what's on it, and Jackson is my best bet.

JACKSON'S HOME

Cleveland Park
Saturday, 4:00 a.m.

On the kid's bike, which I've now officially stolen because I didn't return it like I planned, I pedal through the mostly empty streets of D.C. to my friend's house. I need to tell somebody like Frank about Britta's phone call and the flash drive, but right now my dad's words counter everything else. *Your mother thinks this is coming from someone on the inside.*

Reality is, the inside person could be anybody.

Ten minutes later, I turn into Jackson's neighborhood. He lives five houses down on the right in a small, two-bedroom, two-bath brick home with his mom, who works for the CIA as a support officer. As I always do when I come here, I head straight through the side yard and around to the back.

Dropping the bike, I rap on the door, and he opens it. He takes one look at me, and his bloodshot hazel eyes widen in surprise before cutting behind me, obviously looking for Frank.

"I, um"—I give a guilty shrug—"pulled an Erik and ditched my security."

"Holy shit."

"I know." I slip past him and into his cave, already taking the device from my pocket. "I've got a lot to tell you."

He closes the door. "How did you get here?"

"I stole a bike."

"Jesus, who are you right now? Are you nuts? You picked the absolute worst time to pull an Erik."

With a sigh, I head over and plop into the oversize yellow-and-white checkered bean bag sitting in the corner. Closing my eyes, I take a second to just breathe and center myself. As I do, the slight creak of his chair resonates through the air as he sits back down. But there is no clicking of his keys because he's watching me, waiting.

This time last week I sat right here playing card war with Jackson.

"Oh!" Jackson slams his cards down. "I totally nailed you!"

I make a face at him, and we both laugh.

With a knock, Frank opens the door to Jackson's cave. "All right, you two. Wrap it up. Sophie has a luncheon."

Playfully, I narrow my eyes at Jackson. "Next time," I warn him.

"Blah, blah, blah," he teases.

Forcing my eyes back open, I look beyond him and his industrial-size desk to the wall covered in flat-screen monitors—international news on one, local another, market trends, diagnostic tests, code, hacking software...

My friend is definitely "Big Brother." If he ever

wanted to take over the world, he probably could.

He spins his baseball hat around and it makes a bunch of sandy hair stick out the front. "You done with the dramatic pause?"

Despite the late hour and the weariness in my bones, I manage a little chuckle. If there's one thing I can say about him, he never fails at making me smile.

Pushing up out of the bean bag, I cross his tiled floor over to the corner where a mini-fridge sits. I grab a water bottle, unscrew the top, and take a long gulp.

I begin detailing the last few hours, starting with what Dad told me before we were separated and ending with how I came to have the flash drive I'm currently holding in my hand.

When I'm done, his response is very simple. "Phew."

"I know." I hand it to him. "So, let's find out what's on that."

He grabs a spare laptop from under his desk and plugs in the device. As his fingers click away, I take another gulp of water and wish, instead, it was Mountain Dew. I could use a good caffeine and sugar rush about now.

"Got anything to eat?" I ask.

Without looking at me, he waves his hand in the air. "There's some hummus in the fridge."

My lip curls. "No thanks."

He clicks some more keys, grunts, clicks some more. Then he sits back and studies the screen.

I move in. "What is it?"

"Well, first of all, it's a trigger drive."

I search my brain, trying to remember what that is. Jackson and Callie are the techno wizzes, while Zeke and

I are more the tactical people. So while I can do basic stuff, computers really aren't my thing. "And that would mean…?"

My friend shakes his head. "Do you not pay attention in TIA classes?"

I shrug. "Why, when I have you?"

He rolls his eyes. "Meaning, if I remove it from this laptop, it will trigger a data meltdown."

I snap my fingers. "That's right. Trigger drive."

"Anyway, there's that. But it also has layers of encryption. It might take a while." He motions over to the fridge. "Make yourself useful and grab me a green tea."

Gluten free, sugar free, this free, that free, he's always eaten way too clean. My lip curls again. "You're too healthy."

"Yes." He motions down the length of his long and lean body, all cocky. "But just look at the amazing results."

With a laugh, I grab his tea. "Can we at least trace the IP address it came from?"

"Look at you all computer speak and everything."

"Yeah, yeah, yeah." I hand him his tea, and while he focuses again on the screen, I worry about my brother and his girlfriend. A cloud moves back over my momentarily lightened mood.

I tell myself I made the right decision in coming here. If anyone can find out what's on that device, it's Jackson. My brother and his girlfriend are somewhere hiding, and I'll find them. Whatever it is they're trying to tell me, I'll figure it out.

Yes, I tell myself all of this to mask the overwhelming fear and doubt. I'm just a seventeen-year-old girl, and this is more serious than anything I've ever faced in my life.

"Francis Arzman," he says. "That's the IP this was created on."

I move back over, look over his shoulder at the screen, and frown. "Francis Arzman…that has to be a mistake."

"Why?"

I keep staring at the screen, trying to work it through in my mind. "Francis Arzman is Frank."

My friend cringes. "That's not good."

I shake my head. "That has to be a mistake." Though I'm not sure how. His IP address is right there on the screen. You can't fake something like that. Whatever is on that device came from his computer, and somehow my brother and his girlfriend ended up with it.

"That doesn't mean he's the bad guy."

"It means it came from his computer."

"Right."

"And you know, as well as I do, that he never lets anyone use his laptop. Not even me."

Jackson doesn't respond to that, and we both keep looking at each other, trying to process what we just learned. Why would this have his IP attached?

The laptop dings, and we both jump. "Something just decrypted," he says, clicking a few keys. "It's only one chunk, but it's something." He leans in closer. "It's an address."

He moves away from the laptop and types the address into his mainframe. On the screen in the center of his wall a satellite image of a deserted warehouse pops up. He clicks some more keys, and as he does, I study the dark warehouse. Nothing about it seems familiar.

"It appears as if the building has been sitting empty for years," he tells me.

"What do you think is in there?"

"No clue."

He clicks some more keys, and the screen in the top left corner flicks. It's the security footage of the safe house that I ran from. "Oh my God, how did you get that?"

My friend just looks at me as if that's the most ridiculous question I could've asked. "You called from there, remember? I did a simple trace, and when I figured out where you were, I hacked the system. Though, this is the first time I've looked at it, otherwise I would've known you'd run."

"My God, am I happy you're on my side. I'd hate to have you as an enemy."

He lets out a silly evil giggle.

The screen flicks again, from the hallway image to the garage, and Prax, the Director of the CIA, climbs from his car. As always, a tall and loping giraffe comes to mind.

"What's he doing there?" Jackson asks.

"I'm missing. What do you think he's doing there?"

Frank walks across the garage to greet him. It's common knowledge that they don't like each other. I don't know what the whole story is, but I do know it goes way back. Frank is about to get in some major trouble over me being gone. I hate it, but I just don't know what else to do right now.

Until we know what's on this drive, the fact that it came from his IP is a bit moot. It's what in the TIA we learned is called a back-burner fact. A fact you put on the back burner to simmer until you know more.

I understand the importance of not jumping to conclusions and waiting for hard evidence before making final decisions. But I also know the importance of trusting my gut, as Frank has told me time and again. My gut led me to the device. And now my gut is about to lead me to the warehouse.

"If you're going to that warehouse," my friend says, "I'm going with you, or we're calling Zeke. Either way, it needs to be now because I have a feeling the director is about to make all of our lives difficult."

As usual, Zeke's name alone makes all kinds of girlie flutters dance through my stomach. But I push those down and focus. My never-ending crush is the absolute last thing I need to be thinking about right now. "Okay, you call and fill him in. Tell him to meet me there."

Jackson tosses me his keys. "Take my truck."

As I walk out, Zeke's groggy voice comes over speaker. "The world better be ending for you to call me at this hour."

DESERTED WAREHOUSE

Washington, D.C.
Saturday, 5:30 a.m.

I duck behind a tree, and when I glance beyond, I see Zeke just feet away, holding his fake bloody side and staring right at me. His breathing becomes labored.

I love that Frank takes us through simulations outside of the TIA. This one is a course set up off of 207 that special ops uses to run drills. It's my first time on this course and it's unique in that it's elevated in the trees.

Zeke holds up one finger and does a half circle with it, telling me our opponent, Frank, is at my six o'clock.

I nod to let Zeke know I understand. Then I take a stone from the course and toss it beyond him. It does the trick, drawing Frank's attention, and his head peeks out of hiding. I get him in my sight, and I don't hesitate a second in pulling the trigger.

The paint pellet connects with his shoulder, and he grunts. Then before I know it, he turns and runs, leaping off the platform. I race across, but when I reach the edge and look over, Frank has already landed on the ground *and is sprinting into the trees.*

I don't waste another second on him as I spin and race back across to Zeke.

He's still in the same spot, and I stand for a second looking down at his dark hair. He inhales a raspy breath, and I drop to my knees. Fake blood oozes from his stomach wound to darken his gray tee. His eyes meet mine, his head rolls, and he loses consciousness.

He's now seconds from dying.

I know this is a simulation, but my heart still lodges in my throat. What if this wasn't fake? I would be watching Zeke take his last breaths.

He opens his eyes, startling me. "You should have left me and gone after Frank."

That happened three months ago, and it was in that moment that I realized choosing between a teammate and a target would be my greatest challenge. Logic tells me that, yes, I should have gone after Frank. But emotion wouldn't let me.

Fake or not, I had to be there for Zeke.

After driving the truck through the early-morning streets of D.C., I meet Zeke a block from the deserted warehouse. He's already standing outside in the dark, dressed in his usual camo pants and snug gray tee, leaning up against his old Land Rover and looking like he stepped off a billboard for the military. At nineteen, he's one of the oldest participants in the TIA.

Jackson, Callie, and I all assumed he'd join the marines when he turned eighteen, but he opted for college first.

I'm not complaining, because I definitely wasn't ready to say goodbye to him.

When I first met him, I asked Mom if there was such a thing as love at first sight. She laughed and said it was possible, but it had never happened to her. She and Dad found their way to love through being friends first.

I'd asked my brother one time, too, and in his usual joking way, he said, "Who you got the hots for?"

That effectively ended that. I should've known better than to go to him. Though, he and Britta were a love at first sight scenario. At least, if I were to ask her, she'd probably say it was.

Cocking his head, Zeke gives me a quizzical look, and I open my door and climb out. "Sorry," I say. "Lost in thought."

I make my way toward him, and his dark green eyes pull me in. "Jackson told me everything. How you holding up?" His deep voice vibrates across my skin.

"As good as can be." My gaze trails across his clean-shaven cheeks. Last week he had a goatee. The week before that—stubble. Does he remember my different looks? Hair in a ponytail this week. Hair down last week. Jeans. Skirt. Makeup. No makeup.

No, he probably doesn't think of those things.

Turning away, he surveys the alley and the warehouse. "I walked the perimeter and looked in all the windows, but the place seems empty. Still, let's go in prepared." He reaches inside his Land Rover and pulls out several small throwing daggers. "Your favorites."

I love that he knows this.

For the first several months of TIA classes and

trainings, I liked the program and what I was learning, but admittedly, I was a little lost. Jackson and Callie excelled in gadgets and technology, Zeke in pretty much anything.

Have I mentioned how perfect he is?

But for me, it wasn't until I was handed a set of throwing daggers that I found my groove. Hand-to-hand, mixed martial arts, simulations, obstacle courses—anything tactical is my favorite.

He goes about strapping one of the small daggers to his ankle and the other to his thigh, and I do the same. "There's a broken window on the second floor. We'll go in that way."

We've done a ton of simulations over the years, but nothing real-life. The fact is, we're about to enter a deserted warehouse based only on an address taken from a flash drive created on Frank's computer, which my brother wanted me to find.

It appears as if these terrorists plan on bombing random places until your mother is delivered to them. Jackson's words come back to me as I stare at the warehouse. What if this is one of those places?

What if that's the reason why its address is on the device? We could be walking to our deaths.

But most likely not. When extremists bomb places, they are packed with people. This place is empty.

Zeke moves into my line of sight. "Do you want to stay out here?" The corners of his eyes crinkle a bit in understanding. He can tell I'm starting to freak out.

"No, you're not going in there by yourself." There is no way I would let that happen. He is here for me. If anything, I should be the one to go in while he stays outside.

Reaching around, he grasps the back of my neck, just like he's done so many times before. Gently, he squeezes, and the warmth of his fingers bolsters me.

"Don't doubt yourself," he says. "Don't hesitate. Remember, your first instinct is always the best."

With a nod, I make my feet move forward with purpose. "Second-story window. Let's do this."

Side by side, we scoot down the alley that runs the length of the vacant building. As I do, I scan the roof and the numerous windows dotting the three-story warehouse. I stare hard at each window, looking for signs of anything unusual. Even though he said the place was empty, I still look for movement, a flicker of a shadow, anything.

But other than our destination—the broken window on the second story—nothing seems off. Still, I listen intently as Zeke checks out the area behind us.

My chest tightens on a spike of new nerves. Fear is a good thing. But I can't imagine why this warehouse's address was on the flash drive. I wish a team of Special Ops were here instead of just us. But my dad's words ring through my ears, and I truly don't know who to trust.

I can't do this alone, and so I'm placing faith in my closest friends.

Silently, we cross the alley to duck under the metal steps that lead to the second story and the broken window. I scan the steps, looking for anything odd, like a trip wire or something, because in the simulations we've done, there are always trip wires on stairs.

Zeke taps me on the elbow, silently telling me to go, and with a deep breath, I take the first step up. Surprisingly, the metal stairs only creak slightly as I climb, and soon

I'm on the second-floor landing. Behind me, he begins his climb, and I wait, barely breathing, for his arrival.

With my back plastered to the brick wall, I shift my head to look through the broken window and inside. From this angle, I make out dusty, broken factory equipment, some random drop cloths, odds and ends of furniture, but nothing else. Just like Zeke said.

Shards of broken glass litter the landing, and one large chunk juts out of the window sill. I pry it loose and lay it aside before crawling through the window and stepping onto the dark factory floor.

I breathe deep, working past my nerves, and inhale a good drag of dusty air.

Zeke comes through the window, and his eyes narrow disapprovingly at me for coming in ahead of him. I brush the look off, and with two fingers I motion him to go left. While he does, I go right, stepping my way through the room. As I do, my nerves transition from those stemming from anxiety to the ones that invigorate me, just like they do in training. I welcome the familiar energetic alertness that they bring.

I have no clue what I'm looking for, but I suspect I'll know it when I see it.

A shadow shifts over to the right at the exact second a gun goes off to ricochet through the quiet warehouse. Panic spikes through me, and I dive forward. Holy shit. Not only is someone in here, but the person has a weapon, and I would 100 percent bet it has real bullets. This is not a simulation.

I come up against a large piece of equipment, and, breathing heavy, I scan around it to see the shooter dart off into the shadows. Another bullet pings through the air, and it hits the floor somewhere over to my left. Whoever it is, he's shooting at Zeke!

I surge to my feet as a pebble bounces across the floor, followed by the sound of another shot. A pebble to draw the fire. Of course. He's not shooting at Zeke. He's shooting at the pebble.

Whoever the man is, he doesn't even know I'm here.

Running footsteps come next, as the person moves farther into the abandoned warehouse.

As quietly as I can, I slide from behind my cover and slink up against a nearby wall. I catch sight of Zeke on the other side, and he signals me that he's okay. I signal him the same. Then he moves his index finger in a counterclockwise motion, giving me the sign that the guy is coming up to my left. With a nod, I slip the small dagger from my ankle holster, and my body pulses with the anticipation of what I'm about to do.

He counts down with his fingers—*five, four, three, two*—and on *one* I spin from my hiding spot, point down and throw, and the person yelps.

Sirens echo in the distance, and my heart slams against my chest. Someone's called the cops. We only have a few minutes before this place is taken over.

I lunge forward into the shadows to see the guy—I'd say probably in his early twenties—curled up on his side and clutching his knee where my knife is seated. I can't believe I just stabbed this man.

On the dirty floor beside him lies the weapon, and I knock it out of the way.

Zeke moves in beside me. "Good job," he whispers.

The sirens get closer, and their high pitch ricochets through my head. We don't have much time.

He wraps strong fingers around the guy's neck and squeezes. "Who are you?"

The guy shakes his head, and I try desperately to figure out if I know him. He focuses on me, and his eyes widen a little with recognition, much like the asset's had back at the safe house. The asset who is now dead.

"You're Sophie Washington," the guy says.

My heart skips an alarmed beat. "How do you know me?"

"From…from TV," he quickly replies, but he's lying.

I grab the guy by the front of the shirt. "How do you know me?" I demand.

"If you want to see your brother again, you better let me go."

I snap to attention, jerking the guy up. "What did you just say?" I get right in his face. "You think that knife hurts now? You haven't felt pain yet. Now, you better tell me where Erik is, and you better tell me now."

The sirens close in, and I estimate they're within a few blocks of us now.

"Talk," I demand.

"I don't know anything," he rushes to say.

"That's not going to work for me."

I can't believe what I'm about to do.

I grip the small handle of the dagger and give it a little twist. His screams echo through the warehouse and throb through my blood. Yes, I've just crossed a line and am officially torturing this guy now, but I'll do what I have to for my family.

"Stop!" he yells, and I ease up.

"Talk," I say again.

"I'm just doing what I was told," he whimpers. "I was supposed to come here, get a phone they hid, and take a call."

Zeke tightens his hold on the guy's neck. "A phone that *who* hid?"

"I don't know!" The guy grapples for a cell phone and holds it up. "This one. It was hidden over there. I just found it when you two came in."

As if on cue, it rings, and for a second, my brain comes to a screeching halt.

"Put it on speaker." My fingers hover over the small dagger still seated in his knee. "Do not tell them we're here."

Frantically, the guy hits the speaker. "Yes?"

A garbled voice speaks, "There's a car on the corner of Summit and Todd. Keys are in it. There's something in the trunk we need you to dispose of. Your payment is in the glove compartment."

The line clicks dead. The sirens are outside now. This is it. "What else were you supposed to do?" I ask.

The guy shakes his head. "That's it. I was hired to take a call and do whatever it was they said."

"How do you know about my brother?"

"I overheard a conversation."

Downstairs, footsteps pound across the warehouse floor, indicating the cops are inside.

"We've got to go," Zeke urges.

Yes, but this guy knows something about my brother. "Where were you when you overheard this conversation?"

"I was at a party. I needed some extra money. I really don't know anything."

"Party? What party? Was my brother at this party?"

In the far corner, a door bangs open and cops enter, guns drawn. But they don't see us yet.

Zeke yanks me up, and despite everything in me wanting to question this guy, I have to run. Staying free is the best chance I have of finding my brother.

I rush after Zeke to the window we came through, back out onto the second-story landing, and I barely touch the steps as I fly down. My feet hit the alley's pavement, and I take off in a full sprint. Behind me, bullets pop through the warehouse, lighting it in intermittent flashes. The guy probably got stupid and fired at the cops.

This is real. This is happening. This is not a simulation.

My shoes seem to catch air as I break from the alley and jump back into Jackson's truck. Ahead of me, Zeke leaps into his Land Rover, but I don't wait on him. I yank the steering wheel to the right, push the gas, and shoot right past.

Summit and Todd. That's my destination, along with whatever is inside the trunk.

ABANDONED CAR

Washington, D.C.
Saturday, 6:00 a.m.

L ike a possessed demon, I navigate to the corner of
Summit and Todd, and as I do, a phone rings from
somewhere inside of the truck. I don't bother looking for
it or answering it and instead keep my eyes on the road.

Over Bluetooth comes a voice. "Sophie, it's Jackson."

I look around like he's going to miraculously appear.
I don't know how the hell he does half the stuff he does.

"What happened at the warehouse?" he asks. "Please
tell me it was a lead."

"It was, but I don't have time to explain."

"Director Prax has put an all-out search for you."

"I don't care." I whip around a corner and head east,
going straight through a yellow light about to turn red. I
catch sight of a camera mounted to the light and other
than knowing I'm on film, something else occurs to me.
"Traffic cameras. There've got to be traces of Erik and
Britta."

"I'm already on that and nothing yet. Please tell me

Zeke is with you."

I totally forgot about him in my race to get to the car. In my rearview mirror I note that he's right on my tail. "Yes, he's with me."

"Be safe," my friend says. "And seriously, watch out. The director is tracking you." With that, he clicks off.

One more corner and I brake to a stop behind a car that I assume is the one the guy in the warehouse was talking about. I leap from the truck before it's barely in park, and I'm already trying the locked door handles when Zeke catches up.

"Wheel wells," he says, dropping down, and I follow his lead, feverishly looking for a magnetic key holder, more than aware we are possibly about to be caught.

My fingers brush across a small box. "Got it." Quickly I slide the key out as I rush around to the trunk. It's an old car with no fob, and I fit the key into the lock and turn it.

The trunk releases at the exact second unmarked cars careen down the street, piercing us with their lights.

"Fuck," Zeke says, and I whip around, looking for somewhere to run, but we're completely surrounded.

We put our hands in the air, backing away from the trunk, and the cars squeal to a stop.

A door opens, out steps Director Prax, and dread burrows into my gut. He struts toward me in all his cockiness, with his loping giraffe stride. I fight the urge to glare at him, knowing that will only insult him and egg him on.

Somewhere beyond him, I hear, "Taffy Pop secured."

He comes to a stop right in front of me and puts his hands on his hips as he takes in first me and then Zeke.

"This is exactly why I have always hated the idea of the TIA. You kids get it in your minds that you're trained agents when all you're doing is playing cops and robbers."

I lower my hands. "You have no idea what you're talking about."

His brows lift. "Oh? Why don't you enlighten me?"

The last thing I want to do is tell this man everything, but at this point, I don't know what other choice I have. "May we speak privately?"

He gives that considerable thought, and my teeth clench hard with strained patience. Finally, he leads me a few paces away and up onto the curb, and I lower my voice as I tell him everything—the words my dad said to me when the threat first came in, the text I got from Erik, the phone call from Britta, the device I found and took to Jackson's, the guy in the warehouse, and the information that brought me here to this car and whatever is in the trunk.

I finish up, saying, "My mom thinks there is an inside person. Whoever created that flash drive did it on Frank's computer, and whatever is on it has something to do with what's going on."

He digests everything I just said, and I remind myself he is the head of the CIA and a person I need on my side. He can make my life very difficult. "It is important for us to keep this as small as possible," he tells me. "The fewer people who know the details, the better we can contain the situation."

I agree.

"Who have you told?" he asks.

"Just Jackson and Zeke."

"Good." He turns toward the car, nodding one of his guys to the trunk. "Let's see what's inside."

He doesn't move closer, so I don't either. One of his men opens the trunk all the way and shines a light inside. Even though I'm several yards away, I'm up on the curb and have a clear view of the trunk's contents.

The sight renders me temporarily mute. Somewhere in the back of my brain, I register what I'm looking at. I want to move away from it, but my feet stay where they are. My eyelids freeze in place as I stare at the clear plastic bag and the curled-up dead body within it.

Something foul and bitter claws up my esophagus. I turn away, ready for whatever is in my stomach to come up, but nothing does. I cover my face with my hands, and I concentrate on taking deep breaths.

In. Out. In.

I sit between Callie and Jackson as the TIA international relations instructor cues up the video. Across the table from me sits Zeke along with a few other TIA members.

With a slight frown, he reads through the document we just reviewed. It contains declassified information on a bombing that occurred six months ago in Turkey.

His forehead creases even more as rereads the lines. He does that frown thing when he's concentrating.

"Okay," the instructor says. "What you're about to see is graphic. There is no shame in responding to this. If you want to cry, cry. If you need to leave the room, please feel free."

The giant screen flicks, and an image launches of a man running through smoke carrying a small child with bloody stumps where her legs used to be.

If I thought we'd be eased into this, I was sadly mistaken.
"Oh my God," Callie gasps and I reach over and take
her hand.

I've seen a lot of things in my TIA classes and training, but it was all recorded, nothing in real life. The videos and photos are shocking enough, but this body in the trunk... *This* is horrific.

Frank puts his hands on my shoulders. I'm not even sure where he came from, and I don't think about the fact the device came from his computer and what all that means.

I simply step into his arms and lay my cheek on his solid chest just like I've done for as long as I can remember. His arms go around me warmly, safely, and I close my eyes and take a few minutes for myself.

When I feel ready, I step away and whisper, "Do they know who that is? Did they ID them?"

"Not yet," he says, sternly leading me a few steps away. "What were you thinking, taking off? And what's this about a flash drive that came from my computer?"

I assume he must have overheard me and Prax talking. "Yes, an encrypted one that led me to the warehouse and then to here and that body in the trunk."

I look up into his light blue eyes, searching them for a hint of anything. A truth. A lie. This is the man who has been with me since I was a little girl. The one person other than my parents who I have looked to for guidance. Ex-marine, bodyguard, trainer, advisor, and now possibly connected to all of this?

I don't know how that could be. It makes no sense. "What's on that and why did it come from your computer?"

Without a response he stares down at me. To say he is huge puts it lightly. His mere presence tends to make people uncomfortable. But I keep my eyes locked with his curious ones.

Curious, or suspicious?

"Prax says you got it from Britta?" he asks.

"Or Erik. One of them left it in the fort for me to find."

His eyes narrow. "And it's encrypted?"

"Yes, according to the IP trace, it came from your computer. You never let anyone use your laptop. So hypothetically, you created it and should know what's on it." I'm stepping over a line with him. I don't care. There are more important things to worry about than my respect for him and for boundaries.

His narrowed eyes glint with a warning that I did, indeed, step over a line, but I keep going. I might as well get my questions answered. "Where did you go earlier when you got that phone call back at the safe house?"

His glint transitions into a glare. "That's none of your business."

He's right. His whereabouts are usually not my business, but this is different. "My brother and his girlfriend are missing, a cell has put a hit on my mom, and as of right now, that device is our only link to what's happening. It came from your IP. So, yeah, it is my business."

Frank arches an incredulous brow. "You're right, I never let anyone use my laptop. But it isn't on my person every minute of every day. Clearly someone has hacked my password to make me look guilty. It would take a certain level of expertise to do that. Someone like

Norman, for example. Or your friend, Jackson. Perhaps that's where your witch hunt should be focused—a person with the tech ability to do such a thing. Not on your personal bodyguard."

I open my mouth to respond, but nothing comes out. He's right. My focus should be on someone with the tech ability to pull this off.

A couple of tense and quiet beats go by, then he turns toward a town car. "Enough of this. Let's go."

I just made a huge mistake.

M inutes later, I'm in the back of the town car, and we're driving away. The air conditioning kicks in, and it soothes my heated skin. I'm still in the tank top and jeans from when Frank got me out of bed. I could really use a change of clothes, a shower, and some food.

If I can't trust him, then I'm at a complete loss. He has always been the one person to have my back.

My breath stutters on a sob. "She said the only reason she invited me was because her mom made her."

Kneeling down in front of me, Frank tucks my hair behind my ear. "Sophie, you are a kind and sweet girl. I know you don't see this now, but not everyone will want to be your friend. What's important is that you maintain your generosity of spirit. Be above them always."

I sniff. "What's generosity of spirit mean?"

Franks smiles. "You're happy and caring and you never expect anything in return. It's who you are naturally, and it's a wonderful trait to have."

I was five then and crushed to find out my supposedly

best friend didn't like me after all. But Frank was there. For as long as I can remember, he's had my back.

Lifting my eyes, I look at his reflection in the rearview mirror. He's not looking back, but the hard lines of his jaw tell me he's irritated. Having my parents upset at me is one thing, but him? I don't know. It's different.

"Britta called me. She said someone was following her. She was scared and hiding in the fort. She was adamant that I come alone. She said Erik told her to call only me. I freaked. I'm sorry.

"And I had just gotten a text from my brother that he was partying. A text that he obviously didn't send. All that right on top of the threat, Mom thinking there's an inside person, and Dad telling me not to trust anyone. I'm sorry. I just didn't know what to do, and I made a bad choice."

"If you can't trust me, then who? I'd like to think our relationship isn't just about me guarding your life. You know how much I care for you. You should have called me."

Guilt over the whole thing weighs my shoulders down, and with a sigh, I look away. "I know. I'm sorry."

We lapse into an uncomfortable silence. Danforth and Britta were the last people to see Erik. I have no clue if Danforth ever got that message I left him, or if he is being followed, too.

I straighten up. "Will you try Danforth's number again?"

Without a reply, he dials the number. The call comes on over Bluetooth but goes straight to voicemail like it did before.

"Can we go to his house?" I ask.

He hesitates, glancing at the car's digital clock. "Is that what you really want to do?"

"I don't want to go back to the safe house, or wherever else. I want to find my brother," I implore. "Please. It's just in Bethesda. We're not far."

His expression softens with understanding as he stares at me in the rearview mirror. It rolls over me, giving me much needed comfort.

With a nod, he clicks his blinker and exits to Bethesda.

DANFORTH'S HOME

Bethesda, Maryland
Saturday, 6:45 a.m.

I ring Danforth's doorbell, and it's answered with silence. Raising my fist, I knock before ringing the bell again. This time yesterday, his parents would've already been up and on their way to the Medical Plaza where they share a pediatric practice.

A dog barks from somewhere in the back of the house. The barking gets louder, a few lights flick on, and through the glass panels on the door, shadows move as someone crosses through the house coming toward us.

With the morning sun beginning to shine off to our left, we are clearly visible, so when his dad moves the curtain aside, it doesn't take him any time at all to recognize us and open the door.

His eyes go from sleep to high alert as he surveys us. I haven't looked in a mirror, but I must look horrible. I've been up for hours and running around the city. I'm a sweaty, tired mess.

"What's going on?" Danforth's dad asks.

"Dr. Kendrick," Frank addresses him. "Did Danforth come home last night?"

"I-I assume so."

"Can you please go check?" Frank calmly asks.

Dr. Kendrick's shoulders stiffen. "Why, what's going on?"

"Unfortunately," Frank says, "we can't say, but we do need to find out if your son came home last night."

Dr. Kendrick doesn't move. He might be in shock. But once again Frank calmly addresses him. "We just need you to go look."

With a jerky nod, he steps back from the door, letting us in before hurrying up the stairs toward Danforth's room.

We hover at the door, waiting, and I hope beyond all hope that Danforth is here and is okay and can give us anything at all to help find Erik and Britta.

My gaze drifts through the archway that leads into the family room. A few weeks ago I laid right there on the floor watching a silly zombie movie.

Standing in front of the TV, Danforth rubs his hands together. "Okay this one is from 1943 and it's called 'I Dreamt I Was a Zombie and Then I Became One'. It's a classic."

Erik and Britta are cuddled up on the couch and she giggles. "That's a stupid name."

"It's the stupid-named ones that are the best," Erik says.

"Totally," Danforth agrees.

I toss a kernel of popcorn at him. "Let's get on with it!"

Danforth flicks out the lights. "Get ready to be scared."

We watched that movie, laughing pretty much the

whole time. The guys were right—stupid name but the best.

Dr. Kendrick returns. The worry and alarm he held before has transitioned into full-on panic. My skin prickles like a live wire.

"He's not in his bed," Dr. Kendrick whispers.

Frank inclines his head, again calm. "Stay by your phone. I'll call you as soon as I know something."

DUNKIN' DONUTS

McLean, Virginia
Saturday, 7:15 a.m.

We climb back into the town car. My hand grasps the flag pendant on my necklace while my brain clicks through the facts. Max Grayson said he left Erik, Danforth, and Britta at the river drinking beer, and then he thought they were going to some party.

Then the guy at the warehouse said he saw my brother at a party. So where was this party? Because somewhere, either at the party or after, my brother and his friends got separated.

With Erik being the son of the president, I understand why someone would want to take him, but why his girlfriend and Danforth? What do they have to do with anything? Or maybe they were just in the wrong place at the wrong time.

I glance around the interior of the town car, just now realizing this isn't the one we normally drive. "Where's our car?"

"Wouldn't start." Frank's phone rings, and he picks up,

taking a second to switch it off Bluetooth. I hate when he does that, but of course I get it. As much as I want to be involved in everything, I understand the need for security.

It's funny how the older I get and the more classes and training I do with the TIA, the more I'm convinced I want to be in the clandestine division of the CIA. I say funny, because years ago I was sure I was going to be an elementary school teacher. But several rounds of babysitting taught me that kids are definitely not my thing.

Elementary teacher to covert ops. That works.

Years ago, when I first talked to Dad and Mom, they were surprisingly supportive.

"I know I've only been in the TIA for a few months, but I really like it." I look between my parents. "Like, I think I might want to do it for real someday."

Dad smiles. "It's why I encouraged you to enroll. I suspected you might take to it."

"But not Erik?" I ask.

Dad nods. "Erik and I talked, but it just wasn't his thing. I knew it wouldn't be. You are two different people and there's a restlessness in you that needs channeling."

I laugh because "restless" isn't a word I would use to describe me. Of the two of us—me and Erik—I've always been the one to accept and know my place.

"I think contained restlessness is a better way to describe you," Mom says. "Just remember that real life experience will help you excel in whatever you decide to do. I know you love school and you love your new TIA classes and training, but I encourage you to explore the world. Take chances. Maybe even break a rule."

Take chances. Explore the world. That has never

been me. That's much more who Mom is and who Erik is, though secretly, I do wish that was a part of my personality. Maybe that's what Mom means by "restless energy".

I wish I was more adventurous like them. Heck, when Mom graduated high school, she was traveling the world with a volunteer organization, helping to rebuild communities. She was making a difference from day one. "A natural-born leader." She's been described that way over and over again, and it's true. There's no one I admire more than her.

I can only hope that one day someone will say something like that about me.

I'm not sure what I expected those years ago—for them to be worried about my safety, perhaps? But Dad was right in that I took to it. He was hoping I would discover a new interest, a new direction, a channel for my "restlessness".

Take chances. Explore the world. I wonder if Mom wishes she could take those words back. I should remind her that she said them. Because now that I'm older and trying to do those things, she's not letting me.

Maybe even break a rule. Well, I did do that tonight. And even though Mom said those words to me when I was fourteen, she would be very angry that I did. But I don't care. I'll take an argument with her because that means I'll hear her voice, and I could use that right now.

My attention goes back to Frank. I strain my ears to hear something, but I can't make out what's being said on the phone call.

He clicks off, lifting his eyes to look at me in the rearview. "That was the lab."

I brace myself, ready. "And?"

"They said the body in the trunk had no fingerprints or face. Whoever killed him put acid on him postmortem."

Meaning the person was already dead.

I process that, looking at it from different angles, very much like I'm in one of my TIA classes and in problem-solving mode. "This might be a delay tactic, because with dental recognition, it won't be long before we know the victim's identity."

He cuts me an impressed look.

"I know the body was covered in plastic," I say, "but you didn't catch anything, did you? Hair color, by any chance?"

"No, and they also said the estimated time of death was one a.m."

One a.m. "That's when all of this started."

"I know."

I lean forward— "What do you think is going on?"

"I don't know. But I will say, wherever Erik is, I believe he's okay. If the terrorists had him, they would be making a big show of it."

Though he doesn't come right out and say it, he means the body in the trunk is not my brother. And he's right— if they had Erik, they would be making a big show of it. Kidnapping the son of the president is huge. They'd have his capture on live video feed, or something equally impressive.

They wouldn't just put his body in a trunk.

Still, uneasiness turns through my stomach, and the devil's advocate side of me comes out. "But what if they're holding him for some sort of leverage to use against Mom—" I don't finish that sentence because the United States does not negotiate. It doesn't matter if we're talking about my brother or not.

Frank shakes his head. "Don't let your mind go there."

I try not to imagine my brother being held somewhere, tortured, threatened, but I can't help it. I do imagine it.

The enormous weight of the past several hours slumps through me. Outside the window, the interstate zooms by, and we take an exit into McLean. Soon we're pulling off at a Dunkin' Donuts. "You need caffeine and sugar. We both do."

He's right, and I smile at the kind gesture. "Thanks."

He climbs out, locking the doors behind him, and disappears inside.

From somewhere close by, a phone buzzes, and it takes me a couple of confused seconds to find it. It's in the back pocket of the passenger seat in front of me. I pull it out and look at it, and it stops buzzing. That's weird. I go to slip it back into the pocket, and it buzzes again.

I have no idea who this phone belongs to, but I answer. "Hello?"

"Do not move," says a garbled voice. "Do not speak. Do not show any expression. I have your brother, and if you do not do exactly as I say, he will die."

My hand holding the phone trembles. Inside Dunkin' Donuts, the worker smiles at Frank as he places his order. He peers through the glass and into the car where I still sit in the back.

"Smile at him," instructs the voice in my ear.

I force myself to do just that, and he turns away to answer a question the worker just asked.

"Good girl," the distorted voice says.

Through the car windows, I search for a camera, and I locate one across the street and mounted on a light pole. It rotates to point directly at me, and my muscles tighten.

"Yes, I can see you," the voice confirms.

"Wh-what do you want?"

"Turn the phone off and put it under the tire. Under the passenger seat in front of you, you will find our new mode of communication."

Our new mode of communication? What does that mean? "H-how do I know you really have my brother?"

A text buzzes the phone, and I pull it away from my ear to check the display. It's a live video feed of Erik pacing nervously back and forth in a small area. My heart stops for a second and then kicks back in.

He's wearing the same thing as last night before he sneaked out—a yellow graphic tee I gave him for his birthday, cargo shorts, and black flip-flops. I take note of his dark curly hair, his face, and his arms and legs, all of which look okay. No cuts or bruises or anything. I note his surroundings. He's in a windowless room, like the inside of a garage.

I have a quick image from a few days ago…

He pokes me in the ribs.

"Stop it!" I laugh, shoving him. "You know how ticklish I am!"

"All the more reason to torment you." He bear-hugs me, poking me again.

I squirm and laugh. "Uncle!"

A few more pokes. "You make it too easy," he teases.

The memory sends a pang through my heart.

In Dunkin' Donuts the worker now pours coffee.

But what if they're holding him for some sort of leverage to use against Mom. I just said those words. This extremist, whoever he is, has my brother, and that is exactly what they're planning.

"Do what I said," comes the voice, and it jerks me into action.

I unlock and slit open the back door, crawl out, wedge the phone under the back tire, and get back inside. Another quick peep into the shop as Frank slips his wallet from his back pocket.

Leaning down, I fumble around under the passenger seat until my hand brushes a plastic bag. I give it a tug and pull it free. Inside are three things: a red thumb drive, a blue one, and an earpiece.

Someone on the inside… It's the only way these things could have been hidden here. Someone tampered with our usual car, forcing us to use this one.

Taking the earpiece, I wedge it deep into my ear. A little bit of static comes across, and then that same distorted voice. "Nicely done."

The car door opens, and I jump.

Frank casts me a curious look. "Everything okay?"

"Yes," I assure him, nodding to the bag. "Need this more than I realized."

With a nod, he settles in and puts the car in reverse, and the phone barely makes a crunching noise as he backs over it.

"His phone is about to ring," the distorted voice continues in my ear. "He is going to be told Erik has been found and is at a secure location."

On cue, his phone rings, and he answers it.

"Eat the donut," the distorted voice reminds me. "Drink the coffee. Make sure you act surprised and relieved to hear the news."

Lifting the coffee cup to my lips, I try to take a sip, but my unsteady hands make me spill more than I manage to get into my mouth. I put it in the cup holder, and I stare at Frank in the rearview mirror. He gives me a little smile that I try my best to return, but it comes across awkward and forced. I make myself take a bite of the donut, but it lodges in my throat in a thick and dry clump.

He switches to Bluetooth. "I have her here."

"Sophie, this is Director Prax."

"Yes?" I croak and clear my throat. "Yes?"

"I just received word that Erik has been located."

"Oh," I breathe. "Thank God."

"Not bad," the voice in my ear says.

"Thank you," I say, trying to put real gratitude into it. "Thank you."

Frank takes the director off Bluetooth and they continue their conversation. I have three things I want you to do," the voice says in my ear. "If you do not execute those three tasks, I will remove pieces of your brother and deliver them to you in a box."

The line goes dead, and I don't move. That body in the trunk is the first thing to pop into my brain, and I don't doubt for a second that whoever has Erik will do exactly what they say. This isn't some bluff.

Take the root out, and it won't grow. That's what Mom says, and that statement hits me hard right now. She's right—there is an inside person. They've orchestrated this day down to the very last second.

Do not negotiate with terrorists. Forget that. I'm negotiating. I'm doing whatever they want to keep my family safe. As of this moment, I am officially their puppet. My dad said not to trust anyone. Well, that's exactly what I'm doing. I'm now trusting whoever owns that garbled voice not to hurt my brother.

I don't know what else to do.

COVERT FACILITY

Tyson's Corner
Saturday, 7:45 a.m.

I lay in my bed, willing myself to sleep, but restless energy
gnaws through me. Throwing the covers aside, I pad
across the hall to Erik's room, and I knock on his door.

"Erik," I softly call. "You still up?"

His music filters through the door, and I tap on it again
before turning the knob and cracking it open. I don't have
to step fully inside to know he's gone. Dampness permeates
the room from where he opened the hidden door in the
wall and disappeared through the secret passage.

My gaze automatically tracks over to the wall where the
concealed door sits flush with the rest of the wood planks.
A stranger would never know the door is there, but I do.
I'm pretty sure I know where all of them are. So far, I've
counted twenty-one, and they connect the basement to the
master suite to the innermost rooms of the estate.

This particular one leads from his room through the
passageways, down into the kitchen, and from there outside.
It's been years since our parents secured the secret doors

with locks. To this day they still don't know that Erik snuck a master key so that he can come and go.

As I always do, I curl up in his bed and wait for his return.

Sometime later, he jostles my shoulder. "Hey, wake up."

With a yawn, I open my eyes to see him already moving into his bathroom.

"You don't have to wait on me. You know I'm coming back." He unwinds floss and begins working it between his teeth.

"I know. Just need peace of mind, I guess. Where'd you go?"

"I met Britta at the park."

He's been officially dating Britta a few months now. He used to sneak out to hang with Danforth or Max. Now it's all about Britta. "You don't have to sneak out. You know Dad and Mom like Britta."

Erik throws his floss in the garbage and grabs his toothbrush. "It's not that. It's just a pain. You know what I'm talking about. I have to have a friggin' army trailing my wake just to see my girlfriend."

It's true. We can't go anywhere without security. Privacy. It's just not part of our life.

Yet if I'd told our parents that he was sneaking out, he'd be safe right now and I wouldn't be taking orders from a terrorist. Does that officially make me one, too?

Unfortunately, it does.

"A person who uses violence or intimidation, especially toward civilians, in pursuit of political gain. Or a person who complies with such acts." According to the TIA, that is the official definition of a terrorist. And I am now the second part of that.

There are several covert facilities throughout D.C. and Northern Virginia that the intelligence agencies use. Frank takes me to one housed in Tyson's Corner. It's a nondescript building a few blocks from the Galleria Mall, and I've been here a few times with the TIA during our classes.

As we pull into the underground garage, all my attention goes to the thumb drives in my pocket. They either want me to retrieve information, load something, or perhaps both.

The garbled voice said I'm to do three things. They have to involve something only I have access to, otherwise why use me?

Whatever they are and whatever the reasoning, it doesn't matter. I'm doing them.

Frank parks, and leaving my coffee and donut behind, I follow him inside. The moment we clear the elevator, the voice in my ear speaks. "The red USB drive—replace it with the one that is currently in Jackson's computer. The one you found in the fort."

But that doesn't make any sense. I'd have to go back to his house. "But Jackson's not here," I say.

Frank turns, giving me an odd look. I don't bother explaining why I was just talking to myself. I don't say anything at all. "He's here," Frank says. "They brought him in. He's in the lab."

Now I see—because the device that I found in the fort turned out to be a trigger. Once it's in a computer, you can't take it out or you lose the information. And Jackson's laptop has fingerprint technology, so once he began working on it, he was stuck with it. The director couldn't leave it and Jackson in his cave.

"I'm going to go say hi." I veer off to the stairwell that leads up to the computer lab. As I do, I run smack into Zeke.

He grabs my upper arms to steady me, and despite everything going on, heat warms my cheeks.

"Um, hi. Hey." I wince.

A smile tiptoes across his face. The last time I saw him was at the car where everyone found us. I was so preoccupied I didn't even think to ask what happened to him. The truck, too. Crap, I just left it there.

"Happy birthday," he says.

"Oh, wow, that's right." I chuckle. "Happy seventeen to me, right?" I look beyond him and up the stairwell. "What are you doing here?"

"Prax decided I would be 'easier to watch' if I was here."

"Oh." I groan. "I'm sorry. And I also just remembered that I left the truck."

"Someone drove it here. Don't worry." His hands slide away from my arms, and coolness creeps into my skin where his fingers just were.

"So you're here, and Jackson, too. Please tell me they didn't haul in Callie."

He chuckles, and the deep sound of it hums through me. "She's hiking Old Rag this weekend. Did you forget?"

I did.

This is one of the things I envy about her. She loves the outdoors and disappears for days on end hiking, rafting, and climbing. Number one, I'd never get away with that, considering who my mom is. I would have to have a whole team of people go with me. But more importantly, even if I snuck out like Erik, I'm too scared to do something like that by myself.

Though I'd never tell Mom that.

In the stairwell, Zeke shifts, and with a sigh full of something dark and regretful, he says, "I'm assuming you didn't hear?"

I don't like the sound of that. "Hear what?"

"The body in the trunk." He slides his hand around to the back of my neck. He's about to deliver bad news. "It was Danforth."

It takes a second for that information to register in my brain, and when it does, I bend forward, bracing my elbows on my knees, and squeeze my eyes shut.

I shake my head as memories flash by. One of me, Erik, and Danforth camping out in our living room—another of him laughing as my brother dunked me in the pool—and then that time we fed Danforth's dog peanut butter…

Danforth laughs. "Watch." He holds out a spoon and his Boston Bull Terrier happily licks it up.

And licks.

And licks.

And licks some more.

And even after the peanut butter is gone and Danforth takes the spoon back, his dog continues to lick the air for the next five minutes.

Me and Erik both crack up.

Then of Dr. Kendrick standing in the hallway earlier, alone and worried but holding on to hope that his son was okay.

Danforth was very much a silly guy just like my brother. He was going to med school and planning to join his parents' pediatric practice.

Was.

My head swirls, and I put my hand over my mouth, muffling a moan. He was the last person to see my brother and his girlfriend. The image of that body in the trunk hits me again, and I gulp in a breath. They poured acid on him. Whoever did that to him has Erik now.

Gently, Zeke squeezes my neck, but I don't open my eyes. Why kill Danforth? He's just an innocent boy. A boy I've known my whole life. One who traps any bugs in the house and releases them outside. He brought me a cupcake when I broke my wrist a few years ago. He'd never harm a thing.

"That's right," the voice speaks in my ear. "Danforth is dead, and your brother will be next if you don't do exactly as I say."

Opening my eyes, I clench my teeth, and I shove back up to a standing position.

"The drive," the voice says. "Now."

"I'm fine," I assure Zeke, pushing past and heading the rest of the way up the stairs and into the computer lab.

"Sophie," he calls, but I ignore him. I need to do this.

As I enter the lab, Jackson squints at me through bloodshot eyes and with a soft smile says, "Hey, I'm sorry about Danforth."

"Thanks," I mumble, tears pressing in, and I concentrate on blinking them away. The device sticks out of his laptop. How in the hell am I going to make the switch? I look around the empty room. "You're alone?"

"Not for long. Norman is on his way."

"Mm-hmm." I study the flash drive, trying to figure what to do. "Um, anything on the decryption?"

"The address to the warehouse, the body in the trunk, and something about an earpiece. Makes me think whatever is on here contains the exact details of the things yet to transpire."

A nervous swallow moves down my throat. "Earpiece?"

"That's all I've got so far. This is hyperspherical encryption. It's the most layered I've ever seen." He shrugs. "I'll figure it out, though."

"Sophie," the garbled voice says. "If he deciphers that information, your brother *will* die. I promise you that."

My friend goes back to typing. The terrorist can hear what I'm doing, but he can't see. I can quickly jot a note and give it to Jackson, so he'll know what's going on. We can pretend to make the switch, but not actually do it.

Yes, that's exactly what I'm going to do.

Crossing the lab, I come to a stop in front of the supply desk. I grab a pencil and paper, and I scribble a note.

"Put the pencil down," the voice warns me, and my hand pauses. "That's right. I've got eyes and ears everywhere."

Up in the corner, a security camera sits mounted, and I imagine whoever is in my ear smugly looking back. This extremist, whoever he is, has infiltrated the private network. Or he's here right now, somewhere in this building.

Watching.

Tracking.

My gaze zips back over to my friend and to the device

sticking out of his laptop. I don't know what's going to happen when I make the switch, but I don't have a choice. I could be loading a virus, or I could simply be switching drives so no one discovers what's on the real one.

"You're wasting time," the voice says.

With a deep breath, I make my way over to the water dispenser sitting in the corner, and a plan falls into place. I fill a small cup, and as I cross back to Jackson, I slip the replacement from my front pocket. He doesn't notice me as I get closer and closer, and when I'm right up on him, I make my toe catch on the wheel of his chair and water goes flying.

"Sophie!" My friend leaps to his feet, throwing his body over the laptop, and the water sloshes across him as planned.

I cringe. "Sorry."

After he checks to make sure the laptop is okay, he stomps over to the water cooler to grab some napkins, and quickly, I make the switch. He turns, wiping his neck, and he throws the napkins away before coming back.

"I'm sorry," I apologize again, and he ignores me as he plops back down.

He gives the laptop a good study again, making sure none of the water hit it, and I stare at his screen, waiting to see what happens.

But…nothing does. It's like I didn't even make the switch.

"Move," the voice says. "Go to the bathroom."

"Um—I really am sorry." I take a step back. "I'm going to the bathroom."

He doesn't even look at me as he goes back to typing.

I scurry out of the lab and down the hall into the bathroom. When I'm safely inside and have checked that I'm alone, I whisper, "What now?"

But the voice doesn't answer me, only static.

Even when I complete these three tasks of his, there will be something else. I'm kidding myself thinking this is over.

He showed me a video of my brother. But what if that was an old video the terrorist somehow got his hands on? What if that wasn't a live feed? In my panic and alarm I was quick to believe. But what if they don't have Erik?

I step up to the mirror hanging above the sink. I take in the dark circles under my light brown eyes, my dark curly hair in a lopsided ponytail, and the scrape on my cheek. My wide eyes look petrified.

I straighten up and channel determination, instead. "I want to hear my brother's voice," I demand, proud of myself for sounding and looking strong.

The person doesn't respond, and I don't look away from the mirror while I wait, hoping to God I didn't just make an enormous mistake. The static in my ear stretches my nerves, but I keep quiet, waiting for his move.

There's a crackle, then, "Sophie?"

"Erik?" I gasp. "Are you okay?"

"I'm fine," he assures me, but the emotion in his voice closes in on me.

My brother laughs a lot, but rarely, if ever, have I seen him cry. In fact, the last time was two years ago at Pop-Pop's funeral.

Erik's breath catches, and I glance over right as several tears leak from his eyes to trail his cheeks.

I sit beside him in the church with Pop-Pop's closed casket at the front and Mom standing at the podium speaking.

Wrapping my arm around him, I lay my head on his shoulder. I don't say anything. I simply hold him as his shoulders shake with quiet tears.

My brother and I don't say anything else as we listen to each other breathe, and I'm caught up in the maddening thought, *What if this is the last time I ever hear his voice?*

He sniffs. "Tell me you're safe."

"I am. Don't worry about me."

"Sophie—" But his words are cut off by a painful yelp.

"Erik?" I nearly shout.

"You have your proof," the distorted voice says. "Now, destroy the drive. I want it gone. Remember I can see everything you're doing."

I break the drive open and take the memory chip out, flushing the plastic pieces away before leaving the bathroom. In the copy room, I go straight to the industrial shredder, and I glare up to the camera in the corner. I want to make sure whoever is watching can see me throw the chip in and hit the on button.

"Good," the voice says. "Now for tasks two and three. Senator Gostler and the vice president."

find Frank in the hall, talking with Norman, the CIA analyst.

My voice is audibly tense when I say, "I want to go to the speech today."

Frank's expression remains blank, but there is no void in that head of his. "There is a confirmed domestic crisis. That's not a good idea. We're trying to keep this thing as down-low as possible. You heard the director. Being out in the public puts not only you at risk but elevates the threat."

"The School Math Initiative is something William and I have done together for years. It would look weird if I'm not there. The public will wonder, especially since it's my birthday and that was going to be part of it."

The plan was the speech, zip-lining with my close friends, piercing my own nose. That was supposed to be my day today.

Not all of this.

"Hey, happy birthday," Norman says, and I nod my thanks.

I look back at Frank. "Normalcy is the best way to go. Even you have said that."

"No." He shakes his head.

Norman quietly excuses himself, and I take a step closer to Frank, lowering my voice to a tone that I hope comes across respectful, reasonable, and not panicky. Because if he doesn't agree to this, I don't know what I'm going to do. "Please. I know Erik is safe now, but I'm so wigged out about everything else going on, I need to get out of here and do something to take my mind off of things. With the vice president there, security will be tight."

He studies me as he works it through in his mind. I keep my eyes on his, concentrating hard on looking honest and earnest. "I'll have to clear it with Prax," he tells me. "And he is not happy after what happened earlier."

There is no way the Director of the CIA will agree to this, and so I'm ready with my counter. "Or," I humbly suggest, "you could clear it with William. The director can't argue over something the VP has approved." I'm counting on his inherent dislike for the director to drive his response.

He thinks about that, and then, with a sigh that has me blowing out a quiet breath of relief, he relents. "Okay, go get cleaned up. I brought your bag in. Be ready to leave within the hour."

F rank always keeps a small suitcase packed with things I might need. In the women's locker room, I'm too paranoid to shower with someone possibly watching, and so I clean up the best I can.

As I do, my brain ping-pongs between Danforth, Erik, Britta, the flash drive, the inside person, the warehouse, the piece in my ear, and back to the device.

I don't know how my brother and his girlfriend ended up with it, but Erik must have suspected something was going to happen today. Somehow, he found out there was going to be a threat, and he was either trying to stop it or to find out who the inside person is.

How did he find the info and why didn't he say something sooner?

There's a soft knock on the door. "One minute," Frank calls.

"Coming!" I slip into ballet flats, dress pants, and a white blouse. I double-check the clasp on my vintage American flag necklace and make sure the earpiece is still firmly in. I note my hands are steadier than before and am glad to see it. "Are you there?" I whisper.

"I am," comes the garbled voice, and it provides me a weird comfort. Hearing that voice means there's a possibility Erik is still alive.

"What do you want me to do once I'm at the Ripley Center?" I ask.

"No, your first stop will be Senator Gostler's house, then the Ripley Center."

The senator is like a grandfather to me. What does he have to do with this?

"Gostler's away on business," the voice says. "Say you have to feed his fish."

I don't know how the person in my ear knows I sometimes water Gostler's plants and feed his fish, but he does.

Frank knocks again. "Let's go. You can do your makeup in the car."

"Go," the voice instructs. "I'll talk to you again once you get there."

SENATOR GOSTLER'S HOME

Eastern Market, D.C.
Saturday, 9:30 a.m.

Frank is behind the wheel, and as he drives, I go through the motions of doing my makeup. I swipe powder foundation on my T-Zone, brush mascara on my lashes, add a bit of tinted gloss for my lips, and I'm done.

Another agent occupies the passenger seat where Karen usually sits. I was told she was transferred off of my detail and put onto my father's. It's not unusual to move agents around, especially during a crisis.

Her replacement is a woman, too, and she's new. She introduced herself, but, honestly, I don't recall her name. I'm a little preoccupied with whatever the voice in my ear wants me to do at the senator's house.

Since it's a Saturday morning, the usual jam of D.C. commuters is absent. The people who are out this morning are clueless.

No one knows what a crap-fest my life has become overnight or how much danger they're in.

Over the years, there have been numerous threats on

my family. Some idle, some dangerous. Regardless, Mom has always been adamant about keeping things out of the media and going about our lives as normally as possible. She's right, and as much as I hate to admit it, the director is right to follow her mandates and protocol. If the media gets wind of anything, this whole thing will blow up.

Frank takes the exact route I knew he would, and when we're one street over from Senator Gostler's place, I say, "Will you make a quick stop at the senator's house? He's out of town, and I told him I'd feed his fish."

Holding my breath, I wait for his response. I've taken care of the senator's fish and plants before. It's not an unusual thing for me to do, which I bet is the exact reason why the terrorist picked me to do whatever he wants me to do when I'm in the house.

He gives me a quick look. "You only have a few minutes."

"I know. I'll be fast." Now I just have to make sure he stays on the porch and doesn't go in with me. He normally does, but with everything happening today, I'm not sure he will this time.

A few minutes later, we pull into the short driveway. We all get out of the car. A pebbled walkway leads up to the small stone and brick house with a wraparound porch. I've always loved this place. Except the senator makes the weirdest food...

In the backyard, Senator Gostler stands over by the grill, flipping salmon and pimiento patties.

I lean in to whisper to Frank, "Salmon and pimiento?"

Frank whispers back. "I know. Just pretend to eat one. I'll stop and get us something on the way home."

Elizabeth, the senator's granddaughter, sits down beside me on the deck. She mumbles, "I heard that and I'm totally coming with you."

Frank winks. "Got your back."

Yes, I've known the senator for as long as I can remember. Elizabeth and I are the same age, and when she visits from his home state of Pennsylvania, I usually come over and hang out. Or as she likes to say, I rescue her from starving to death.

I gave him one of the fish that I'm here to fake feed.

Moving forward, I step my way across the path. Frank nods to the other agent, indicating she should wait by the car, before trailing behind me up the steps and onto the porch. I have a copy of the house key that he keeps, and he hands it to me.

As I fit the key into the lock, the air around me vibrates with uneasiness. I don't know what I'm walking into, but it's not going to be good or easy. I can't imagine what the extremist wants with Gostler, but I'm about to find out.

I unlock the door, and blowing out a quick breath, I turn to Frank. "I won't be long," I say and pull the door closed before he has a chance to follow me inside.

Through the window I see him turn to take a guarding position on the front porch, as I'd hoped he would.

"Senator Gostler?" I call out, just to be extra sure he's gone.

But only silence greets me.

"Okay," I tell whoever is on the other end of the earpiece. "What now?"

"Take the blue drive and put it in the CPU."

I head straight into the office where his computer is. I boot it and press the Win key to bring up the Run dialog box and bypass his password. Jackson and Callie would be so proud.

I almost put the blue one in, but I pause. Unlike where I just was at the covert facility, there are no cameras in here. There's no way I can be seen. I can very quickly bring up the senator's history and see what files he's been working on. Maybe something will jump out at me. Because there is obviously a reason I was sent here. Gostler knows something.

I do just that, quickly scrolling, and various things appear, none of which seem odd. There's one particular file that he's recently worked on several times, though. It's labeled LONE EAGLE. I'm not sure if it's anything, but I go to click on it—

"Stop!" the voice in my ear says. "You click on that file, and I will maim your brother and let you listen."

Lifting my hands away from the keys, my heart surges so hard that it thumps in my ears. "I'm sorry."

"You know what? You need to hear that I mean business."

Fear grips my gut and I hold my hands higher in the air. "Please," I whisper. "I'm sorry."

"Too late."

My brother's scream echoes through my ear, and my heart suspends beating. "Stop." My voice cracks. "I'm sorry. Please." His scream quiets to a muffled cry, and the sound of it wrenches through me. "You can't do this," I croak.

A deep chuckle resonates in my eardrum and curls

down my neck. "Oh, but I can. Put the drive in," the garbled voice says. "Now."

With fumbling fingers, I take it from my pocket and wedge it in, and the virus loads to eat away at the computer.

"Now go," the voice says. "Time for task number three."

Pushing away from the computer, I turn around and freeze.

There in the dimly lit corner of the office sits Senator Gostler. Dead. His body slumped in a chair, his arms limply lying over the armrests. On the floor, just inches from his dangling fingers, lies a gun. My gaze darts from it up to his unseeing eyes and over to the gaping bloody hole in the side of his head.

I stare, unable to comprehend. My heart pounds faster, and I'm scared it might give out on me.

He's...dead. Suicide? Tears fill my eyes, not only for him, but for Danforth, too. Nausea climbs my throat to fill my mouth in a horrifying bitterness.

I take a hesitant step toward him. "Senator Gostler?" I whisper, though of course he's not going to answer me.

Was he in on it? Does it have something to do with that Lone Eagle file—whatever that is?

"Well, that's convenient," the voice says, and I spin in a circle, looking again for cameras. He obviously didn't know about this.

"Sophie?" Frank calls from the front door. "We need to go."

"Do not tell anyone what you just saw," the voice warns.

I manage to turn away from the senator, and my chest

burns like someone is poking it with a hot blade. He was such a good man. Danforth was such a good boy. Why? *Why?*

I make myself move.

Frank takes one look at me, and concern flashes through his eyes. "You okay?"

I don't answer because I don't think I can use my voice even if I tried. I nod and stiffly head to the car.

Two people I cared for deeply are now dead.

Erik's scream ricochets through my brain, followed by, *I will begin removing pieces of your brother and delivering them to you in a box.* Please, God. Please let him be okay.

RIPLEY CENTER

Washington, D.C.
Saturday, 10:15 a.m.

"You sure you're okay?" Frank asks as he pulls onto Jefferson Street and into a slot reserved for us.

"Yes," I say, but Danforth's body in that trunk flashes through my mind, followed by the bullet hole in Senator Gostler's head and then Erik's scream.

I'm losing my mind. I shake my head, trying to get the chaos out. I have to focus. This is the last task, the third thing, and then my brother goes free.

But even as I tell myself this, I know it's not going to be that easy. Still, I have to try.

The press is already here and snapping pictures as we walk inside, flanked by additional security. I do my usual smile and wave. Everything is okay.

Happy birthday to me.

We make our way through the crowd and down to Sublevel Three where the math exhibit is on tour. I catch sight of a K9 unit up ahead, just turning the corner. The yellow patch on the dog's harness tells me he's sniffing for bombs.

"Go to the bathroom," the garbled voice instructs me. "The one on Sublevel Three near the water fountains."

We're already near the water fountains the voice is referring to, and so I turn to Frank. "I'm going to pop into the restroom real quick."

With a nod, he and the other agent stand outside, and I walk in.

The door closes and the voice in my ear speaks. "Second stall. Bottom left corner. There's a loose brick. Take what's in it and put it in your pocket."

Not a second is wasted as I rush into that stall, kneel down, and work the brick loose. Inside the small area sits a tiny brown bottle with a single pill inside of it. I take the bottle and wedge the brick back into place.

I hold the brown bottle up, and it's like lead in my hand as I look at it. The pill inside appears identical to an aspirin or any other number of round white tablets.

"Put it in your pocket and go," the voice says.

T he vice president greets me with a warm hug. I hug him back, lingering a little to enjoy the safety it provides me. I've always liked William. He and my mom made history with her being the first female POTUS and him the first gay VP. They make a powerful and dynamic team. To quote many a reporter, they "move mountains" for the American people.

"USA! USA!" the crowd chants.

Smiling, Mom and William clasp hands and hold them up in the air. The crowd becomes louder before gradually quieting.

Mom nods him on, and William steps up to the microphone. When they appear together, they always share the speeches. "This great country will not destroy itself under second-rate leadership. America will once again be one of the most admired places in the world. We will be at peace." William looks across the crowd. "America is full of hope and there are great things ahead!"

The audience erupts in cheers again, and the energy buzzes through me. Last week they won the election, and this is one of many speeches they've given in their weeklong tour of America.

I glance over to Dad to see him smiling proudly. Erik, too.

William has been my mom's best friend since the military, and when the two of them get together, it's always a snort-fest—they get to laughing so hard at each other that they end up snorting. Him first, then her, then back to him.

I like his husband, too. He's a law professor at Georgetown and makes the absolute best pecan candies.

"How are you?" William whispers.

"I've had better days," I honestly tell him.

He curls a warm and secure hand around my elbow as he leads me over into the corner of the hospitality room to give us a private minute. He's not much taller than me, and as I look straight into his friendly and welcoming brown eyes, a sense of peace settles over me, as if everything is going to be okay.

"Prax has been keeping me up to date on everything. You did not have to come today," he tells me.

"I don't want anything to seem off. Plus, I needed this."

He squeezes my elbow. "We're going to nail these sons of bitches. Count on it. The director knows a lot of the ins and outs of what's going on."

I go on instant alert, and the next words come out of my mouth before I remember the extremist in my ear can hear everything. "What are you saying? Do you know who the terrorists are?"

"We have some viable leads."

I want to ask for details, but I keep my mouth shut. This cell already knows too much. I let out a frustrated sigh, wishing I knew what these viable leads are, but also not wanting him to say anything more with the terrorist listening.

"It's for your own safety," he says, somewhat reading my frustrated thoughts.

What would he do if he found out I have this in my ear?

"I can tell you our Intel indicates the first bombing is going to occur while we're on stage giving our speech."

Hence the K9 unit. I don't want him to say any more, so I just nod, though I wish I could follow up with questions.

Gently, he clasps my shoulder. "We've practiced this speech several times. You feel good?"

"I got it," I assure him. Truthfully, I haven't thought about the speech. But I've never had a problem speaking in public. Everything comes to me when I get up there. "You do your thing, and I'll follow with mine."

He smiles. "You're a natural, just like your mother."

Sure, Mom and I have been at odds lately, but I do

love the comparison. Still, I roll my eyes with a chuckle. "I wouldn't go that far."

With another kind smile and one more hug, the VP wanders off.

"You see those water bottles over on the table?" comes the distorted voice again. Where are the cameras? How the hell does he know there are water bottles in here? "I want you to take one, put the pill inside of it, and offer it to your friend William."

I whirl away from the crowd to face the wall so no one can see me talking. My hands shake, and I tighten them into fists. "What do you mean? What is that pill going to do?"

"Need I remind you I have your brother?"

His scream resonates through my brain, and panic spikes through my blood. I catch my breath and press the pads of my fingers into my temple, like the weight of my head is too much for my neck to hold. "Okay, okay. I'll do it."

Behind me the people in the hospitality room shuffle around, signaling we're about to leave and go on stage.

"Do it now!" the voice commands.

Shoving my hand down inside my pants pocket, I retrieve the tiny bottle, and with fumbling fingers, I twist off the cap and get the pill. I spin away from the wall, the pill clenched in my fist, and head straight to the water table.

Dread burns through me as I grab the first bottle, twist the cap off, drop the pill inside, and recap it.

I give the water bottle an uncoordinated swirl, making sure the pill is dissolved, before spinning back toward the crowded room. I spy William over near the door, about to exit. He runs a big hand over his thin hair and gives me a nod, signaling it's time.

Forcing my lips to smile, I walk over with weighted and sluggish feet, almost as if I'm dragging them through mud. When I reach his side, I shove the bottle toward him before I have time to rethink this. "I-I know you always get thirsty when you speak."

A smile dances through his face. "How thoughtful. Thank you."

We walk beside each other from the hospitality room and down the long hallway that leads to the stage. Security flanks us on all sides, and my heart thunders so loudly everyone around me must hear it, too.

Out of the corner of my eye, I look at the water bottle in his hand. I don't know what's going to happen when he drinks that, but it's not going to be good. *It's probably going to render him unconscious, not dead.* This is what I tell myself in an effort to justify my actions.

We reach the steps leading up to the stage, and the crowd applauds as we enter the room. William smiles at me, but all I can do is stare at the water bottle. What am I doing? I can't let him drink that.

He unscrews the lid. The bottle gets closer, and right as it's about to touch his mouth, my world rockets back into place, and I lunge.

smacked the water bottle from his hand, the place went dead quiet for less than an instant, then cameras flashed, secret service moved in, and the whole place erupted into chaos.

That was fifteen minutes ago, and now, here I am back in the hospitality room with Director Prax in my face. I didn't even know he was in the building.

"You are out of control," he grinds out through a clenched jaw.

I look over to the tech who is currently testing the contents of the water bottle. "Wh-where's William? Is he okay?"

The director moves even farther into my line of sight. "The vice president is out there right now giving the speech and covering your ass."

Turning my face away, I pinch the bridge of my nose. Static fills my ear. Tears clog my eyes, and I squeeze them shut. I may have just killed or horribly maimed my brother. I both want to hear and dread to hear the garbled voice. I need to know what he just did to Erik.

"What is this?" Prax demands, grabbing my face and turning it farther away to dig in my ear.

"Stop it!" I try to yank away, but he still manages to get the earpiece out.

Frank moves in. "Leave her alone."

The director studies the piece closely, and my stomach pinches tight. If he was pissed before, he's beyond pissed now. "What is this?" He holds it up in front of my eyes. "Who's talking to you?"

Covering my face with my hands, I inhale a choppy breath. "I don't know," I tell him, miserable to my very soul. "But I may have just killed Erik."

"What are you talking about?" Prax asks.

"He's not safe," I mumble, looking up into his angry

yet perplexed face. "They have him. The cell has him."

He and Frank exchange a confused look, and it's Frank who gets out his phone and turns away to punch in a number. It connects and I hear, "Bit-O-Honey"—Erik's code name. Frank is calling whoever is supposed to be guarding my brother.

My knees give out on me, and I lean back against the wall.

"Sir?" the tech says, and Prax waves her over. She hesitates. "We should talk in private."

"No," the director tells her. "I want Sophie to hear this. Several people saw you give him that water bottle," he reminds me.

Dread drops in my stomach as I stare at the tech, waiting to hear what she says.

She casts a nervous glance between me and Prax before saying, "It was saxitoxin."

He spins on me. "Where did you get your hands on saxitoxin?"

I shake my head, and my back merges even more heavily with the wall. "What's saxitoxin?" I croak.

"It is the most lethal drug on the black market," the tech says. "It works on the nervous system, effectively paralyzing every muscle until a person's insides liquefy and they smother to death on their own bile. There have been a few incidents over the years where it's popped up, all of which involved the"—the tech shoots the director an uneasy look—"the CIA."

"I repeat. Where did you get saxitoxin?" he demands.

Unable to speak, I shake my head. I almost killed William, and whoever has Erik tried to frame me for it. They knew I was the only one who could make that happen. If I had any doubt of there being an inside person, this right here is further proof that there is a conspiracy coming from within. And with the VP now threatened, too, it's clear my family isn't the only target.

The director waves over several members of his team. "Take her."

"What?" I gasp, straightening up. "Take me where?"

Frank hangs up the phone as he steps in. "*I'll* take her wherever you need her to go."

Prax holds up his hand. "You are officially off her detail."

"You can't do that," Frank firmly states. "The president would not want this."

A man I don't recognize grabs my upper arm, and frantic terror hammers through me. "No." I pull at his hold. "I'm not going with you."

Several other men move in toward Frank, and he gives them a threatening glare before turning to me. For the first time ever, I note desperation and helplessness in his expression.

"Do what they say," he says in a calm voice, which is forced, but does manage to keep me somewhat level. "You're going to be okay."

I look at his phone because, really, my brother is the only one I'm worried about right now.

"Erik?" I ask, holding out a minuscule hope that this is all a horrible mistake and he's safe and being guarded by his agents.

As a response, he presses his lips together and shakes his head. "I'm sorry."

Tears press in, and tightening my jaw, I swallow them back.

"Don't worry," he says, again with the calm. "We're going to figure all of this out."

But I don't have time to respond, because Prax's men forcibly lead me from the room.

THE NATIONAL MALL

Washington, D.C.
Saturday, 11:00 a.m.

The man on my left squeezes my arm a little too tightly, and I flinch. I don't recognize him or the man on my right. I tell myself this isn't too odd, as there are a lot of people who work for the director. But as I peek over my shoulder and see nothing behind us but an empty hallway, everything in me screams that something isn't right.

"Where are you taking me?" I ask.

"Just walk," the man on my right responds.

My Spidey senses prick even more alert. Straight ahead of us sits a doorway that leads out into an alley, where, I assume, there is a car waiting to transport me wherever these men are supposed to go.

I am not going anywhere with these two men. I don't care if they do work for Prax.

The door at the end moves vertically, controlled by a red button on the right side. The last time I was here, Frank accidentally hit it twice instead of once, and it got stuck at the one-foot gap. But one foot is plenty of room for me to roll under.

Not these guys, though; they're too big. They'll have to wait until it rolls down and then back up.

By then I'll be gone.

Once again, I'm about to break protocol. A few hours ago, the thought of running terrified me, but now it settles through me with resolve. It's what I need to do.

Moving only my eyes, I look to the man on my right and see his weapon in a shoulder holster inside his suit jacket. I do the same to the man on my left, but I don't see a weapon. That's not to say he doesn't have one; it's just hidden.

To my right, the man is shorter, and I put him at five-eight. To my left, he's around five-ten. I'm five-five.

Our TIA martial arts instructor holds up a one and three-fourths inch thick board. Given the fact Callie, Zeke, and Jackson all broke theirs, I better be able to break mine.

I get in position, planting my feet firmly, and spread slightly with one ahead of the other. I shift my weight, allowing my back foot to support. Palm facing downward, I make a fist, placing my thumb on the outside. I line my wrist so that it's even, twist my hips, and with a yell, I deliver a straight punch.

It ricochets back and up my arm to jar my shoulder. Crap, I can't believe I didn't break it.

"Release all fears," Jackson says. "Commit to breaking the board. Clear your mind. Tell yourself you will break it."

Callie rolls her eyes. "Zen master over here."

"Focus on speed, not power," the instructor says. "Aim at a point beyond. Don't think of the board as your final target."

Zeke steps into my line of sight. "Try striking with your left."

I glance across the oversized mat and over to where Frank stands off to the side. He nods. "Agree."

Zeke was right, I throw a stronger punch with my left hand. I broke the board without an issue by simply switching.

With the knowledge of my dominant hand, I visualize my moves, and as I do, my fists clench tight. No hesitation. Quick. Effective. Efficient. Still, my pulse thunders through my veins.

I squint to the man squeezing my arm. "I'll walk without the vise grip. Plus, I'm sure no one is going to like the fact you're squeezing my arm so hard you're leaving a bruise. Especially the *president.*"

With an annoyed look, he lessens his grip. "There, Princess."

And if I was determined before, that condescending "Princess" just sent me over the edge. Without another second, I yank my left arm from his grip, spin, and I punch the man on my right in the Adam's apple. Thrusting my right hand into his jacket, I grab his weapon and whip back to sidekick the man on my left in his groin.

Like an electrical prod jabs me, I take off in a full sprint down the hall toward the door. I have no clue what the men are doing behind me, and I'm not pausing to see.

With my fist, I punch the red button twice, and like it did last time, the door clanks up and stops with a one-foot gap. I drop and roll under and come to my feet.

Quickly, I survey the area. There's a dark car parked right next to a dumpster, presumably the car they were going to put me into. A small red box sitting on the hood catches my attention. There's a white card taped to the top with SOPHIE printed in bold black marker. The shock of seeing my name curls terror through me, and with shaking hands I grab it, and I go.

I make a demon dash through the daylight and down the alley, away from the National Mall. I don't know what I'm going to do next, but I have to run.

I could jump in a cab or hop the Metro, but I don't have any money, and frankly my identity is more of an issue. Someone will recognize me, and my picture will be all over social media within seconds.

I sprint down Ninth Street, my senses heightened, trying to develop a plan. And then I spy this little old lady getting into her car.

She closes her front door at the exact second I open her back door and dive in. She screams, and I do the first thing that comes to mind: I point the barrel of the gun at her head.

Her eyes go wide, her hands up, and she violently shakes.

Fighting the urge to comfort her, I snap out, "Drive." But even I can hear the rawness and the panic in my own voice.

With fumbling fingers, she pushes her key fob into place and starts her car. As she does, I poke my head up and make sure we're clear.

"Wh-wh-where?" she stutters out before catching a breath that transitions into a sob.

The sound of her distress clenches through me. My God, I hope I don't give this lady a heart attack. "I don't care. J-just go away from here. I have to think."

She puts her car into gear and carefully pulls out, like she thinks if she makes quick movements, it'll set me off.

"P-Please don't hurt me. You can have whatever you want. My purse is right here. There's maybe a hundred in there. I can stop at an ATM and get more. Just don't hurt me."

I close my eyes, and my stomach pinches with what I've just done and the scare I'm giving this poor woman. "Just move," I painfully say, and she does.

CLEVELAND PARK

Washington, D.C.
Saturday, 12:00 p.m.

iggling, I race down the hall of our family home. "I'm going to find you!" I yell.

"No, you're not!" My brother yells back, and his voice and laughter echo from the guest room on my right.

I follow the echo, ducking inside, and his curly dark hair disappears through a secret door.

Covering my mouth so he can't hear me giggle, I tiptoe across the room, press the release panel in the wall, and the secret door pops open.

As quietly as I can, I slip inside, and the door closes behind me, shutting me in the small dark space. Some of the passages in our home go from one floor to the next, or they follow the length of a hallway. This particular one goes nowhere except to the next guest room. It's kind of like adjoining rooms in a hotel.

In the dark I fumble around and find the interior release lever, but when I press it, the door doesn't budge.

I press it again, but still it doesn't budge.

I try the one I just came through, and it doesn't work, either.

"Erik?" I call, but he doesn't hear me.

I bang on both walls. "Erik!" I scream.

But still he doesn't hear me.

"Erik!"

That day from so many years ago comes back to me with complete clarity. I was five, my brother seven. I was stuck in that dark space for three whole hours. It was Mom who finally found me, and when she did, I was so shaken up and scared that I had worked myself into a state of shock.

My parents took me to the emergency room. Aside from peeing myself, physically, I was fine, but emotionally, I have never been the same. I've come a long way since I was five years old, but small spaces still terrify me.

Six months ago, we did a drill in the TIA that involved each of us being closed inside a tank. I lasted all of ten seconds before I went into an all-out panic attack. Thankfully, it was just an exercise, the teacher let me out, and my friends were there to help me ride the panic attack out.

But that's not always going to be the case. If I truly want to be in the clandestine division of the CIA, I'm going to have to face, and get over, that fear.

Luckily, today is not that day.

Shoving all of that away, I tune in to my surroundings. I'm in the back seat of a car, crouched in the floorboard, and the car is stopped. I become aware of a gun cradled loosely in my right hand and a small red box gripped in my left.

Then it all pops back into place.

With a jerk, I grasp the weapon and lurch up to see the old lady staring curiously back at me. She hesitantly smiles, and through the car's windows I note that we are stopped along the side of a curb in an old historical neighborhood.

Oh my God, did I just fall asleep? How did I lose track of time? I've done this before—been so sleep deprived and stressed that my body gives out on me. Or my brain zones out. I can't believe it just happened in this lady's car.

"You're Sophie Washington," she says, and I don't nod. In fact, I don't do anything except stare back. I kidnapped an old lady at gunpoint.

"You can put that down," she says. "You're not going to have to use it. At least, not on me."

She's a lot calmer now than she was before. I scared her so bad she was shaking and nearly sobbing. I'm not sure why the change. Maybe because she knows who I am now, or because I just conked out in the back of her car. Either way, I lower the gun.

Yes, she obviously knows who I am, and she's clearly more curious at this point than anything. Curious, and perhaps also wants to help.

"I love your mom," she says. "I voted for her."

"Th-thank you."

The lady gives me a kind, sympathetic smile. "Now, why don't you tell me what's going on?" She motions to the box. "How about you start with what's in that."

I stare down at it and my heart thump-thump-thumps as I recall the garbled voice's threat. *I will begin removing pieces of your brother and delivering them to you in a box.*

I don't believe it. There is not a piece of my brother in this box.

I couldn't kill the vice president. Don't they realize that? Killing William is like asking me to kill my brother or parents. William is a part of our family. And if there is a piece of my brother in this box, how will I know it really belongs to him? They could've cut up anybody and put it in here. Like Danforth, before they mangled his body with acid.

Or—my thoughts grind to a halt—Britta.

Wait, what if this is the bomb that is supposed to go off, and I'm the casualty? But then, that doesn't make sense. Why would they bother having me target William with the saxitoxin?

Three tasks. That's all they wanted me to do. I did two of the three.

Scenarios tumble around in my brain as I stare at the box. One second goes by. Two. Then three. I can't just stay here crouched in the back of this lady's car. I need to find out what's in here.

Before I can rethink my resolve, I grasp the small box, and my stomach roils with what I'm going to see.

I lift the lid in one jerky, quick movement, and the lady gasps. Somewhere in the back of my mind it registers that I'm looking at a toe and that the severed skin is clean. The cut was quick.

I'm not sure if it's the intensity that is currently my life, this severed toe, or the fact my actions may have just caused my brother's death…but sharp pain shoots through my chest.

With a gasp, I press my palm to my heart, fearful I

might be having an attack. The sharpness brings tears to my eyes. They roll down my cheeks, and they don't stop. They become big, blubbery, and snot-nosey, and I welcome the release that they bring.

When the old lady reaches over the seat and rubs my shoulder, it only makes them come hotter and heavier.

Several beats of time pass before I get myself back under control enough to breathe and blow my nose in a tissue the lady hands me. When I'm done, and only a few sniffles are left, I unload the whole story on her while she pays close attention.

I start at the very beginning, and I don't leave a single thing out. It brings me such relief to tell the whole thing to someone else.

When I'm done, she takes no time at all to think through it all. She simply says, "Honey, have you tried calling your mother?"

It seems like such a simple question, but with everything that has happened, calling my mom didn't factor into things. Honestly, I wasn't sure if I was allowed. "No, ma'am," I answer, feeling like I'm five years old again. "I don't even have a phone. I don't have anything."

Over the leather seat, she hands me her phone. "Here."

I stay crouched in the back, and I dial my mom's phone. It goes straight to voicemail. I try Dad next, and it goes to voicemail, too.

On a normal day it's not odd to get their voicemail. Both of their schedules are jam-packed, and they usually call me back as soon as they can.

But this is far from a normal day. I don't leave a message on either one. I'm so paranoid, I don't know who might have hacked their lines.

Next, I try Zeke, who thankfully picks up after the first ring. "Zeke here."

His voice flows through me in a soothing warmth. "Hey, it's me."

"What the hell is going on? You're all over the news for knocking that bottle out of the vice president's hand. He covered for you, saying that you didn't mean to, that you swiveled your arm up a little too forcefully and accidentally did it, but hell, it looked real to me."

A sigh heaves out of me. "I'll explain it later."

"You're not going to believe what's happened here. Norman's in holding."

I frown. "Why is he in holding?"

"He was caught talking to one of the terrorists."

My eyes pop wide. *"What?"*

"One of the director's guys caught Norman on a disposable phone talking to a person named Bain, who, from what I understand, is the lead. But Norman doesn't seem to know anything. Not the real identity, where this person currently is, or what his ultimate agenda entails. Because the bomb that was supposed to go off still hasn't."

"Well, what *did* he say?"

"Just that he didn't have a choice. Bain wanted access to video surveillance at several of our covert facilities, and Norman gave it to him."

"Oh my God. That's not good."

Norman was there at the safe house I was taken to. He was also at the covert facility. Hell, he's the CIA's top analyst. If there was ever a good person to have on the inside, he would be it. He could've easily hacked Frank's computer to make it look like the device I found came from his IP.

But if Norman said he didn't have a choice, I believe him. Just look at what I'd been made to do today.

"So does that mean this is over?" I ask. "If he's the inside person, it's just a matter of time to flush out the rest, right?"

"I don't think it's that easy."

Yeah, me neither. "Is Jackson there with you?"

"Yeah, he's still working."

"Tell him to stop. I'll explain later, but it'll go nowhere."

"That's been forty-five," he says and clicks off.

It takes forty-five seconds to trace a call. He's making sure no one knows where I am. Thank God he thought of that, because I sure as hell didn't.

"Do you want me to take you back to my house?" the elderly woman asks, glancing hesitantly at the box and the tiny appendage.

"Sorry," I mumble, wedging the lid back on and sliding it down inside my pocket.

Truth is, I don't know for sure if this toe belongs to my brother. I've never taken the time to analyze his fingers and toes. Either way, it's going with me.

I look up into the elderly lady's bright eyes, realizing I don't even know the name of the person I kidnapped who is turning into my ally. "What's your name?" I ask.

She smiles. "I'm Edna."

I smile back. "Edna, I appreciate the offer, but I don't want to drag you any further into this than I already have. But if you don't mind, can I use your car and phone, and perhaps that hundred dollars you mentioned?"

Her thin gray eyebrows pinch together. "Are you sure it's safe?"

I don't respond to that question because I'm not sure of anything.

After I drop Edna at her house, I use her phone to call Zeke back.

He answers on a rush of breath, "Erik called me."

Relief slams into me. "He's alive!"

"Yes! He said he stole a phone and tried to call you first, then decided on me. He was talking too fast, but he said this thing goes deep and he wasn't sure who all was involved. But by the time Jackson and I tried to trace it, he ended the call. Wait a minute... Oh holy hell, he's calling back."

My heart leaps. "Patch him through if you can."

Zeke mumbles something to Jackson, a few clicks come across the line, and then, "Sophie?"

Relief slams into me again, and I nearly sob out his name, "Erik."

"Oh my God," he whispers.

I talk quickly. "There is so much going on, and I don't know who's in on it and who's not. Norman is. I can't even reach Mom or Dad, or for all I know they've been kidnapped, too. Senator Gostler committed suici—"

"Okay," he says in a voice much calmer than I feel. "You have got to breathe and settle down. I don't know how much time I have before my kidnappers come back. We need to focus."

"You're right. You're right. Are you okay? My God, I

have your toe in a box!"

"I'm fine. My toe is the least of our worries. This has everything to do with Lone Eagle. I tried to stop it from happening, but they caught me."

"You tried to stop what from happening? What is Lone Eagle?"

"It's all on the drive I gave Britta." But before I can tell him she is missing and the information has been destroyed, he whispers, "They're outside the door."

The line goes dead, static fills my ear, and I want to scream.

Zeke comes back on. "I got everything but still no trace. The signal is triangulating between Silver Spring, Rockville, and Potomac."

Which means I've been triangulated, too. I've got to get out of here. "You and Jackson need to leave. I don't care how you do it but go. You aren't safe there. Norman's on the inside and there's no telling who else.

"Danforth is dead. Senator Gostler is dead. Britta is missing. Erik has been kidnapped. Neither of my parents are answering their phones. Someone could be eavesdropping on us at this very second. Drag Callie off of whatever mountain she's climbing. We need her. It's just the four of us now. We are the only ones we can trust."

"Okay," he says, not even questioning. "I'm moving to my burner phone. You know the number."

He clicks off, and as I put Edna's phone on the seat beside me, I see the two men who the director put on me now running toward me.

My heart stops for a frantic second before kicking back in. How the hell did they find me? Even with cell tower triangulation, they shouldn't have located me so fast.

I crank the engine and jerk the car into motion.

In the rearview mirror, I spy one of them talking into the cuff of his sleeve, presumably giving my license plate number to whoever is on the other end. Which means I need to ditch Edna's car ASAP.

Picking up speed, I pass a delivery truck and swerve back in front of him to hang a right onto the next street. I take a left and then another right.

It's one way, and—I quickly peep up—there are no cameras.

Wedging Edna's car into an empty spot along the street, I catch sight of some loose change in a cup holder and grab it all up. I open up her glove compartment and rifle around, and I'm more than surprised when I spy a pearl-handled pocket knife. I grab it, leave the key under the seat, and with her phone and the gun tucked under my shirt, I take off on foot.

I need to ditch her phone, but until I find another one, this will have to be it.

There's a gated and locked park over to the right, and I jump the small fence to cross through it to the other side. A line of cars sits parked on the next street over.

"Always look for the oldest car," the TIA instructor says. *"Old means easy to hot wire."*

I race down the row of them, heading toward the one at the end that appears the oldest. Of my friends, I excelled at last year's hot-wiring lesson.

The instructor continues, "Check for unlocked cars. If someone leaves a car unlocked, they often times hide a key under the seat."

I try the door handle and find it open. Okay, maybe a little too easy. I take my chances and quickly check for a key. But as I look around, I find nothing.

Hot-wire it is.

"Locate the steering wires. Strip and twist red. Spark it with green. Rev. Pop the key hole. Crank hard." The TIA instructor demonstrates.

Grinning, I look at my friends. "This is going to be fun!"

With Edna's knife I remove the plastic cover on the steering handle and find the wires leading straight to the steering column. I strip the red battery wires and twist them together. The green starter wire comes next and I spark it against the red as I rev the engine. Then with her knife, I pop off the metal key hole and break the lock.

I crank the wheel hard to the right, releasing it, and pull out.

As I do, a little thrill zips and zings along my skin, having everything to do with the fact I just successfully hot-wired and stole a car.

This time yesterday, I would have never imagined I'd be on the run, stealing a car, and holding an old person at gunpoint. I don't even recognize myself right now. Twenty-four hours ago, I was looking forward to piercing my own nose, and now I've broken more laws and rules than I can count.

Bain. My brain latches onto that name as I merge into traffic. Norman claimed someone named Bain contacted him. Whoever he is, he is involved in this day that is becoming more and more twisted as the minutes and hours tick by.

Why does that name sound familiar?

No, not a who, a what.

Holy crap.

I grab Edna's phone. "Siri, please find B-A-I-N."

Siri answers, "Brotherhood Alliance International Network. 2001A International Drive."

I dial Zeke's burner. He doesn't answer, but I leave a message he'll get once he picks it up. "BAIN is Brotherhood Alliance International Network. Meet me there. Ditching phone now."

Tossing the phone out the window, I expel a breath, hoping to God that I'm right and that for the brief time I just used the phone, I wasn't triangulated.

BAIN BUILDING

Tyson's Corner
Saturday, 1:30 p.m.

I pull into the underground parking garage of BAIN, and I spy Zeke's old black Land Rover all the way in the back, taking up two spots. From the moment he bought it two years ago, it matched him. Black hair. Black shades. Black Rover. Dark windows. Camo pants. Tight gray tee. When he opened the door and climbed out, a sweet burning awareness crawled across my body.

I pull my stolen car into a slot a few down and get out. The tiny red box in my front pocket wedges into my thigh, reminding me that I have my brother's toe with me. This is insane. We need to talk through everything that's happened so far, compare notes, and brainstorm.

But I don't have time. None of us do. I have to find Erik.

Zeke is already out and coming toward me, and the sight of his strong body and purposeful stride brings me security and relief.

He doesn't say a word, just closes the last few feet

between us and pulls me in for a firm and warm hug. In all the years we've known each other, he has never once hugged me.

My arms don't hesitate in wrapping around his muscular sides as I lay my cheek on his strong chest, close my eyes, and inhale his clean scent—soap, mixed with fabric softener, and something uniquely and only him.

All too quickly he pulls back, stepping away from me, and I get the sense he's as shocked as me at what he just did.

He clears his throat and slides a look toward my stolen car, as if to give himself something to do other than look at me. Though he's not flushed red, I detect embarrassment in him, and that makes me love him even more. Maybe this thing I always feel in his presence is not so one-sided after all.

"Hey, you got my message," I say.

With a nod, he brings his dark green gaze back to mine. "So, um, how you holding up?"

I latch onto that "um" because that tells me he's not as unaffected by me as I always assume.

I huff a laugh. "How do you think?"

A tiny smile pulls at his lips, and though I'm trying very hard not to, I'm fully aware my stare is eating him alive. So, I close my eyes, breaking contact, and refocus. "Any problem getting out of the facility?"

"No, Jackson looped the security feed and we went straight out through the garage."

My eyes open back up and I'm pleased to be more in balance. "Where is he?"

"Trying to locate Callie."

With a nod, I take a second to look around. We're in an empty section of the garage with a service elevator about twenty feet away. There's a Cadillac parked in a reserved spot right beside the elevator. I look at the posted sign and read:

HENRY GENTRY
PRESIDENT AND CEO
BAIN

Zeke opens the back door of his Land Rover. Inside sits a toolbox and beside that a dart gun already loaded with tranquilizer. I don't bother asking him where he got the tranq. He's got his connections.

He checks his watch. "Good ole Henry Gentry is coming down that elevator in just a couple of minutes. He's going to be meeting his wife for a late lunch, so he'll be by himself. There are no security cameras in this area because he doesn't like his comings and goings archived."

Zeke holds up the dart. "We'll tranq him from right here, put him in my Rover, and go to a more private area."

I can't help but smirk. "And how did you get all of this information?"

He returns the smirk. "It's amazing what an assistant will share if you ask the right questions."

"Seems like she gave it a little too easily," I point out.

"True. But we're out of options, and if this is somehow a trap, we're just going to have to be on alert."

"I ditched my phone, but who the hell knows if I was triangulated?" The fact is, I don't know what else to do to find my brother and hopefully Britta, too. As of right now, this Henry guy is our best and only connection. Well, other than Norman, but he's in holding and there is no way we're getting to him. "I also still have the weapon I took off Prax's man."

With a nod, he engages the dart he brought. "We're going Jason Bourne on their asses."

With a slight laugh, I turn and look at the toolbox in the back of his Rover. "Let me guess—our method of persuasion?"

His brows lift. "It's there if we need it."

I try to imagine either one of my parents in this situation. They were both in the military. There are certain things they haven't told me about. The United States does not condone torture, but everyone knows it happens. What would Mom do in this situation? How would she make Henry talk?

She'd bluff him out, make him think imminent danger lies just ahead. But what if it didn't work? I honestly don't know. I've never seen her pushed to that point. I'd like to believe she'd do what was needed. Especially for family.

Either way, I'd rather not, but I have to be ready. The thought of torturing someone for information makes me physically ill.

The elevator dings then, and my spine straightens as nerves kick through me. Here we go.

The door opens, and a middle-aged man steps out. He's not at all what I envision from the word "terrorist."

He doesn't even look our way as he points his fob at the car and presses the lock release. He's a big guy, as in heavy, not tall, and I hope Zeke has enough tranquilizer to take him down.

With both arms, he lifts the gun, holding it with his right hand and resting the hilt in his left palm. Of the four of us, he's the best shooter. He won't miss. He never does. Still, my breath catches and holds as he sights down the length of the barrel. The muscles in his arms twitch, and he pulls the trigger.

Henry's key fob hits the ground, bouncing a few times, and then his body slumps to the cement in an oversize, balled-up heap. Okay, the tranquilizer worked a little too well. I hope Zeke didn't overestimate the amount.

"Get in," he tells me, and we coast the short distance to Henry's now-drugged body.

CONSTRUCTION SITE

Tyson's Corner
Saturday, 2:00 p.m.

It took everything in us to drag Henry's body up into the back seat of the Land Rover, secure his wrists and ankles with zip ties, put duct tape over his mouth, and tie a bandana around his eyes. We then drove around Tyson's, found a vacant construction site, and now here we sit in the Rover, waiting on the big guy to wake up.

I just kidnapped, tied, taped, and gagged a man. At this point, nothing I'm doing should surprise me, but my brain still struggles.

Did Zeke give him too much tranq? Because I would think Henry should be awake by now. He's breathing, though, so there is that.

God, we may have the wrong guy here, but he is the President and CEO of BAIN and our best bet in finding something out.

My gaze moves down to where the closed toolbox sits. My palms get a little damp with what I might have to do. Though, I did do okay with that guy in the warehouse and the knife in his leg. When it came right down to it, I didn't think. I just did what was needed. I have to count on that happening here, too.

"Remember," Zeke whispers, "the threat of pain is sometimes all it takes."

On the monitor, we watch as a man sits strapped to a metal chair, sweating, shaking, his eyes fixed on the interrogator.

Dressed in a suit and with her hair smoothed into a severe bun, the interrogator calmly lays a black leather pouch on the table directly in front of the nervous man. The pouch appears cared for and well used.

Slowly, she unties the straps keeping it closed, and just as slowly she unfolds the leather. A row of shiny silver tools is revealed—a knife, scissors, a hook, a few dental tools, and items I don't recognize taken from a medieval torturing book.

Though I'm not there and only watching this on a screen, I still swallow.

She trails her fingers over the row, teetering between the medieval-looking fork and the hook, before selecting the latter. She slides it from its holder.

Holding it up in front of her, she rotates it, catching the light. Then she pricks her index finger on the tip, drawing blood. She smiles at the result. Turning to the shaking man, she takes exactly one step, and he opens his mouth and begins rattling off information.

The TIA instructor pauses the video. "That man had viable information on the recent hits placed on our agents. Note that she didn't lay a finger on him. The threat of pain is a powerful motivator."

"I would have talked, too," Callie mumbles to me. *"That woman was scary."*

The threat of pain. Let's just hope that's true for Henry.

Next to me, his phone buzzes and a text comes in from his wife.

WHERE ARE YOU?

I show Zeke the phone. "Forgot about the wife."

SORRY, I text back. GOT HELD UP. NEED TO CANCEL.

OKAY, she responds. NO PROBLEM.

I show him the response. "She's understanding."

Henry moans then, and I snap to full alert. Putting the phone aside, I inhale. *Here we go.*

Reaching across the space, I give his cheek a little slap. "Wake up."

With a sharp breath, he jerks, and his sudden movement startles me. I expected him to be groggier coming out of the tranquilizer. I reach over, and with as much force as I can, I rip the duct tape right off of his mouth. I grimace.

"What the hell is going on?" he demands, craning his neck, trying to see beyond the bandana wrapped around his head.

Well, okay, I wasn't expecting him to be angry. Scared, sure, but not this.

"Where is Erik Washington?" I demand, putting just as much anger into my voice.

"Who?"

I take a breath, hoping I'm right about this man, and

I slap his face. "Erik Washington, the son of the President of the United States."

"Who are you?" he barks, tugging at his holds.

Silently, Zeke passes me the dart gun, and I don't hesitate as I take the weapon from his hand.

I engage it, even though there's nothing in it, but make sure our captive can hear the slide of metal on metal. I force it past his lips and teeth and straight into his mouth. With a groan, the big man shakes his head. "No," he pleads around the barrel.

Good, he's scared now and hopefully realizes that we mean business.

I slide the barrel free from his lips and leave it resting on his chin. "Erik Washington?"

"Please," he pleads some more. "I have a wife. I have kids."

"And won't it be a shame if they never see you again," Zeke speaks softly, darkly.

Henry yanks away from the voice, surprised, I'm sure, to discover two of us are here and not just one.

"No." I tap the barrel to his chin before setting it aside. "A little something else might be in order."

When we tied the bandana around his head, we left a sliver of an opening in the lower part for what comes next. I take a Ka-Bar from the toolbox, and gripping the handle, I sweep it side-to-side across his gut. I rotate the blade, giving Henry a real good look through that opening in the bandana, and making sure he can feel the whisper of the blade.

His entire body quivers. He's good and scared now. He sees and feels exactly what I'm doing. "Erik Washington?" I ask again.

Henry inhales a choppy breath. "I don't know anything. I'm just a figurehead. This wasn't part of the deal," he whimpers.

Zeke and I exchange a curious look. This man may not know all the ins and outs, but he definitely knows something. We made the right decision doing this.

With the tip of the Ka-Bar I continue with the taunt, popping one of the buttons on his striped dress shirt. "How about Lone Eagle. Want to tell me what that is?"

His body goes still, making it more than obvious that I've hit on something.

"Please," he rushes. "I really don't know anything."

Yeah, we'll see about that. I pop another button. "Let's try Erik Washington again. Where is he?"

The man's bottom lip wobbles. "Oh, God. They're going to kill me."

Zeke touches my arm and shakes his head, and I already know what he's thinking. You can't let the person you're interrogating think they're going to die. If they think that, they stop speaking. They have nothing to lose. No hope.

Good interrogation gives the witness something to hold on to.

I reformulate things in my mind, coming up with the next statement.

"If you tell us where Erik is"—I insert the tip of the blade between the opening in his dress shirt, and I poke his gut with the tip, firm enough to feel it but not hard enough to draw blood—"I'll make sure you live." I can't really make that promise, but it's the best I've got.

Henry doesn't speak, and I hope he's weighing the

options in his head.

He needs a little more incentive. "We'll make sure you *and* your family are safe."

His bottom lip wobbles some more, and his throat works to swallow. His arms and legs shake again. This man is really scared, and I'm part of the reason why. I should probably feel bad about that, but I don't. He may just be a figurehead or whatever, but he's definitely mixed up in this.

Zeke shifts then, grabbing the toolbox and sliding it over until it's sitting right at Henry's feet. He jerks at the sound and what he can see beneath his blindfold. When he does, he nicks his own self on the knife that I still have pressed against his gut. The movement makes me jerk, too, and blood trickles out, staining his striped shirt. I cringe. I didn't mean for that to happen.

The big man sobs, or howls is more like it, in long and deep, stuttering shudders. Despite the fact he knows something, the sound of his wails pangs through me.

Zeke seems unaffected by Henry as he rifles through the toolbox, picking things up, putting things down, revealing a plethora of possibilities in the torture department.

He makes a big show of running his leather gloved fingers over the tools before selecting a pair of pliers.

He lays the pliers aside before reaching down and slipping off one of Henry's dress shoes and the accompanying sock. Five perfectly pedicured toes stare back.

My heart picks up pace as he takes the pliers. He's just taunting, but could he cut off a toe if need be? Could I?

He wedges the pliers between Henry's toes. "Okay! Okay!"

TOWNHOME COMMUNITY

Silver Spring, Maryland
Saturday, 3:00 p.m.

It didn't take but a slight press of the pliers on Henry's delicate piggies to get him babbling about a construction site in Silver Spring, leased by the BAIN Corporation, where the extremists took Erik. Yes, Mr. CEO knows much more than he originally let on.

Zeke's driving now, and I'm in the back with a blubbering Henry, and where his cries were affecting me before, now they're annoying me.

A) I'm not even touching him, and B) he's a liar and, at this point, overdoing the crying thing. I want to tell him to shut up, but that'll just make him whimper even more. I'd rather have back the angry version of him that we started with.

If I'm ever taken and held hostage, I'm not going to blubber. I'm going to be mean and angry.

Zeke exits off 495 and winds his way out into the more sparsely populated area until we're hitting more country than city. Several new construction projects dot the landscape, and I eye each one. Henry said it was a townhome community, but so far, I'm seeing only single-family sites.

Eventually, Zeke pulls over to the side of the road and parks. "Bingo."

He takes a pair of binoculars from his glove box and peers across the road at the construction site and the skeleton of townhomes going up. While he does that, I eye the homes as well. There are only two units that are nearly done, and they sit all the way in the back corner.

Moving in between the two bucket seats that separate the front from the back of the Rover, I lean forward to point. "Those two in the back. One of those is probably where they have Erik."

With a nod, Zeke hands me the binoculars, and I readjust them to get a better look at the area. It's Saturday, so it's not odd that the workers are gone. That'll make things easier on our end. We have the whole place to ourselves.

Spinning the binocular dial, I zoom in on the completed units in the back corner, which are butted up to woods. As I do, Zeke scoots closer to me, and I get a contact high from the slight brush of his forearm against mine.

He points. "There's only one entrance to the community. We can park over to the left and make our way across. No matter what window they're looking out of, they won't be able to see us with that giant crane in the way. Of course, we have no clue what weapons they have."

Lowering the binoculars, I look into his dark green eyes, now just inches from mine, and it takes me a second to latch onto what I want to say next. "You do realize this could be a trap?"

"It's your brother," he simply says, and my heart tumbles around inside my chest.

"Thanks," I whisper, getting a little more lost in the depths of his gaze.

Those eyes flick over my shoulder, and the swift flash of alarm that flares through them has me spinning around. But Henry moves quick, lunging forward, with—holy shit—a knife! What the hell? How did he get a knife?

I dodge his lunge, and the knife nicks my upper arm as I lift the binoculars and whack him hard in the side of the head two good times.

But it doesn't even seem to faze him. Zeke tries to scramble through the seats to help me, but it all happens so fast as the big man makes another pass for me.

I whack him again—once, twice—and on the third time, his scalp splits open and blood spurts. I hit him one more time for good measure, and his body slumps forward, pinning me in place.

My breathing comes heavy as I shove at Henry's passed-out body. "Get him off me!"

Zeke comes all the way through the front seats, and it takes the two of us to roll Henry back into place. We work quickly, re-securing him, and as we do, I find a sheath on his calf where that small knife was hidden. I should've found that earlier.

With one last hard yank on the zip ties, I fall into the seat beside him. "Figurehead, my ass."

Zeke yanks hard on the ties, too, before blowing out a breath and looking across Henry's body at me. "You okay?"

I look down at the tiny sliver where he cut my forearm, but other than that I'm fine. When I look back up, he's smiling.

Smiling.

I laugh. "That wasn't funny."

Zeke reaches over and takes my wrist. He rotates my arm, studying the slight nick, and apparently appeased that it is, indeed, a surface wound, lets his smile turn into a chuckle.

"What?" I laugh some more, trying to ignore his warm and rough fingers on my skin.

Shaking his head, he reaches behind the seat and brings out a first aid kit. "Nothing, just…you are something else."

You are something else. I hope that's a good thing.

He finds a Band-Aid, and I totally expect him to hand it to me, but he shocks the hell out of me when he strips the plastic lining, takes my arm again, and smooths the Band-Aid in place. His fingers linger on my forearm, and all the air in my lungs suspends as I wait for, well, I'm not sure what.

Then he blinks, and still with his smile, he climbs back into the front, puts the Rover in gear, and says, "Let's do this."

We pull through the entrance and park over to the left where we previously identified our best spot. Dragging Henry from the Rover, we triple-check his restraints and leave him propped against a pile of construction pavers.

There's no love lost between me and Mr. CEO, and he's served his purpose. We need the Rover free in case we have to get out of here fast.

We strap on small throwing daggers like we used at the warehouse—one on my ankle, another on my thigh, and a third on my forearm. Zeke does the same.

There are fifty or so townhomes, all at various stages of construction. As I look them over, my stomach cinches tighter and tighter. Blood pounds through my veins, circling back to my heart in a restless rhythm. Just last month we did a search and rescue simulation in the TIA.

With straps secured around their chests and under their arms, Callie and I work together to first drag Jackson to safety, then Zeke. All around us debris is scattered from the fake bombing that just occurred.

"Time!" the instructor calls. "Locate. Stabilize. Extract. Well done, team. You earned first place."

Jackson and Zeke jump to their feet, and laughing, we fist-bump our success. One of the other TIA teams throws down their gear.

Callie does a little jig. "That's right. First place!"

"Yeah, well, we'll get you next time," one of the other teams says.

But that was fake, and this is real.

All of this is real.

I wish it were dark. At least then we'd have some measure of cover. But the sun beats down on us, elevating the anxious heat pulsing off my skin. As usual, Zeke appears focused and driven. I could use a lesson in that.

But he doesn't nod a go-ahead. He's waiting for me to.

If I give it too much thought, my anxiety will ramp up even more. So before I overthink things, I give the nod he's waiting for and dart off to the right. Zeke will go left, and we'll meet up in the back corner.

Ducking behind a framed-out home, I peer through the skeleton of wood and PVC, surveying our destination. If there is someone in there looking out, there is no way they could see us from the angle of the home and the big crane in front. In my periphery, I catch Zeke silently moving around a pile of bagged cement and coming down behind a bulldozer.

I cross straight through what will eventually be a living room and a kitchen and come to a crouch beneath a framed window. From this viewpoint, I have a clear shot of the townhome where my brother likely is, now just twenty feet away.

I squint my eyes, surveying every crevice, crack, and opening—knowing Zeke is doing the same from his vantage point—but I don't see anything unusual.

Across the way, we make eye contact, and with one last nod, we scurry the twenty feet and come up against the townhome, each of us on opposite sides. I wish our friends were here, that we were right beside each other, and that there was some sort of cover.

Heck, I almost wish a rifle would go off. At least then I would know for sure someone is in there. As it is, though, we're going in blind. But we're doing the best we can.

He tosses a rock, and it clears the side of the townhome, signaling me he's ready. I'll go in the front, he'll go in the back, and we'll make our way through.

I blow out a long, steady breath, and then I crack open the unlocked front door, and I slide inside. Sunlight beams in the new windows, and dust floats in the bright rays. They tickle my nose and throat, and I fight the urge to cough.

For a second, I don't move or breathe as my fingers hover over the dagger strapped to my thigh. I cock my head but hear nothing.

Swiftly, I move into the empty living room on the right, circle through it, and come out in the kitchen that only has a refrigerator, disconnected and sitting on a trolley.

Zeke comes through the other side of the kitchen, and our eyes meet. Sweat rolls down my back, and I almost shiver as it trails my spine. It is beyond hot in this house. He points up.

We slide across the pass-through bathroom and back out into the hall where the stairs lead up. He goes first, and with my fingers hovering again over the dagger on my thigh, I follow.

Twelve wooden steps up and we hit the landing, repeating what we did downstairs, me going right and him going left to meet back up at the top. This is a duplex, and Erik could very well be in the unit connected to this one. I really don't want to do this again.

The video of him comes back to mind. He was in a windowless room.

Zeke touches my arm, and his fingertips nearly sear me—he's even hotter than I am. I look into his questioning face and I mouth, *garage*.

Back down the steps we go. The garage will be empty, or my brother will be there. Either way, the sensation that this is a trap hits me hard.

My senses prick to overdrive as I become acutely aware of every tiny detail—of the sawdust sprinkling the floor and the three nails lying over in the corner; of the scent of fresh paint and the dampness of my skin; of the slight rustle of Zeke's camo pants and the pinch of hair stuck in the clasp of my necklace.

We move through the downstairs and over to the door that leads out to the garage. Slipping the dagger from my thigh holster, I put my hand on the knob and turn it.

It's unlocked, and I crack it open, leading through with the dagger up and ready, my fingertips on the blade in a throwing position.

Unlike the rest of the townhouse, it's dark in here, but a ray of sun filters in behind me to gradually illuminate the room. It takes a second for my eyes to adjust, but when they do, my heart stops.

"Erik," I whisper.

In the center of the room sits my brother, a hood over his head, and his arms and legs strapped to a metal chair. For a terrifying second, I think he's dead, but then his head moves, his chest rising on an inhalation of breath, and joy surges through me.

"Erik," I cry, rushing over and yanking off the hood.

Violently, he shakes his head, and I grapple with the gag in his mouth, tugging hard to get it free.

"No!" he shouts the second the material leaves his lips.

I grab him. "It's okay. I'm here. I'm here."

"No!" he sobs. "B-bomb. Bomb!"

I jerk away, smacking right into Zeke, and I go numb when I spy it mounted up in the corner—a bomb with the faint glow of a timer.

A timer that reads 00:00:54.

It's the bomb the cell promised to set off, and we're the target.

WOODS

Silver Spring, Maryland
Saturday, 3:30 p.m.

My gaze lands on the trip wire attached to the door handle, before darting up to the C4 secured near the ceiling. I trail to the right, following the wiring that attaches to yet another pack of C4. I turn 180 degrees and see the next C4.

I don't bother following the wiring to the next one. I don't have time.

This whole townhouse — and the one attached to it — is about to blow. My brain scrambles to remember any tiny detail of the things I've learned about bombs, but nothing pushes to the front, except… *We're about to die.*

00:00:39

"Hurry," Zeke urges, whipping out a knife and slicing through the ties around Erik's wrists.

00:00:29

Dropping to my knees, I slide a knife under the ties around my brother's ankles, but my hands are so shaky, I end up nicking my own self.

"Just go!" my brother cries. "There's not enough time."

00:00:19

I refocus, and feverishly, I saw at the ties. "Goddammit," I hiss, accidentally cutting my brother this time.

Zeke brushes my unsteady hands away and finishes the last cut.

00:00:09

Together we yank Erik from the chair and make a mad dash from the garage, through the house, across the kitchen, and the three of us scramble for the back door.

Zeke bursts through first, reaching back for me. Behind me, Erik shoves me forward at the exact second a buzz resonates across my skin. The air around me sucks in and the explosion that follows comes loud and hot, vibrating around and through me.

The power of it lifts me off my feet and propels me. My entire world slows to an animated pace as my arms and legs scramble through the air. I land on my stomach and roll a few yards, and another explosion slams into me, picking my body off the ground and flinging it another few yards.

Something pings me — glass, metal — I'm not sure, but I squeeze my eyes shut and cover my head.

My ears buzz. They ring. They go mute.

A flash of heat rolls over me, and I try to get up, but a wave of dizziness rocks me, and I dig my palms and knees into the dirt, sluggishly coming up on all fours. Lifting my head, I look through the smoke, dust, and flames.

"Erik!" I scream, barely hearing my own voice. "Zeke!"

Zeke barrels toward me, emerging through a cloud of dust and haze. His lips move, shouting something, but

I can't hear him. *Run!* I read his lips.

He doesn't lose momentum as he snatches my arm, yanking me up, and keeps going straight into the woods. Frantically, I fight him, looking over my shoulder for Erik, but Zeke keeps going.

My hearing comes back with a clear and distinct pop, and something whizzes right past my head to ricochet off a nearby tree. It takes a second for my brain to catch up with my hearing and when it does, I register that whizzing object is a bullet.

Someone is shooting at us!

That realization kicks in my speed, and I pull my arm from his grasp, signaling him I'm okay. I can run on my own.

We sprint into the woods, weaving through the trees, bullets pinging all around us. I don't think, I just run. And run. And run, concentrating on losing whoever is shooting at us. The farther in we go, the less and less the bullets come, and gradually they stop. We've lost whoever it was.

My brain, my heart, and my soul all war with one another. My heart wants to go back and look for Erik. My head tells me I need to keep going forward. My soul knows he's already gone. He pushed me out that door. He knew there wasn't enough time for both of us.

In front of me, Zeke darts to the right, and I automatically follow. Some irrational part of me hates that he's the one with me and not my brother.

Whoever planted that bomb knew I was coming. They meant for me and my brother to die. How stupid of me to fall for this trap.

Zeke comes down behind a thick clump of trees,

breathing heavy, and I kneel beside him. Together we gasp for breath, and as the seconds tick by, our breathing gradually slows back to a somewhat normal state.

Grabbing my arm, he shoves my sleeve up and pulls a chunk of glass from my skin. He tosses it aside, and his hands rove over the rest of my body, looking for anything else. Any other day I would be lost in the sensation of him touching me, but I barely register what he's doing as I close my eyes and rock with silent grief.

My mind blurs, and all the air in my lungs hangs. A slight tremble courses through me, squeezing my heart.

The pain hits deep, hollowing me out and completely robbing me of real tears. It burns in my chest, festering, aching. It hits my bones, going deep, pressing in with suffocating thickness.

Time stands absolutely still as the real-life nightmare of what just happened replays in my head. Agony, then, sharply slices through. My lungs contract with a searing breath. My heart thumps. My brain clicks.

Wildness replaces the emptiness, and a harsh laugh escapes me. I open my eyes, searching for anything to hit, and see Zeke staring at me.

I don't know exactly what happens, but everything in me just snaps. I shove him hard in the chest, and his back hits the tree. There's so much swirling inside of me—fury, vulnerability, a million other things—that I can't grasp just one.

I punch the ground. I want to scream, but somewhere in the back of my mind I know we're hiding, and I have to keep quiet. I punch the ground again, and it vibrates up my arm and into my shoulder.

"Sophie," he quietly speaks. "It's okay. I'm here."

Red-hot anger licks across my skin, and I zero in on the ground as I punch, and punch, and punch some more. All thoughts leave my head, replaced by a blinding white haze.

"Sophie," he tries again, his arms wrapping around me.

"Please," I whisper, struggling against the hold, but my voice sounds strange and empty.

"It's okay," he quietly says. "I'm right here."

The center of my chest burns, and my brain shifts. I struggle to regain the fury of a second ago, but it won't come. I try to take a breath, but it won't come, either. My lips tremble, and I dig my fingers into his forearms as guilt claws up my throat.

"He's dead, and it's all my fault." My voice cracks.

"None of this is your fault." His arms tighten even more. "This is their fault."

I shiver, and the image of my brother being blown to pieces ricochets across my mind. A sob hitches through me.

"It's okay," he whispers. "Right here."

Memories wash over me—me and my brother racing motorcycles across our property; making homemade butter on our grandfather's farm; raking our yard and getting into a leaf fight; and all the times we snuck cake...

"Sophie," Erik whispers from beside my bed.

"What?" I grumble.

"I need a partner in crime."

One of my eyes open and I stare blearily at the digital clock on my nightstand. It flicks to two a.m. "Let me guess, the chocolate cake."

Erik grins. "You know it."

With a sigh, I throw the covers back. "The things I do for you."

"You're the bestest sister in the whole wide world." Handing me my robe, he nearly skips back across my room to the door.

For as long as I can remember, Erik has done this. His sweet tooth attacks him at the oddest hours and always when I'm dead asleep. But I don't mind.

Down in the kitchen he drags the four-layer chocolate cake from the refrigerator and I pour two glasses of milk. He hands me a fork and we don't bother slicing off a piece, we just dig in.

"Mm," he moans, smacking his lips.

Playfully, I roll my eyes. "You think we'll do this even when we're in college and back for the holidays?"

"You kidding me? We're going to do this always. Even when we're old and gray."

Smiling, I fork up a bite. I like that thought.

"He's gone," I quietly moan, burying my face in my palms.

Gently, Zeke's hand grasps the back of my neck, and he squeezes. "I know."

My shoulders hunch forward, and my fingers dig into the skin on my face as more memories flood me. My entire family going sailing. Dad and Erik building a tree house. Mom teaching him how to sew a button.

Chocolate cake.

I cry silently into my hands, wanting the memories and not. They burst through my head rapid-fire—the two of us sprawled on the floor watching *King Kong*; making

Mom breakfast for Mother's Day; rigging my room with a trap to catch the Tooth Fairy.

And that damn chocolate cake.

Bitterness burns in my chest, and I rock harder, trying to soothe a pain that will be with me the rest of my life.

Zeke stays where he is, silently holding my neck, not speaking, just letting me grieve. *Erik's gone*. The words slam into me even harder, pounding through my head. Over and over again. Like a nightmare.

Air clogs in my throat, and my stomach cinches. I try desperately to ignore the hollowness spreading through me, filling me with loss, but I can't.

My brother is dead.

With a sniff, I wipe my nose with my shirt. When I finally lift my swollen eyes to Zeke, he's looking over his right shoulder. Silently, he reaches for one of his daggers. Someone is there.

No, whoever it is. He's mine.

Touching his arm, I slide my ankle dagger free and the one strapped to my upper arm as well. As I do, something shifts in me—a darkness that wasn't there before, a determination, a focus, a desire for vengeance.

A man steps into view then, dressed in all black with a dark skull cap and carrying a rifle.

This is for Erik. The man's head turns my way. His gaze lands on Zeke and me a fraction of a second before he whirls the barrel in our direction.

I don't hesitate a second, simultaneously flinging both daggers, crossing them in front of me as I do. One pierces him through the wrist of the hand holding the weapon, and the other sinks straight into his neck.

The rifle topples from his fingers, and he drops to his knees in the dirt and leaves. Blood gushes from his neck, and the sight of it fuels my fury. I could've hit him in the jugular, but instead I aimed right below. I want him coherent for questioning.

Zeke rushes out first, scanning the woods around us, and I follow, racing straight over to the man. I shove him hard, and he goes all the way down to the ground.

With a pained groan, the man grapples for the knife sticking out of his neck. I let him as I walk over and retrieve his rifle. Zeke yanks the dagger from his neck and takes a step back, giving me room. He knows I need this. This man is mine.

With a foot braced on either side, I stand over him, pointing the barrel of the gun at his head. I give his face a good, long study—the light eyes and blond hair sticking out from under the skull cap, the scar cutting through his bottom lip, the blood gushing from his neck, and his other arm twisted at an odd angle beneath him.

"I know you," I say. "Where do I know you from?"

As a response, he gurgles a chuckle.

I'm not messing around with this idiot. Leaning down, I slam the butt of the rifle into his shoulder. To his credit, he barely twitches. "I am a patriot," he says, "and I will do whatever I must to save this country."

"What the hell does that mean? Who do you work for?" I demand. "How many people are involved with this?"

His mouth works, trying to form words. I watch his

lips, waiting, and a second later a little bit of foam appears.

"No!" I drop to my knees on top of him. But it's too late. He's already popped the suicide capsule hidden in his teeth.

"You son of a bitch!"

But he doesn't answer. He's already dead.

DESERTED PARKING LOT

Silver Spring, Maryland
Saturday, 4:15 p.m.

I *stand at the entrance to the indoor obstacle course, and adrenaline tickles through my veins as I stare straight ahead at the digital clock. I have to stay under 00:03:59 to meet the fitness requirement for the TIA.*

First challenge—The Cargo. A ten-foot net climb, followed by an equal-distance log walkway to a ten-foot ladder, then an immediate ascent, and finally a twenty-foot mesh descent to the safety padding.

After that—The Slide. A climb up a thirty-foot tower to a platform where I'll grasp the rope, swing my legs up, and crawl/slide all the way back to the ground.

Then—The Climb. A twenty-foot vertical climb up a wooden ladder, over the top, and back down the other side.

And lastly—The Belly. A low crawl through thirty feet of sand, with only sixteen inches of clearance under the web of barbed wire stretching to the other side.

Excited, I bounce on my toes, and when I flex my fingers, I feel the stretch of the leather gloves that are cut off at the second knuckle for dexterity. A few pieces of dust float past, and I track them with my eyes.

"Let's do this, Sophie!" Erik shouts.

My gaze flicks to where my brother stands at the side of the course. He lifts both fists in the air and pumps them, and I smile. Beside him are my new friends—Zeke, Jackson, and Callie. As it always does, my silly heart flutters when I look at Zeke.

They all just finished this course, coming in under the expected time. I'm the last to go.

Widening my stance, a little, I rock right, left, right. I glance again at the flashing red clock. 00:00:00.

Beside the clock stands Frank and my parents. Dad squints his eyes and gives me a determined nod.

I crouch, ready. The air horn goes off, and I erupt from the start line.

Three minutes and twenty-one seconds later, the lights in the training facility flick on, and I let out a huge whoop. I did it!

My brother picks me up and spins me around. "Sophie, I can't believe it!"

"I know!" Laughing, I look around for Frank and my parents and see them coming across the course straight toward me. Mom's proud grin says it all.

Yesterday I nailed the terrorist simulation and today the obstacle course. Yes!

"Looks like the four of us are officially TIA," Zeke says, and my grin gets even bigger.

Erik swings his arm around my neck. "So proud of you, sis."

That was three years ago, when I first joined the TIA.

Since then, I've had many thoughts about saving the world. I would graduate high school, go to college, and enlist in the military. Then, after years of experience, I would join one of the agencies. I would be the patriot, not that man who just killed himself.

Honestly, though, all of this TIA stuff has always seemed like fun classes and challenging training. The obstacle courses, the rifle range, the simulations, along with studying profiles, analyzing cold cases, learning about new technologies... I knew one day I might use my new skill set. I just never imagined it would be today.

Zeke and I now sit in his Rover in an empty lot a few miles from the townhome community. Gripping the American flag pendant on my necklace, I stare at the splatter of blood covering my dirty blouse and dress pants—the same clothes I wore to the speech with William. I have no clue whose blood it is. It could be...Erik's. My brother was blown to pieces, and these spots on me could be from him.

My heart turns over heavily, and I close my eyes, like that will somehow shut out the bad stuff.

When we returned to the car, Henry, who we left tied and propped against those pavers, had a hole in his head. The man who chased us into the woods is probably the same one who shot Henry. These terrorists are doing a good job of cleaning up everything connected to them.

I've seen more dead people in the last twelve hours than I care to see for the rest of my life. This whole thing, it's too big. These extremists really do have eyes and ears everywhere.

The gunman—wait a minute, I do know him. He was Senator Gostler's aide. My God, there's no telling how many people are working on the inside.

No wonder the director is keeping this thing as contained as possible. Too many people involved leads to chaos, disagreement, and leaks. Fewer people mean efficiency and action. But even Prax's inner circle could be part of this.

Zeke shifts, turning toward me, and I say, "That man in the woods, that was Senator Gostler's aide."

"You do realize we can't go back."

"I switched out the device in Jackson's computer. I loaded a virus on Senator Gostler's system. I tried to kill the Vice President of the United States. I assaulted two of Prax's men. I carjacked an elderly lady. I kidnapped and threatened torture of the CEO of BAIN, who is also dead. I infiltrated a townhome community and set off a bomb that killed my brother. And I stabbed a man who then committed suicide." With a tired sigh, I close my eyes and press the pads of my fingers into my forehead. "Yeah, I realize we can't go back. What the hell are we going to do?"

He sighs, too, heavy and deep. "We need to eat, wash all this blood off us, get some clean clothes, and find a safe place to sit and think through all of this."

"Do you think my parents are okay?" I mumble.

"I don't know," he quietly responds, sliding his fingers around to grasp the back of my neck. Gently, he massages, working his fingers up and down the tight muscles. "I know a safe place we can go."

"Where's that?"

"My brother's." He grabs his burner phone. "Let's hope Jackson has found Callie. We need as much help as we can get."

EMPTY APARTMENT

Chevy Chase, Maryland
Saturday, 5:00 p.m.

Zeke drives to his brother's apartment, which is currently empty while he's deployed overseas. He showers first, and I barely move from my spot on the couch while I wait.

With my stare fixed on the beige carpet beneath my shoes, I think of Mom that time she walked through a spider web and squealed. Of Dad when he stepped in dog poop and gagged. Of Erik when he hid a fake snake in my parents' bed. Of all of us laughing when Pop-Pop did the chicken dance.

Of me arguing with Mom over the dress I wanted to wear to a state dinner.

With a sigh, I close my eyes. I'm never arguing with her again over anything. I'll cherish every moment. I promise I will.

The bathroom door opens, and Zeke emerges dressed in his brother's clothes. "All yours. I laid shorts and a tee out for you. They're big, but it'll get you through until

Callie gets here. Hopefully, she'll have extras in her van."

I don't even look at Zeke as I trudge to the bathroom to take my own shower.

"I'll put some food together," he says and with a nod, I close the door.

Sometime later I emerge to join Zeke at the kitchen island where he's assembled spaghetti and Coke. I slide up onto a stool and begin eating. On any other day, this would be normal—sitting next to Zeke and sharing a meal. But life as I knew it is now gone. And the hole in my heart left by Erik's death—

I stuff more food in my mouth. I need strength. I will avenge him.

My parents—they're going to lose it when they find out.

I need their arms around me right now. We need to grieve. I want to hear their voices…

If I can just figure all of this out. Yet every clue leads to more unanswered questions, and just when I think I'm about to solve the puzzle, something else happens.

We need a person on the inside. Like Frank. But I can't call him. Staying rogue is the safest bet.

Rogue. My God, I never thought I would apply that word to myself. But that is exactly what I am now.

William's smile filters through my mind, the genuine kindness behind it, the familiarity. He's like family, and I almost killed him. He was my third task. If I'd gone through with it, my brother might still be alive.

Pressure pushes behind my eyes, and I shake my head. I don't have time for this. I have to focus.

Zeke's disposable phone buzzes with a text, and he

quickly checks it. "Jackson and Callie are on the way up."

A moment later there's a knock, and he slides off the barstool to answer.

In strolls Callie, looking like she literally just walked off the trail, complete with boots, cargo shorts, a white tee, and an outback hat. Shuffling in behind her is Jackson, and just the sight of them soothes my raw soul. Neither one of them says a word as they cross the linoleum floor over to me.

"I'm so sorry," she murmurs.

She hugs me hard, not letting go, and for several minutes we stay right where we're at, me sitting on the barstool, and her standing beside me, hugging tightly as I breathe in the scent of campfire sticking to her clothes.

Two years ago, Callie lost her aunt to breast cancer and it hit my friend hard. I held her, just like she's holding me now, letting her decide when to pull back.

"You picked the worst time to go on one of your adventures," I grumble, and she chuckles softly.

Eventually I let go, and Jackson moves in, folding his tall body to hug me, too. "We're going to find these bastards," he whispers, and with a sniff, I nod.

Over to my left, Callie and Zeke talk softly as he catches her up on what's been going on. I grab a napkin off the kitchen island and blow my nose.

If Jackson is "Big Brother," Callie is definitely "Big Sister." The two of them together could rule the world if they wanted to. There really isn't anyone better than them when it comes to tech stuff. Or maybe there is, but I'm damn lucky they're on my side.

As Callie listens attentively to Zeke, she fiddles with

the tips of the short blond hair sticking out from under her hat. I used to think it was a nervous habit, but it's just the way she thinks.

When he's done, she and Jackson exchange a long and silent look. The two of them do this all the time, and it's a bit freaky. It's like they're having a whole conversation without actually speaking. As usual, Zeke and I don't say a word as we wait for whatever brilliance they're about to produce.

Then they nod in some kind of agreement, and Jackson turns his blue baseball hat around as he leans down to retrieve the backpack Callie carried in. From it, the two of them pull out an industrial laptop and a signal-jamming device. They set them side by side on the kitchen island.

Giving me a little smile, she opens the laptop. "We couldn't go to Jackson's cave, so we're limited to my supplies. But no worries. I've got some good stuff stored in my van." She presses her index finger on the print scan.

"Hmm," she grunts as the computer boots up.

Jackson peers over her shoulder at the screen. "Huh," he agrees.

"Okay," she says, rubbing her hands together. "First order of business. There is something in this apartment sending out a signal." She reaches back into her backpack, pulls out a signal detector, and hands it to me. "Find it."

I take the square object from her hand, and it beeps.

Jackson grins. "Well, that was easy. It's you."

I jump off the stool and look down at my body. I have on a pair of too-big gym shorts and an oversize T-shirt. "What do you mean?"

Reaching over the kitchen island, Zeke's fingers brush my neck as he grasps my vintage American flag necklace. My eyes lift to his, widening. Quickly, I take it off and hold it up to the detector, and the beeping gets faster.

I look at all my friends, and dread settles through me. "I've had this on the whole time. This is how they've been tracking and watching everything that I'm doing."

"Well, that, in addition to the cameras they've hacked." Callie cringes. "Sorry."

My friends know how much this necklace means to me, but before I second-guess anything, I shove it at Zeke. "You do it."

With a nod, he rushes into the bathroom. A flush echoes out, and my gut sinks. That necklace belonged to my grandmother, passed down by her mother, my great-grandmother. She gave it to me when I turned thirteen, and I've worn it every day since.

Which means… "Only someone on the inside would have access to that necklace," I say. "How long do you think that's been active?"

Jackson shrugs. "Could be just today, or weeks, or you could've been wearing that around for months and never known it."

I press the pads of my fingers into my forehead. "My God, if I've truly been wearing that for months, I've been showing them the insides of everything, including the White House." I look around. "Including this place."

Callie snaps her laptop closed. "Which is why we need to move. Now."

CALLIE'S CAMPER

Chevy Chase, Maryland
Saturday, 5:45 p.m.

We're inside Callie's Volkswagen camper, which she tends to live in more than she does her own home. Her dad's a janitor at CIA Headquarters and works nights. As long as she checks in every day, he's fine with her doing whatever.

That kind of freedom boggles my mind.

Mom was much like Callie when she was younger. Full of wanderlust. The adventurer. The fearless one.

Why then has Mom had such tight reigns on me lately?

"Does she not trust me?" I ask Erik.

"No." He shakes his head. "Mom trusts you a hell of a lot more than me. Maybe she's scared."

"Scared of what?"

He shrugs. "Losing you? I don't know."

I scoff.

Our words come back to me now and with them, new insight. I think my brother may have been onto something and he didn't fully realize it. Because now that I've lost him,

I would do anything to rewind the clock and do things over.

If Mom were here, she'd feel the same way.

Her path, though, led us to today. Military, college, politics. Her choices mapped out Erik's life and mine.

Because of her, not me, Erik is dead. That thought prods my brain like a rusty knife. It's the wrong way to think, but it momentarily takes the weight off my shoulders and puts it onto hers.

The rational side of me knows the terrorist cell is responsible for my brother's death, but my heart won't let me accept the logic.

Callie pulls on the vinyl blinds covering the camper's windows to let in the late afternoon light, and I automatically shrink away from whoever might see inside, since we're parked within sight of the apartment building.

"Don't worry, the windows are treated with privacy film. We can see out, but no one can see in." She takes a small reflector and mounts it in the window. Then she opens her laptop, disengages the lock screen with her print, and keys a few things. "The bad guys will think we're in Africa."

She opens a drawer under her seat and pulls out another industrial laptop. Where hers is silver and purple, this one is riddled with flowered stickers. That's the laptop she used last year. She hands it to Jackson. "There, now get to work."

He takes it. "I thought you traded this one in for that one."

She shrugs. "Sentimental, I guess."

"Flowers," he grumbles, and she smirks.

She plops down at the tiny table, and he scoots into the seat opposite her, leaving Zeke and me nowhere to sit but the unmade bed. Like everything else in here, it is miniature, and my whole right side brushes his left as we sit down.

We've sat beside each other a million times over the years, but never on a bed. I try not to look down at our touching thighs and to hold still and not lean my shoulder farther into his. But he's a magnet, and I have no control over his pull on me.

He shifts, and my attention moves from our touching thighs up to his dark green eyes. I expect him to look away, or maybe smile and break contact, but he doesn't.

We stare at each other, and my heart pounds so fast it pulsates in my neck. I swallow, and his eyes leave mine to trail down to my throat.

Sliding his hand over, he gently intertwines our fingers, and together we look down at our joined hands. A faint tremor courses through me as he caresses my wrist with his thumb.

Everything around me fades, and I am no longer racing against terrorists, nor am I the daughter of the president. I'm just me, sitting here beside the boy I love, holding hands and sharing a moment.

This isn't one-sided. He feels something for me, too.

"Okay, so, the good news is I sent Callie the data off the flash drive before Prax came and got me from my cave," Jackson says. "The bad news is she didn't know it, so she's only just begun decrypting."

Zeke slides his hand back over onto his lap, and he shifts forward on the bed to focus on our friends. He takes a second, probably working through things, before responding. "Why didn't you tell us that before?"

Jackson glances up. "Um, hello? Like any of us have

had time?"

Callie clicks some keys. "And seeing as how he's been working on a fake device, and I've been out of the loop, we're not as far as we could be decrypting this info."

"What do you have so far?" I ask.

"The thing about a cell is that it doesn't just pop up overnight. There is always a history there. A motivation. Brotherhood Alliance International Network. They pride themselves on peacekeeping, world relations, and global unity. At least that's their front." She grabs a piece of paper from her backpack and hands it to us. "For such a 'peaceful' organization they sure do business with a lot of international terrorists. They do like their bombs."

My eyes trail over the paper and the list of names. I recognize them from our TIA classes. "Did you hack their system?"

"Yes, and the thing is, I located a string of data that seemed off to me. I did a few variations and finally figured out it simply means August the fourth. BAIN was created fifteen years ago, and so I focused on that particular August fourth, and would you like to know what happened on that day fifteen years ago?"

"Yes," we answer.

She keys a few strokes and turns her laptop around for us to see. On the screen are several pictures of a small community that has been bombed. I scoot off the bed, closer to the laptop, and my stomach clenches. Dead bodies, some are kids.

"*That* is Lone Eagle," she says. "Your parents and the VP were all in the military together. That's how they met."

"Yes," I whisper, unease pooling in the pit of my stomach.

"They did that," she softly tells me. "They were involved in weapons testing out in Nevada, code name Lone Eagle, and one of the drones went off course and bombed that community."

I suck in a breath. "No."

"There were a lot of innocent lives lost," she says.

I look over at Zeke. "I've never heard about this. Have you?"

He shakes his head. "No clue."

"It was covered up," Callie tells us.

"And my parents were part of this? You're sure?"

She takes a second before quietly saying, "Your mom is the one who accidentally mis-programmed that drone."

I put my hand over my mouth. "My God."

"There was a small military group involved in that day," she says, "and though they weren't allowed to do anything official for the survivors, they pooled their resources and did what they could."

I look away from the laptop and the bodies, and rawness claws across my chest. Mistakes happen, sure, but a mis-programmed drone and a bombing are huge. Mom would never have been voted president if the public knew this story. For fifteen years, Mom and Dad have lied to me and Erik. They lied to everybody.

I ask, "Are we saying the BAIN organization is run by the survivors of that community? The survivors are the domestic extremists who are doing all of this?"

She nods. "Yes."

"And the CEO, Henry?"

"From what I can tell, he was the leader in name only, a puppet. Not innocent, but certainly not the mastermind of everything going on." She looks between us. "They have people working on the inside of the United States government. That's how they have so much privileged information. Guys, this shit's real."

"'Your mother will get what she deserves.' There was an asset at the safe house, and that's what he said to me."

"This is revenge then?" Jackson asks. "The survivors are trying to off the military team involved that day? We accidentally bombed them, and so they retaliate by bombing us? Why pick today, though? Why not on the August fourth anniversary?"

"Because that would have given it away too easily?" Callie suggests. "Who knows?"

"Erik knew there was something going on. He was trying to work it from the inside and stop all of this from happening." I look between my friends. "We need a list of everyone who had anything to do with Lone Eagle, on our side and the community survivors."

"No." Zeke motions out the windows. "We need to move. Now."

Our heads swivel in sync to see two men dressed in jeans, windbreakers, and ball caps approaching the entrance to the apartment building where his brother lives. One of them shifts, and I catch sight of a weapon in a shoulder holster.

That one says something to the other, motioning him to go around back. We may have flushed my necklace, but before we did, it gave off a signal that they're following up on.

As Callie climbs behind the wheel and pulls away, I study the men now entering the building, one in the front and one in the back. And like that man in the woods who shot at us, these men seem familiar, but I can't place them.

We're now safely in the parking lot of a grocery store. While Callie and Jackson work in sync on their laptops, Zeke and I look through pages of photos and information, everything tracing back to that day fifteen years ago.

There is a picture of my mom and dad and another of William and Senator Gostler. A lot of names and photos I don't recognize. There's a black and white photo of the director wandering through the desolate community after the bombing. He's dressed in military fatigues, and his face appears hard and exhausted.

Prax was part of Lone Eagle, too. That's why he's trying so hard to keep this controlled and private. If news gets out, it'll lead back to that day and the subsequent cover-up and lies. His ass is on the line.

"From what I can tell, there were eight ops involved in the misfire. The president and VP, your dad, Senator Gostler, Prax, and the others are civilians now..." Jackson's voice trails off, and I suspect he's realizing what I am. Those civilians are targets, too.

Zeke nudges me, pointing to a name on a document he's reviewing. "Max Grayson came from that community. Isn't that your brother's friend?"

"Yes...that's odd."

"He was with Erik, Danforth, and Britta last night," he reminds me. "You even called him at one point, right?"

I nod. "Yes, and we just found our next lead."

MAX GRAYSON'S APARTMENT

American University
Saturday, 6:15 p.m.

Callie lends me clothes, and as she drives, the guys keep their backs to me so I can change.

"Strategy," I say, slipping out of the oversized gym shorts and into camo pants. "It has to be me who goes in. I'm the one Max knows. We need an audio device planted in his apartment."

"Agree," Jackson says.

I take off the big tee and push my arms through a small, gray racer-back tank top.

"Tracker, too," Zeke says. "On his body."

"Okay," I tell the guys. "Done."

Zeke turns around, and as I lace up the boots Callie lent me, I'm aware of his stare. She's shorter than me and a bit lighter, so these clothes are snugger than I usually wear. But it's not like I have a ton of choice.

She glances in the rearview. "You look like the female version of Zeke."

I look at Zeke, and we smile. Finishing with the laces, I

say, "Audio device planted in the apartment and a tracker on his body. The first will be easy. The second, not so much, but I'll figure it out."

Callie parks outside of Max's college apartment and cuts the engine. "I'd love to outright question him."

"Me, too," I agree. "But if he's linked to the terrorists, then that'll just set off alarm bells."

A few students stroll by. They have no idea our nation is under threat and my parents are in hiding. That my brother is dead and I'm on the run. And that my mom, a woman I've greatly admired and respected, is a liar and responsible for many, many deaths.

My mom...anger courses through me, followed by deep-rooted disappointment. *Admired and respected.* Despite our recent differences, I still thought in present tense when it came to those two verbs. I never imagined I would use the past form of them when thinking of her.

Callie moves from her seat to the back of the camper. From a cabinet above Jackson's head, she grabs a metal box and begins rifling through it. Her camper is much like Jackson's cave in that it's full of various techy things. She's got several surveillance items that'll do the trick.

Jackson opens the flowered laptop. "We'll monitor you from in here."

You continuously exceed my expectations. Frank has said that to me many times over the years.

Standing beside me, Frank adjusts his sunglasses, surveying the small crowd gathered on the hospital's lawn. He's quieter than usual.

I am, too, because something is off. This Children's National fundraising event was last minute. The twenty-five kids and their parents were pre-screened. We're about to begin the picnic and magic show.

But the tenseness in my shoulders tells me something is off.

My eyes carefully track across the kids, the parents, the nurses and doctors scattered about, before landing on a doctor standing to the side. He's smiling, watching the kids, giving every appearance of enjoying the mild, sunny day.

Mild, sunny day.

Why then is he shivering? There's twenty-five sick kids here and none of them are shivering.

"Two o'clock," I say to Frank. "Doctor in green scrubs and white coat. Short gray hair. Sunglasses."

Frank flicks his attention to the doctor, and apparently agreeing with me, calls it in. Secret service surreptitiously moves in to guide the doctor off the lawn. He is searched and a gun is found.

Taking his sunglasses off, Frank turns to me. "You continuously exceed my expectations, Sophie. Not even I caught that one. Thanks to you these children are safe."

The memory bolsters me. Later we found out that man was in disguise as a doctor and had intended on shooting up the crowd, children and all.

I wish the events of today were as easy to figure out as that shaking man. I'm sure Frank feels the same way.

Frank…

The last time I saw him was in the hospitality room back at the Ripley Center, and the director had just relieved him of duty.

I've known Frank for as long as I can remember, and I don't think I've ever seen anything like the expression on his face as those two men escorted me out. Love. Care. Stress. Worry. There was a lot going on in his eyes.

Outside of the TIA, he has taught me a lot, personally. Does he regret teaching me to basically be a fugitive? But he'd do the same thing in my shoes.

"Be as normal as possible," Zeke says. "Remember we have no clue if Max is actually involved, and if he is, to what extent."

New nerves kick in. "I know."

"You don't have to do this," he says quietly. "We can think of another way. We can always out ourselves to the director and give him everything we know."

I take a second to look at each of my friends, and I don't hesitate with my answer. "No. Until we have an idea who all the inside people are, we are keeping this to ourselves. Max's name was on that list. He's our lead, and I'm following it."

Callie hands Zeke a silver bracelet. "That's the transmitter she'll wear."

He levels intense eyes on me as he clips it around the same wrist that he caressed earlier. "If at any point you're uncomfortable, just say the word." His fingers linger on the bracelet, and the heat from them seeps into my skin. "Remember, we're listening."

From the metal box, Callie hands me a black disc. "That's the audio device you'll plant." Next, she hands me a clear tab. "And that's the tracker you'll put on Max."

I slip the black audio disc inside my front pocket. I already have an idea of where I'll put it. I remove the backing on the tracker and stick it to my index finger. I have no clue how I'll transfer this to his body, but I'll figure it out.

Jackson clicks a few keys. "Everything is synced."

I take a second to breathe, and no one says a word as they wait.

I got this.

I can do this.

"Okay, I'm ready."

Zeke opens the camper door for me, and I step outside. He holds my wrist. "Remember we're right here." With an encouraging nod, he lets go and closes the door.

I've been to Max's place before. Two years ago, Max had just turned eighteen and moved in. He'd invited a few people over, including my brother. My parents insisted I go, too. They think if I go places with him it'll keep him out of trouble, and usually, he never seemed to mind. But that day he did. He was giving me the major cold shoulder.

Max had opened the door, and Danforth was already inside. Britta and Erik hadn't met yet, so she wasn't there. And though he tried to hide it, Max sort of curled his lip when he saw I was tagging along. It didn't exactly make me feel welcome.

"Sorry," my brother had mumbled, and Max shrugged. I wished I could turn around and go back home.

Then they disappeared through the crowd and back into the kitchen, and I hung awkwardly in the living room with Frank. There were a lot more people there than expected, and I knew none of them. Many of them cast me curious stares. Being the daughter of the president, I was used to that.

Frank handed me a drink from the cooler and tried not to hover. I attempted to blend in and talk to a couple of girls, but I really just wanted to go. Then my brother had disappeared into Max's bedroom, leaving Danforth back in the kitchen. They were in the room for a while, and when they opened the door, another person came out with them. Someone who had not initially gone in. A woman who had obviously already been in there waiting.

But at that point, the crowd was even thicker, and no one seemed to notice. Not even my brother's guard. Not even mine.

"You ready to go?" Erik had asked me, and I nodded.

Later that night, I brought up the mystery woman with my brother, but he adamantly denied I had seen anybody. I had, though.

That was two years ago. Did my brother know something was going on even back then? Maybe.

I focus on my objective as I raise my fist and knock on the apartment door. Max has the music up loud. The door swings open, and surprise flicks across his expression.

"Sophie?" Pushing his dark-rimmed glasses up his nose, he glances beyond me, obviously looking for Frank.

If he's innocent in all of this, then he has no clue what's going on. He doesn't know my brother and Danforth are dead and Britta is missing. If this guy isn't innocent, then I'm about to find out how good of a liar he is.

Behind his glasses, he fingers the inside corner of his right eye. "I was just studying."

The last time I talked to him was on the phone when I asked him if he knew where my brother was. I stay with that and don't tell him anything else. "Can we talk?" I ask.

"Um." He peers over his shoulder, and I follow his line of sight down the hall to where his bedroom door stands open on the left. To the right is the living room, and straight ahead, the kitchen. The entire place smells like pizza and old socks. Hesitantly, he turns back.

"Frank's in the car," I say. "I told him I'd be just a minute."

I step into the apartment, not giving him a chance to say no. He laughs nervously as I shut the door, and we stand awkwardly in the small hallway. He scratches his patchy auburn beard, and I try to read his twitchy body language. Honestly, he just seems wired on caffeine.

"I still haven't heard from Erik," I fib, "and was wondering if you had?"

He frowns in honest-looking confusion. "No, I haven't."

My eyes track back down the hall to his open bedroom door and the loud music coming out of it. "Mind turning that down?" I ask.

Anxiously, he rubs his palms on his jeans. "Uh, sure."

He hustles down the hall and into his bedroom, and I don't waste a second bee-lining it over to a light fixture attached to the wall. I pull the tiny black listening device from my front pocket, rise up on my tiptoes, and drop it inside.

And though my heartbeat is all over the place, I'm casually leaning up against the wall when he closes his bedroom door and steps back out into the hall.

Down at his waist, I note that he's wearing the same black leather belt he always is around his low riding jeans. If he took the belt off, the jeans would likely fall to his knees. Either way, this is good because I just figured out where to plant the tracker on him. Now I just need to figure out *how*.

He scratches his patchy beard again as he turns toward the kitchen. "You want something to drink?"

"Sure," I say with a nonchalant shrug.

I follow him down the hall. As I pass his closed bedroom door, I itch to look inside, but I'm not quite sure how to accomplish that.

In the tiny kitchen, he opens his fridge, grabs a two-liter bottle of orange soda, and pours me a glass. As he does, I come up with a plan.

Quickly, I peek down at my index finger and at the clear tracker that is still attached. I've never been an actor. I can't conjure an emotion just by willing it so, but I keep my head bowed.

I think of Erik blown to pieces, Danforth's acid-treated body, and the fact Britta is still missing—and just like that, I've worked up an honest reaction.

Max turns. I sniff and wipe my nose. He puts the glass down on the table and takes a few hesitant steps in my direction.

I sniff again, louder.

"Hey," he whispers, taking the bait and closing the gap between us. "What's going on?"

"I'm…I'm just really worried about my brother," I croak.

He squeezes my shoulder. "Anything I can do?"

I shake my head, leaning forward, and then I'm in his embrace. I wrap my arms around his skinny body, tucking my fingers under his belt and pushing the tracker against the leather. I press my cheek into his chest, wincing at his body odor, and my breath hitches.

He pats my back but doesn't say anything.

I let an awkward minute go by before pulling away and wiping my eyes. I smile up at him. "Sorry about that."

"It's okay." He smiles back.

I turn away. "Well, anyway, if you hear from my brother, will you let me know?"

"Of course," he assures me.

He walks me to the front door.

"Thanks again," I say. Without looking back, I stroll down the sidewalk, cutting off to the right in case he's still standing in the doorway. A block down, my friends pick me up.

"I'm not worthy," Callie jokes.

"What?" I look between them all.

"You were almost too good at that," Jackson tells me.

Yeah, I guess that did go a lot better than I imagined.

The flowered laptop crackles, a few clicks echo, and the audio device I planted in the light fixture picks up Max's voice. He's placing a call. "Sophie was here," he says to whoever is on the other end. "Is there something I should know?"

Zeke and I exchange a curious look.

"Meet at the location," comes a woman's voice.

"Thirty minutes," Max says and clicks off.

We were right in coming here, because he knows something, and we're about to find out what.

Bethesda, Maryland
Saturday, 7:15 p.m.

C allie navigates the streets out of D.C., following the tracker.

Max is involved in this, though to what extent I'm not sure. Does he know his friends are dead? He's probably just a pawn in this elaborate plan, manipulated by whoever the mastermind is.

I suspect he and my brother found out about Lone Eagle, but the question is when. Who told them? Was it that mystery woman from a couple of years ago and was she possibly the one on the phone with him?

And why didn't my brother ever tell me any of this?

Because he was protecting me. He was being my big brother.

Callie's laptop dings, and because she's driving, she presses her print to unlock it and hands it back to us. In the upper right corner, a window displays local news where a bombing has occurred in Manassas.

Three dead: a wife, husband, and a son.

The reporter goes on to say the husband is retired military, then his name flashes onto the screen, and it exactly matches one on our list. He was on the Lone Eagle team with my parents.

Eye for an eye. What a shit storm.

With a sigh, I scoot away from the laptop and sit down on the camper's bed. "It's my guess that there are some survivors who want to take down all those involved and expose the cover-up, and there are others who suspected what was going to happen today and are trying to stop it."

"Like Max, and he got Erik on board," Callie says, and I nod.

I ask myself which way I would go, and without a doubt I'd go the way of my brother. Because even though our parents are responsible, this plot of retribution is wrong. Horribly wrong. A gruesome and terrible mistake was made those fifteen years ago, but a mistake it was.

I say, "The survivors who want retribution have built their lives around blending in."

"There's no telling how many of them work for our agencies," Zeke says.

"Which is why we need that list of inside people." I look at the flowered laptop and the encrypted data still scrolling it. I'm no hacker, but it seems to be taking longer than usual to break it.

"It's on a loop," Jackson says. "Most of what it's giving me are details of the events that have already transpired. The chunk we really need, the part that says who the inside people are and what other plans they have for today, is being rerouted to several servers for this exact reason. But I'll find it."

"I know you will." Between him and Callie, one of them will.

But are we doing exactly what the extremists want? By tracking Max, he's either leading us into a trap, like the townhouse bombing, or distracting us from something else that's about to happen.

Either way, he's our only lead. There's no way we're not following through.

We track him to Bethesda, Maryland.

He parks in an open spot and walks down Elm Street.

Callie circles, not having any luck finding a spot of her own, and while she does, we get ready. From her metal box of supplies we grab coms, each sticking one in our ear. I still have the transmitter around my wrist, and the guys both grab one, too. But where mine is a silver bracelet, theirs resemble a leather friendship type.

Jackson's still wearing his baseball cap, and Callie gives me her outback hat. We put on tinted glasses, and that's about as good as it gets in the disguise department.

"Still no luck," she says, circling again. "You jump out, and I'll monitor from in here." Her laptop is set up back on the console, open and running. She gives it a quick scan. "He turned down Bethesda Lane and has stopped midway."

"I'll cut through the garage and come in the back of Redwood Bar and Grill," Zeke tells me. "There are several outdoor tables. That's probably where he's at."

I adjust the outback hat, pulling it down farther onto

my head. "Jackson and I will cover opposite ends of the Row."

She slows to a stop, and we jump out. Zeke heads toward the garage, and Jackson and I take off down the street. Max went down Elm, so I cut across to Bethesda Avenue and Jackson circles around. With Zeke in the center at the restaurant, we'll have our target covered from three directions. Hopefully, one of us will be able to see or hear something.

"His meet is here," Zeke reports, his deep voice curling through my ear.

I come up on the corner of Bethesda Avenue and Bethesda Lane. There are a ton of people, some out shopping, others eating, and I struggle to see through them all, plus the shadows cast by the buildings. Way at the end, I catch sight of Jackson pretending to window shop.

There's a woman who appears to be in her late forties. She's got an athletic build and short, salt and pepper hair. I study her for a second, realizing this is the woman who came out of Max's bedroom those years ago.

Standing in Redwood Bar, Zeke has the best vantage point. "They're speaking in sign language," he whispers. "What the hell?"

"In case someone's listening," I respond. "That's smart. You getting pictures?"

"Yes," he answers, and through my com, his phone clicks a few times.

I step around a family sharing ice cream, and the new angle gets me a better look at the two of them.

I wish I knew ASL.

Wait, Jackson does. His grandmother is deaf. "Jackson,"

I whisper.

"On it," he whispers back. "Max is saying he's done. That this isn't what he thought. He's also demanding to know where Erik is."

I keep quiet and wait for more translation.

He whispers, "The woman is saying not to worry about Erik and that he's fine. Now they're signing an address in Falls Church."

"What address?" Zeke asks.

"Not sure. Hang on…"

Someone steps in my way, and I look around them in time to catch Max shaking his head. A couple of tense beats go by, and with a nod of acquiescence, the woman pushes back from the table and stands.

What happens next is so quick, it takes me a couple of seconds to register it all. From inside her lightweight jacket, she pulls out a gun with a silencer, and as she passes Max, still sitting at the table, she turns and shoots him in the head.

He slumps forward, the woman tucks the weapon away and keeps walking, and the crowd, one by one, begins to notice what has happened. By the time she's reached the spot where I'm standing, the entire pedestrian street has broken out in chaos.

She doesn't notice me as she keeps her head down and passes right by.

Zeke sprints from the restaurant, turning toward me. But the crowd is thick, and if I wait, we might lose this lead. Turning, I spy the woman already up Bethesda Avenue and about to cut across to the trail.

I do the only thing I can, and I take off after her.

CAPITOL TRAIL

Bethesda, Maryland
Saturday, 7:45 p.m.

The woman isn't running, and so neither do I, but she's walking at a quick clip, trying not to draw attention. She weaves in and out of people on the sidewalk, heading past shops and up toward the trail, and I keep pace. She has a loaded weapon, and I definitely don't need to give her a reason to shoot up the crowd.

"Did you see where she went?" Zeke asks in my ear, and the timbre of his steady voice helps me to focus. I'm about to respond when the woman takes an unlocked bike off a rack, climbs on, and pedals down the trail.

"Son of a bitch," I whisper. She had that bike planted and ready to go.

"What is it?" Jackson asks, huffing a bit.

I survey all the bikes, seeing various styles of locks on every one of them. "Crap." I spin away from the bike rack. I could pick one of those locks, given time, but that's one thing I don't have.

I spot an older man just up the trail, dressed in one

of those biker outfits and leaning against a tree drinking water. More importantly, his bike is propped on a nearby bench.

"She just took off on a bike," I tell my friends, running toward the older man and his wheels. He looks at me curiously. "I need your bike," I tell him, jumping on.

He pushes off the tree. "Hey!"

This is the second bike I've stolen in under twenty-four hours, and unlike the first time, I don't promise to bring it back. In fact, I'm not polite at all as I ignore him and take off in a full pedal.

A few trail lights flip on with the shift from day to dusk. I spy the woman up ahead, curving through the trees. I pedal harder, swerving around runners, roller-bladers, and other bikers. Several people yell at me, and I block them out.

The woman must sense my presence because she squints over her shoulder, catches sight of me, and comes up off the seat as she puts all her energy into picking up the pace. Up ahead sits an intersection, and she doesn't bother waiting for a light. She keeps right on going across the busy street, and several cars honk while others squeal to a stop.

My stomach dips as I use the pause in traffic to race through the opening. I catch a wheelie, jumping the curb, and come down with a hard thud that reverberates up my spine to my jaw.

The bike wobbles, and I kick it down a gear, throwing all my weight into the right pedal, and I keep going. For miles we do this, and I thank God for all the various activities Frank always has me doing—running, biking,

MMA. Being fit comes in handy.

We reach a spot in the trail where pedestrians have thinned out, and so have the intermittent lights. My friends are all talking in my ear, but I'm too breathless to respond with anything other than a grunt. They know where I'm at because I'm still wearing my coms and tracker. I have to trust they'll catch up eventually.

My breaths come hard, my thighs scream, but I have to catch this woman.

To the right runs the Potomac, and she veers down the bank toward the dock and dark water beyond. *What the…?* My God, she's going in the river!

Her bike heads down the bank, across the dock, and sure enough, she flies in. I brake to a stop, gasping for air, and watch with about a dozen other people as the woman surfaces and swims downstream.

"What an idiot," someone says.

"That water's nasty," someone else comments.

I jump off the bike and race down the dock. Canoes and kayaks are lined up, but they're all locked together with a long chain. Between the current and her swimming, the woman is way down the river now. But I don't jump in and follow. There's no way to catch her.

Callie stands beside me, her laptop propped in the crook of her left arm, while the fingers of her right hand race across the keys as she tries to figure out who that woman was. While she does that, I look around the group still gathered at the dock and gossiping about what just happened.

The guys trot up the bank to where we stand on the side of the dimly lit path. More than a few people are starting to look at us. Luckily, it's almost dark out, and I'm still wearing the outback hat and amber-tinted glasses, so hopefully no one recognizes me.

Her laptop dings, and I move in. Zeke comes up behind me, looking over my shoulder, and the warmth of him sinks into my back.

Callie says, "Okay, the pictures Zeke managed to grab weren't very good, but one has come back with ten markers on facial recognition and has identified her as Danielle Fox. As in Fox Development. She owns a ton of property in the area, including that townhome community, and she's on the board of directors for BAIN."

Jackson shifts to see the screen. "Let me guess— she's one of the community survivors of the Lone Eagle mission. But that wasn't her name back then."

"Which goes to my point. There's no telling how many of them are out there, planning on getting back at the U.S. government for what happened." I glance between my friends. "For that matter, there's no telling how many they've recruited for their cause."

Zeke whistles. "This thing's huge."

Take the root out, and it won't grow.

I don't know if Danielle Fox is the mastermind, but if she is, we've got to take her out.

"Max seemed somewhat harmless," Jackson points out. "I don't get it. Why kill him?"

"I have a feeling he wasn't completely cooperating. I think he was faking his involvement, trying to work it from our side with my brother. They just weren't fast enough in figuring everything out."

"And they lost their lives because of it," Callie whispers.

My heart squeezes with fresh sadness, and none of us say anything because there's nothing *to* say. There are no words of comfort.

I give my head a shake. I have to stay in the here and now.

"I've got the address they signed in Falls Church," Jackson says. "We need to go over there and see what it is."

Callie's laptop dings again, and she takes a second to read the update. "Another bomb. Civilian target. Retired military. Herndon. They took her out in a car explosive."

Another bomb. And another member of the Lone Eagle team terminated.

LEESBURG PIKE

Falls Church, Virginia
Saturday, 9:00 p.m.

As we drive, none of us speak and I imagine their brains are on the same frustrating loop as mine. Traffic isn't bad, and it takes us roughly thirty minutes to get to the address in Falls Church. It's an acre of undeveloped land off of Leesburg Pike, surrounded by a variety of buildings: single family homes, apartments, even a school a few blocks away.

Callie pulls into an apartment complex across the street, and we sit studying the dark lot through the windows of the camper. I take in the houses on both sides and the thick trees of the vacant acre. Cars zoom by on the Pike, and people stroll the sidewalk. It's definitely busy for nine at night.

Why would they have been signing this address?

I look at the houses again, one on each side of the vacant lot. They're two-story, white wood, with porches. Nothing seems odd about them. I turn from the window. "Up for a little ground recon?"

"Absolutely," Jackson says.

"Flashlights?" I ask Callie and she points to a crate tucked under the bed. I grab three and hand the guys each one.

Zeke gives me one of my throwing daggers, which I strap onto my ankle. "Let's do this."

Callie takes her laptop. "Meanwhile, I'll see what I can dig up on those houses."

We're still wearing our coms from before, and we give them a quick test to see they're still functioning okay. Then we climb from the camper, and after waiting for a free spot in the traffic, the three of us jog across the Pike and over onto the sidewalk. Though it's completely dark now, I don't hesitate in stepping into the thick woods of the empty lot.

We flick on our lights. Jackson heads right, and Zeke left, leaving me to cover the center. But I don't move.

"Always give your body a second to catch up with your brain and surroundings," the TIA tactical instructor says. "I've been watching you in the trainings and have noted you're too quick to respond."

"I thought that was a good thing," I say.

"It is, but sometimes you have a disconnect with your environment. A tiny pause will eliminate that. You'll see."

I stand, my flashlight beam flicking off the trees and thick foliage, giving that tiny pause the instructor said. I wait for my Spidey senses to go on alert.

But they don't.

I inch forward with caution, ducking under branches, moving limbs aside, and toeing away thick underbrush. My breaths come out fluttery and almost too loud in the darkness around me. I have no clue what I'm looking for. Maybe there's nothing here. But they signed this address for a reason.

About halfway in on the lot, I'm no longer crunching foliage and instead stepping over a softer area, like moss. Stopping in my strides, I bounce a little bit, and the ground beneath my boots gives. I shine my flashlight down, but everything appears the same—dried leaves, pine needles, and dirt.

I go down on my hands and knees to sweep away the ground cover, but nothing moves. It's like it's glued in place. Wedging the flashlight in my mouth, I shine the beam on the ground as I explore a crease. It's big, outlining a large square that I estimate to be roughly six-by-six feet.

Moving to the side to get my weight off of it, I dig my fingers in as far they'll go and strain to pull up, but the square won't budge.

I look up and around, hoping to see either one of the guys, but the foliage is thick, and I can't make out their lights. Either that or they turned them off.

I do see a faint green glow, though, and my muscles freeze in place. The glow is coming from a camera mounted to a tree branch. It's disguised with vegetation, just like this door, but there is no mistaking it is definitely a camera.

Pointed right at me.

Whoever or whatever is below this hidden door knows I'm here, and I am officially screwed.

"Turn around," I whisper into my coms, praying the guys hear me. "I'm caught."

I yank my coms off, not even giving anyone a chance to argue, and I use my flashlight to destroy them. If I'm compromised, my friends are not going down with me.

A red dot dances across my body, glowing bright in the darkness of the trees, and the air around me closes in. Panic clenches through my stomach. Someone has a gun trained on me.

A red-headed man dressed in jeans and a black tee steps from behind a tree with a Glock pointed right at me. My hands shoot straight up into the air.

Though my pulse spikes through my veins, I concentrate on staying as still and calm as possible. I recognize him. Years ago, he came with a team of people to update the security on our country home. At the time, I assumed he worked for the security company.

"You will walk to the house behind me." The man speaks slow and deep. "And you will do it calmly and without issue. Do not try anything. Because if you do, my team will not hesitate to shoot you. Do you understand?"

I don't falter in responding, "Yes, I understand."

The man motions for me to get up, and I do. He steps to the side and waves me on, his barrel still trained on me. Using my flashlight, I lead the way across the dark lot, hoping my friends can see what's happening and that they all got free.

I step through leaves and my brain scrambles to latch onto a plan. I can't overpower this man and run. I have to trust my friends won't try anything here in these woods, because I don't doubt there are other weapons trained on me, and they won't hesitate to shoot.

I do have the small dagger strapped to my ankle and

hidden under my pants, and just knowing it's there brings me a tiny level of comfort.

Over to the left, some distance away, runs the busy street, and beyond that, the parking lot where Callie sits. The sight of her Volkswagen camper helps me breathe a little easier. By now, hopefully, the guys are back with her. Whatever happens to me, they know everything, and I have to believe they'll stop this terrorist cell before they find and assassinate my mom.

I step from the woods and onto gravel, now at the big white house. My chest tightens as I climb the steps up to the porch, and I'm more than aware the man and his gun are right behind me. I have no idea what's going to happen when I walk through that door.

The door to the house opens from the inside, and my thoughts polarize. Something tells me if I go in, I'm not coming out.

My feet falter—"Frank?"

"Taffy Pop secured," the man behind me says.

Frank's lips thin into an angry line as he steps aside and waves me in. I'm so dumbfounded to see him standing there that I have no response but to step over the threshold. Somewhere in the back of my mind, I'm relieved to see a friendly face, but the confusion overpowers the relief.

I walk fully into the house and the door closes behind me. Karen crosses through the living room, coming straight toward me. The last time I saw her was when she and Frank drove me to the safe house where I was taken when this horrible day began.

There are a few other agents here, too, and I recognize

them all from the safe house.

Prax kept saying he wanted to keep this controlled. I have a feeling this place is where everyone is now operating from because of Norman, the CIA analyst who helped tap the terrorists into our covert facilities. The director had to relocate somewhere, so he relocated the team here.

It's a good move. No one would think our guys are operating out of a home on Leesburg Pike. But relocation to a private home doesn't seem like something he would approve. Is someone else now calling the shots? Does anyone here know about the Lone Eagle cover-up?

Danielle Fox knows this address. It's been compromised. I need to make everyone aware.

Frank's phone rings. He cuts me a quick, irritated glare before walking a few feet away to quietly take the call.

I strain to hear what he's saying, but I can't make it out. When he catches me watching, he walks another few paces away.

Whoever he's talking to, they're discussing me. I'm in trouble. Major trouble. But all I can do is wait for him to hang up and see what he says.

"Sophie," Karen says as she none-too-gently takes my arm. "I'll take you to your father."

I stare at Karen in disbelief. "My father? He's here?"

She gives a stoic nod. "Follow me."

I look at Frank one last time, and he's still talking on the phone, staring irritably back. I wish he and I could sit down and talk, but we're way beyond that now. It doesn't matter what I say, he's clearly pissed at me. Okay, I get it, he's pissed I ran, but does he know about Erik? I'm not sure he does, otherwise he'd be consoling me right now instead of shooting me these angry glares.

I follow Karen through the house and down steps into a basement that bleeds into a tunnel. It probably leads under the empty lot and over to connect to the other house.

The empty lot... I went down the center, Jackson right, and Zeke left. Thank God, because if one of them had gone down the middle, they'd be in here right now and not me. I'm glad it's me.

As I trail behind her and down the well-lit passageway,

I say, "I don't know how much you know about what's going on today, but my father is not safe here. You need to move him. *None* of you are safe here."

She comes to a stop halfway down the tunnel and turns to unlock a metal door.

"Did you hear what I just said?" I ask.

"I did."

I wait for more, but she doesn't say a word, reminding me why I've never really liked her. Getting emotion from this woman is like getting me to eat liver. Not going to happen.

With a frustrated sigh, I glance up to see wire run across the ceiling and connected to a square piece of metal about six-by-six. That's the door I came across on the empty lot. A metal ladder leads from it, trailing down the wall.

It's an escape hatch. That's interesting.

"Sophie," she says, motioning me inside.

I step into a hallway with three locked doors on the right side, each with a small window. Lifting up on my tiptoes, I peek into the first window to find an empty cell complete with a small cot, metal toilet, and sink. Like solitary confinement.

We come to the next door, and lifting up, I peer inside. Norman lies face-up on the cot, his long body extending over the end. Despite the fact he was working with the terrorist cell, a pang of sorrow moves through me. I always liked him, and somehow, I can't see him voluntarily doing the things he did. They must have threatened him just like they did me.

I turn to Karen. "Have you had a chance to question him? Maybe he didn't have a choice."

Her eyebrows go up. "Everyone has a choice. He made the wrong one."

Well, she does have a point. I had three tasks, three choices. The first two I did, but when it came to killing William, I chose not to.

Now my brother is dead instead.

She keeps walking, coming to a stop at the third door, where she keys in a code. Why is she bringing me down here to see my father? The door opens, and there Dad sits on a cot, his wrists and ankles cuffed together.

He's being held as a prisoner.

"Five minutes," she tells me, but I don't move. My brain can't seem to process that my father is chained up and being held in a cell.

"Sophie," he says, and his voice comes out deep and sure, not at all matching his circumstances.

I take a hesitant step in, and my stunned senses snap into place. I whirl on Karen, jabbing my finger in his direction. "What the hell is going on?"

She peeks at her watch, silently telling me I now have less than five minutes, and my jaw clenches at the passive-aggressive gesture.

"Sophie." He speaks again. "Come here."

I turn from her and cross the cell to come down on the cot next to him. My gaze trails across his light brown skin, his dark and gray hair, and it latches onto his light brown eyes. He smiles then, and I don't waste another valuable second as I wrap my arms around him and hold him tight.

"Dad," I breathe, taking in the familiar scent of his aftershave, and the steadfast comfort I always feel in his presence.

He turns his head and presses a kiss to my forehead. "Are you okay?"

Keeping my arms around him, I croak, "Erik."

"I know," he whispers.

Together we sit here, me holding him, him pressing his head into mine, and we grieve the death of my brother. I could sit here for hours, holding my dad, but the clock is ticking, and too soon Karen is going to make me leave.

I concentrate on getting myself together, and I lift my head to look at him. This is the man partially responsible for the death of so many people.

An accident, sure, but he taught me how to ride a bike, held me while I got stitches, showed me how to change a tire, nursed me when I had pneumonia, came to my tea party...

Dad wedges himself down into the miniature chair. His bent knees nearly touch his chest. With delight dancing in his eyes, he scans the small table set for my tea party with my dolls already in attendance.

I pick up the delicate tea pot and pour him pretend tea. "One lump or two?"

"I'll take three."

I giggle. "Daddy, you can't have three!"

He looks offended. "Why not?"

"Because you'll get cavities."

Playfully, he rolls his eyes. "This one time won't matter." He leans in. "Just don't tell your mom," he whispers, and I giggle again.

My thoughts go from the tea party to all over the place, and I try to grab on to just one, but what happened with Lone Eagle needs a conversation that will require more than our valuable few allotted minutes. I ask, "Why are you in here?"

He straightens up like he's making a conscious effort to be strong. "They think I'm trying to kill your mother."

"*What?* Why would they think that?"

"Planted evidence." He shakes his head. "Just know I did not, and all of this will get sorted out."

The water bottle incident with William comes back to my mind. The extremists tried to frame Dad just like they did me. I want to tell him everything, but I refrain. I don't know who is or is not eavesdropping and how deep the conspiracy runs. It's better if I keep my mouth shut.

Dad glances toward the door where Karen still stands before glancing up to the camera mounted in the top corner. He brings his eyes back to mine, giving me a tender look. "Can I have another hug?"

Something's off about him, and his words come back to me from so many hours ago. *Do not trust anyone.* Those words weren't supposed to include my own family.

"Sophie?" He inclines his head, and I lean forward and give him another hug. He shifts a little, pressing another kiss to my forehead, and the movement is slight, but his lips move against my skin. "They are going to put you in one of these cells," he barely speaks, and my whole body goes still. "You have to run. Mom isn't safe. You have to find her."

The saliva in my mouth dries, and I fight to swallow. What does he mean Mom isn't safe? I was told she was in a secure location. Then again, he was, too, and here he is being held as a prisoner. I need to find her.

My mind sifts through the loose ends: Max Grayson's

apartment, where I'm sure there's something hidden in his bedroom; the identities of the inside people, which still need to be nailed down; and Danielle Fox, who is out there, and who knows this address where my father is.

Yes, I need to run. But what about my father? What's going to happen to him?

"Time's up," Karen says.

"Green, then yellow," he whispers. "The hatch."

The hatch. Green then yellow. He's talking about escape.

I pull back from him, and I look him straight in the eyes, masking any fear and letting him see only determination. How this all ends depends solely on me. I understand.

A proud smile flits across his face. "You are so much like your mother. You're strong. Independent. A natural-born leader."

My breath catches. He's never said anything like that to me before, and his words course through me, bolstering me and giving me the courage to see this through.

"I love you, Dad." No matter his involvement with Lone Eagle, I love him, and I love Mom very much.

With one last quick hug, I follow Karen away from my father, and my brain spins with next steps. They're going to put me in one of these cells. They think my dad wants to kill my mom. They may think I'm working for the terrorists, too, and this time not under duress.

She opens the metal door, and I step back out into the tunnel. Why didn't she try to put me in a cell like Dad said? Maybe because Frank wants to talk to me first. He can't believe any of this.

Dad knew about my brother, which means Frank does, too. I can't believe he didn't console me. It doesn't matter how upset he is with me, that's just not like him. Unless… unless he thinks I'm really at fault in all of this. Surely, he doesn't believe that. But that look on his face—irritation, yes, but also anger and suspicion. He must think I have blame in all of this.

The tunnel to the right leads back to the house we came from. To the left, the other house that—I'm sure—has agents in it, too. Right above me sits the hatch that lets out into the empty lot.

Exposed wiring trails the ceiling. *Green, then yellow.* It's the same schematics as our home security unit. Severing the green wire cuts the electricity; the yellow will short circuit the hatch.

Our generator at home takes roughly twenty seconds to kick in, and I'm assuming the one here will be the same. I can be up the ladder, out the hatch, and almost across the lot before they realize I'm gone. Plus, with security infiltrated, they'll be forced to move my father to a safer location.

Karen turns, ready to pull the metal door closed. If I'm going to do anything, it has to be now.

Right now.

I lunge, body-slamming her hard and shoving her back inside the hallway with the holding cells. She loses her footing, stumbling back, and I throw all my weight behind grabbing the door and yanking it closed. With a muted scream she propels herself forward, and her angry face comes up against the square of thick glass.

There's a keypad on both sides, and my heart bangs

a heavy rhythm as I grab the small dagger from its ankle strap. I work quickly, jabbing the blade behind the keypad and slicing the wires. All the lights on the panel go out, signaling I've disabled it.

When I look at her next, she's got her weapon out and pointed right at the thick glass separating her from me. My gaze briefly meets her furious one. I spin away, and adrenaline flies me up the ladder.

I'm not sure if that glass is bullet proof or not, but I'm not waiting to find out.

Using my dagger, I snip the green wire, and the power winds down as the tunnel goes black. I already have my hand on the yellow wire, but I don't need light to slice that one. The hatch pops open, and I crawl through and make a demon dash across the dark lot.

A tree branch whips across my chest, and it only fuels my flight. Faster I go, tearing through the foliage. Behind me, the generator kicks in and the lights flick on in both houses. I break free from the wooded lot, look across to where Callie should be parked, and find her camper missing.

Shit.

Turning, I take off in a mad sprint down Leesburg Pike. I don't know where I'm going, but I have to run.

I have to get as far away from here as possible.

MAX GRAYSON'S APARTMENT

American University
Saturday, 10:30 p.m.

hail the first cab and dive inside. I give the address of Max's apartment without even thinking, like my subconscious is telling me where to go. I'm still wearing my friend's outback hat, and I tug it down as far as it will go as I slide down in the back seat while the driver navigates traffic.

I don't know where the guys are. I can only hope they made it back to the camper. I destroyed my coms, so they have no idea where I am. I need to call Zeke's burner phone. Which means I need a phone.

I eye the cab driver. "Excuse me, sir. Do you have a phone I can borrow?"

He doesn't respond and instead shoots me a dark and suspicious look. I don't need to set off any alarms, so I simply give him a little smile, mumble, "That's okay," and lower my hat even farther.

Sometime later, he pulls up to Max Grayson's apartment. I stay in the cab a second, surveying the area, but everything seems normal. I don't know what I'm going to encounter inside, but I need to see what's in his bedroom.

I hand the man a few twenties from the stash Edna, the elderly lady that I kidnapped, gave me, and with every muscle in my body tense, I stride up the sidewalk toward the apartment. It's like I'm expecting someone to jump out at me.

There are twenty units in the two-story brick complex—ten on the bottom and ten on the top. Max's sits on the first floor, over to the right. I try the handle and am not surprised to find it locked.

I look around for hide-a-key spots, and I find a spare one under the mat. I take it, but uneasiness curls through me. The key under the mat was too easy. But I proceed anyway, and with another quick glimpse around, I let myself in.

It's exactly the same as a few hours ago, and I stand in the darkness acclimating myself. Ice drops in the automatic freezer, and the air kicks on, stirring up the smell of stale cigarette smoke.

I quietly make my way down the hall. The bedroom door is on the left, and it still sits closed. Before I go in, I peek into the kitchen to make sure it's clear, following with the disgusting bathroom, and then backtrack to his bedroom.

The light fixture still has the audio device I planted, and I speak quietly to my friends, "If anyone can hear me, come get me."

My senses on full alert, I turn the knob to his bedroom, swing the door inward, and am greeted by complete darkness. The only way it could be this black is if Max has his windows covered. My hand slides across the wall, and I locate a switch.

A tower light in the far-right corner flips on, casting the room in a blue glow. My gaze tracks over the double bed with wadded sheets and dirty clothes on the floor, the textbooks spread across a desk, a metal shelf with more books, and several movie posters hanging on his walls. But nothing seems off.

I head straight for his shelving unit and pick books at random, thumbing through them, not really sure what I'm looking for. At his desk, I flip open the laptop. It's not password protected, and I scroll through his files but don't see anything there, either.

In his closet, I rifle through his clothes and some boxes along the top shelf. But that's a dead end, too. With a sigh, I turn to survey his room. Maybe I'm wrong about this and there's nothing here.

A gap separates the bed from the floor. Dropping down to my hands and knees, I dig under but find only dust, more dirty clothes, and a single unsmoked joint. As I scoot away, the floor beneath me creaks.

Hope surges through me as I scramble off his throw rug, toss it back, and finger the wood planks, looking for a loose one. One pops up.

Inside the hidey-hole sits a brown leather journal, and my pulse picks up its pace as I pull it out. It's old and well-worn with cracks in the leather and yellowed pages. I open the cover.

The first few pages are pictures of the gory Lone Eagle scene. After that are photos of the military team involved, my parents included. Under each picture is a detailed timeline of each person, including where they've lived and what they've done, and their families, too. There's even a picture of me.

They've been tracking us for years.

More pictures follow of the community survivors, including children and adults. Though these photos were taken fifteen years ago, I recognize a very young version of Danielle Fox.

I continue flipping through the book, looking for names—old or new ones. There are a lot of first names but no last names, and I imagine that's on purpose, in case someone like me finds this. But that's okay; once we scan these photos, we can use facial recognition and hopefully pinpoint who all these people are.

This book appears old, but how did Max get it? It seems to me one of the extremists would keep something like this. Unless…he stole it.

Yes, that would make sense. Danielle was in this room all those years ago recruiting him to the cause. He told my brother about it, who foolishly agreed to get involved, thinking he could bring this terrorist cell down. At some point, Max must have come across this journal and taken it for evidence. I only wish he would've turned it over.

As I thumb through the rest of the journal pages, I come across random entries and outlines of various bombs. I flip to the last couple of pages, and something slides free. It's a folded piece of paper, and I open it. It's a blueprint, and I lean in close, trying to figure out what it's a blueprint of.

Everything inside of me stills. It's my home. Not the

White House, but our country home, where we were when this horrible day started.

I trace the intricacies of the prints, realizing some key things are missing. Namely, the secret doors and passageways, like the one I was stuck in when I was five years old. Whoever provided this either knew about the passageways and didn't share that information, or didn't know about them at all.

The air in the room shifts then, and the hairs on my arms lift.

Someone's here.

"Well, hello, Sophie," comes a voice from behind me.

My muscles lock into place. I have to move, but I'm afraid to. Like if I move, then whoever is behind me becomes real. Too real. The person takes a slow, measured step, and I make myself turn, coming face to face with Danielle Fox.

Her eyes narrow when they meet mine, and she glances sharply at the journal still gripped in my hand.

Whatever fear I have transitions into something more acute and aware.

Her thin lips curl up.

"You've been quite the pain in the ass today," she comments, and despite the fact something bad is about to happen, I take that as a total compliment. I'm glad I'm making things difficult for her and whoever else is involved.

She chuckles then. Like she truly finds me funny.

My brows come down. This woman is insane.

She lunges, catching me off guard, and before I have time to react, she tackles me to the floor. I go down hard, bouncing off the wood planks. Pain flares through me, but I twist as fast as I can to get free from her arms.

With a grunt, Danielle flips me over, and I try to get to my dagger, but I can't reach it. I swing out, and my fist connects with her jaw so solidly that pain shoots through my knuckles. I swing again, and she catches my wrist and slams it to the floor.

I scream loudly, hoping someone will hear, and the muscles in my throat spasm. She lifts me up and slams me down. My head cracks against the floor and my vision dots.

Fear curls through me, but so does white-hot anger. I buck my hips, and she topples to the side. Scrambling up, I go to kick her in the ribs, and she grabs my ankle and yanks. I land on my butt and kick my legs. One of my heels connects with her face, and she yelps.

Her hand wraps around my calf, and then she's on top of me, pinning me to the floor. She lifts my shoulders and throws me down, and my head bangs against the floor again. Everything whirls, terrifying me. I can't lose this fight. I claw at her face, and she lifts her arm and punches me.

Fiery pain explodes under my eye, and I can't breathe. In my hazy vision, she lifts her fist again, and I bring my knee up, but it only connects with her butt. I grapple for my dagger, but she wraps her fingers around my throat and squeezes. I open my mouth to scream, but she just squeezes tighter.

With her free hand, Danielle reaches down and pulls my dagger free. It glimmers in the dim light as she taunts me with it. My chest clenches as I stare up into her cold eyes and she replaces her hand around my throat with the knife.

"Is this what you want?" she mocks.

A fine shiver of fear works its way down my spine. Fractured memories flow through my brain about how this day started with grand plans for my birthday but then, one by one, everyone I love has been picked off.

I don't want to die. My parents are depending on me.

My fear morphs into deadly rage. My mind dives into dark places, like me slitting her throat and not the other way around. Danielle must recognize the shift in me because she pulls back a little.

I draw in a shallow breath.

I will kill this woman.

Her gaze drifts over my head and recognition flashes across her eyes as she shoves off of me. I go to look back to see who's behind me, and whoever it is crams a hood over my head. Pain erupts in my skull next, and my world goes black.

LOCATION UNKNOWN

Time unknown

A thudding pain is the first thing I register, in my skull and radiating fiery fingers up through my temples. It licks down my neck, and I wince. With a groan, I open my eyes, and I jerk back when I'm greeted with nothing but blackness. There's a hood over my head.

I inhale, and the air comes stagnant and hot. I try to get another one, but it's just as stuffy. I try again—another one—and it's cut short by the cloth. A bubble of panic rises in my chest. I need to calm down. I was breathing fine when I was knocked out.

I can breathe just fine again if I calm down.

A rapid sniffing filters into my senses next. There's a dog crouched beside me, his nose cruising up and down me as he checks me out. My first instinct is to scoot away. But I make myself stay as still as possible, knowing a sudden movement could set this dog off, just like with Erik's Shepherd.

Distant voices leak into my consciousness next, and I turn my head.

"We've got Sophie," the garbled voice says.

I gasp. "Who's there?"

The dog rumbles, and every muscle in my body freezes. A sharp whistle pierces the air, and the dog pounds away from me. From the vibration in the floor, I can tell it's big.

I let out a relieved breath. "Is anyone there?" I whisper.

"Shhh," someone right beside me hushes, and I jerk back.

The sound of footsteps comes toward me, and I try to scoot away. But I'm already up against a wall and can't go anywhere.

Someone nudges me with a shoe, and I jerk again. "Speak," the garbled voice commands.

Beneath the hood, I shake my head. "What do you want?" I hear the unsteadiness in my voice and hate it. I don't want to come across scared, but I am. More than I've ever been in my life.

"Are you satisfied?" the garbled voice asks. "We'll trade her for the president. That is my one and only demand. You have thirty minutes, or she will die via a bomb just like Erik. Thirty minutes."

He clicks off, but he doesn't move away from me, and my heart bangs a fearful beat in my chest.

"The U.S. does not negotiate with terrorists," the distorted voice says. "We'll see about that."

I focus in on that voice, trying to figure out if it was the same one speaking to me hours ago when I had that earpiece and was running around doing their tasks. But I can't tell.

What I do know is that there is absolutely no way

these people are getting my mother. Even if she wanted to exchange her life for mine, that wouldn't be allowed.

In thirty minutes, I am going to die.

L ater, somebody yanks me to my feet. "Let's go," the distorted voice says. "Time to trade."

"What?" I gasp. "There's no way." There is absolutely no way I'm being traded for my mom.

I'm shoved forward, and I stumble to stay upright. Someone grips my right arm, and I try to see beneath the black hood, but all I can make out are my own feet and the boots Callie lent me.

Callie. Zeke. Jackson. I pray they're okay.

We exit a door and enter a garage, and I'm tossed into the trunk of a car. I struggle against the ties on my wrists, but they won't budge. The trunk lid slams shut and my already frazzled nerves snap.

"No!" I yell, kicking my legs. "Please. I'm claustro-phobic!" I scream.

Telling them my fear gives them ammunition against me, but I don't care. I can't do this!

Other doors open and close, the garage door goes up, the engine cranks, and we're backing away.

"No!" I scream even louder, and my voice cracks. "I can't do this!" The trunk seems to shrink in on me, and violently, I thrash around.

Fear moves through me in a very real and crippling way. "Please!" I scream again, but this times it comes out more of a sob.

"Shut. Up," a voice commands with such sharp clarity

that I go still. They put something in my ear.

"Good girl," the distorted voice says, and it vibrates through my eardrum.

They must have put it there when I was knocked out.

This voice is different, though, from the one who spoke into the phone. I can't distinguish gender, but the timbre is different and also the tone. This one is more authoritative. Is it *the* leader of the cell?

I tune my senses to the sounds around me—the tires crunching over gravel, the car's engine slowing down, and my own breathing.

The car rolls to a stop. The doors open, and the weight of the vehicle shifts as whoever is inside gets out. I brace myself for whatever is next.

The trunk opens, and there are multiple hands on me as I'm lifted out. My legs are free, and I want to kick and struggle. But I can't afford to be hit in the head again.

I'm dropped onto the ground, and I wince as the chunky gravel digs into my body. Someone helps me sit up. Someone else cuts the ties off my wrists, and my arms are so numb I'm barely able to move them.

If I'm ever taken and held hostage, I'm not going to blubber. I'm going to be mean and angry.

I almost laugh. There's no way to tell how you're really going to act in a situation until it actually arises. I'm much braver in my head. In reality, things are out of my control.

"There is a rifle trained on your head," comes the authoritative distorted voice. "Do not move until you are instructed to. Do you understand?"

"Yes," I answer.

A clicking sound fills the air. They're taking pictures of me. Hell, they may even be livestreaming right now.

Whoever is out there moves around, walking away. Car doors open and close, an engine cranks, and then they're gone.

Everything in me screams to rip this hood off and run, but I make myself stay. Somewhere there is a rifle trained on my head. A sharpshooter.

If my mom is delivered, I'll go free. If not, I'll die. They said by bomb, so that means there has to be a bomb somewhere around me. Eye for an eye. We bombed them, so they bomb us.

There is no way they are getting the President of the United States. My mother will not be handed over. This is what I tell myself, but she's already lost Erik, and she would give her life for me or for Dad. She would figure out how to go rogue, too. She'd skirt her detail, just like I did, in order to save my life.

Knowing her, she'd think it was atonement for her past mistake.

I *admire* and I *respect* her, present tense, not past, and I love her so very much. I would gladly give my life for her.

Even if the death of innocent people deserves justice, this isn't right. None of this is right.

They can't have my mom.

I am brave. I do have control. I don't have to do what they say.

With a shaking hand, I slide the hood off, and I tense with the knowledge that I may be seconds away from a sharpshooter's bullet in my head, or death from a detonated bomb.

I hold a breath. Yes, I'm ready to give my life for Mom's safety.

But...nothing happens.

A wave of fresh air drifts over me, and I look around the small, dark park. There are swings over to the right, seesaws to the left, and a merry-go-round straight ahead. But I have no clue if I'm in D.C. or Virginia or Maryland.

In the distance, trees bump the landscape. That has to be where the sharpshooter is hiding.

If there is indeed a sharpshooter. Because wouldn't he have done something by now? A warning shot, at least? I look again at my surroundings. Where would the bomb be?

"Take your hood off," speaks the voice in my ear.

My hood is already off.

Which means...they can't see me. They assumed I would follow their orders. After everything that has happened today, I would think they'd know better. And something about this knowledge bolsters me. I might finally be a step ahead.

"Walk through the park and out the other side," the voice instructs. "You'll find a blue car. Wait for instructions."

VACANT PARK

Northern Virginia
Saturday, 11:45 p.m.

It only takes me minutes to run through the park and find the blue car. There's an iPhone set up on the dash, and the screen flicks, displaying a black and white image of my mother.

My guts twist with horror. "Mom?" I whisper.

She's dressed in a T-shirt and jeans, exactly how she looked when she wrapped her slender, strong arms around me and hugged me goodbye. It can't be real, but I swear I smell the homemade coconut soap in this car.

Do not trust anyone. Your mother thinks this is coming from someone on the inside. Those were Dad's words to me as he hugged me goodbye, too, and how right they were.

Mom is blindfolded, and it looks like she's in the back of a moving van. Other than that, she appears unharmed.

"Mom?" I say louder. "Can you hear me?"

Her head twists and turns, like she's trying to hear where my voice is coming from.

"Mom!" I yell. "It's me. I'm looking at you on a screen."

"Sophie!" she gasps. "Are you okay?"

"Yes, I'm fine," I assure her. "I'm in a car right now looking at you. They want me to do something, but I don't know what it is yet."

"No! Absolutely not. Do *not* do what they want."

"Mom," my voice wavers.

"You listen to me good. They have me. They have what they want. Enough. You cannot believe a word that they say. Promise me you'll walk away."

I shake my head. "No, I won't promise that."

"Sophie." She firms her tone. "You must."

"No," I murmur. My brother is dead. If there's any way of stopping Mom from dying, then I'm doing it. Whatever it is.

I throw my hands up. "I don't understand, why can't I go?"

"Pick anything else for your birthday, just not a concert. The risks are too great. Especially at FedEx Field."

"If I were Erik, it wouldn't matter."

Mom sighs. "Erik has nothing to do with this."

"Fine!" I yell and clamp my lips together. I can't believe I just yelled at her.

"How about zip lining?" she calmly suggests. "You and your friends love that and I've already had security look into a few different options."

"Of course you have," I mumble.

"Oh, Mom. I'm so sorry. I'm sorry for everything. I'll be a better daughter. I promise. I love you. I love you so much."

She shakes her head. "Sweetheart…"

A masked figure moves into view, and my heart races as he studies her. He lifts a scalpel and trails it close to my mom's blindfold, not quite touching, but almost. He's taunting me, not her. He knows I'm watching.

He moves a little closer, and she must sense his nearness. Though it's slight, the muscles in her upper body quiver with constrained fear. I have never seen my mother scared, and I hate that he's doing that to her.

"Stop it," I snap. "Just tell me what to do next."

The screen goes black. The voice speaks, "Beneath your seat are the keys to the car and also a phone. Use it to call the vice president. Tell him you want to meet. There's an envelope under there, too. You are to give him that."

My mother's image flicks onto the screen again. The masked man runs the scalpel across her forehead, drawing blood, and with a gasp, she jerks away.

The screen goes black again, and without another wasted second, I jab the keys into the ignition. As I pull from the park and down the first road, a billboard advertising Virginia Drug Cards tells me what state I'm in.

"Where do you want me to meet William?" I demand, but I'm met with silence.

I don't dial William.

Dad is being held as a prisoner by the United States government. William is still alive. The terrorists have Mom, and once again—I'm their puppet.

They used my brother to get me to do the work they couldn't. Swapping drives, entering Senator Gostler's house, and almost killing the VP. And unless Callie's hack has produced results, I'm no closer to finding out who these people are.

Now they're using Mom to put me back together with the VP. Obviously, they want me to finish what I couldn't before. So, this goes two ways. I kill him or I don't kill him. Either way, Mom is dead, because that is the ultimate goal—to kill the military team responsible for Lone Eagle and their families, too.

Or is it?

We're talking about the President of the United States. If they're going to kill her, they'll make a show of it by broadcasting it and demonstrating to the world how powerful they are.

Or they'll auction her off for an enormous price, and whatever future plans they have will be funded for years.

I'd bet anything they're taking her to our country home. Why else would they have the blueprints?

I dial William's secure line, knowing the terrorists are tapped in. He answers on the second ring, and I say, "It's me."

"Thank God," he breathes.

I tried to kill him. The fact that he's answered the phone that way gives me hope. "There is so much that has happened. Please know everything I've done was with the best intentions. I'm just trying to save my family and figure all of this out, too."

"Yes, I really need to hear your side. Because what they're telling me is not good."

"What do you mean?"

"I'd rather talk in person."

He read my mind. "I saw Mom," I tell him.

"Me, too," he quietly says. "I was watching the same

video you were."

I want to ask him about Dad, but I refrain. I don't want the extremists to have any updates on my father.

"Sophie, where are you?"

"It doesn't matter where I am. You saw the video. We need to meet."

"I won't come alone."

"Pick two men that you absolutely trust and come only with them. This is Mom we're talking about. The President of the United States and your best friend. If there is one last chance to save her, I don't want to screw it up."

William doesn't answer.

"I have no ulterior motive," I promise.

"Okay," he finally relents.

I don't want whoever is listening to know where we're meeting, so I say, "Do you remember where we were a few years ago when you got sick off junk food and threw up?"

"Yes."

"Meet me there. Thirty minutes." I hang up the phone. Now I just have to convince him to pretend to die.

EMPTY BASEBALL FIELD

Reston, Virginia
Sunday, 12:15 a.m.

I exit off the Toll Road and pull the blue car into a vacant lot that sits a half mile away from an empty baseball field. Several years ago, Erik was playing here on a community team, and William came to watch. He had a little too much junk food and ended up throwing up in the bathroom. He knew what I was referring to when I said that.

I take the sealed envelope they want me to give him, and I hold it up to the dome light in the car. There's a small piece of paper inside and nothing else. If this is a bomb, I'm not seeing it.

With the K9 units, I get why they used saxitoxin at the Ripley Center, but why a chemical weapon now? Still, I run it under my nose to smell it, but I don't catch the bittersweet scent that is supposed to indicate it's been dusted with poison. But I've never actually smelled poison, so I don't know for sure.

It does appear as if this piece of paper inside is a note.

I leave the car and the phone behind, and taking the envelope with me, I jog down the dark road toward the baseball field.

Roughly five minutes later, I arrive. At this hour, the place sits dark and empty. William is already here and outside near the empty concession. Two of his men are with him, standing at attention, their eyes alert and looking around.

I walk toward him, and as I do, his gaze travels up and down my body, checking—I'm sure—to see if I'm okay. My natural inclination is to hug him, but I'm not sure he would welcome the gesture.

When he opens his arms, I'm so relieved I don't hesitate a second in walking straight into them.

He pulls away first, taking in the bruise on my face where Danielle hit me. His expression hardens. "What else did they do to you?"

"I'm fine," I assure him. "We don't have much time. First, tell me Dad's okay."

"After you infiltrated the facility, they moved him. Or rather, Frank did."

"Good." I sigh my relief. "Dad will be okay with Frank by his side." I really want to hear what William has to say about Lone Eagle. I take a few steps away to get out of earshot of his men, and he quietly follows. Leaning in, I lower my voice. "Will you tell me about Lone Eagle?"

Guilt moves across his expression, followed by shame. He's reliving the whole horrendous event.

Lifting his hand, he rubs his neck. "It was the worst day of our lives. It was a horrible and tragic mistake. We tried to make it right. To this day we are still trying to make it right. But the cover-up goes deep. Sometimes even the president's hands are tied."

"What do you mean you've tried to make it right?"

"We wanted to go public back when it happened, but we were shut down. We did, and still do, what we can. Financial support for the survivors. Jobs for them. Health care. Opportunities where they need them. Some of them, though, have fallen off the grid." He reaches out a hand to me. "Know that your parents were going to tell you and Erik. They never intended to hide it from you. If we could relive the moment, we would've died for those people."

I don't doubt that he's speaking the truth. "Senator Gostler committed suicide over this."

William sighs. "I know."

"I really liked him," I whisper, and a pang of sorrow moves through me.

"Me, too. He was one of the good ones." He nods to the envelope. "We probably better get to that."

I hand it over, wanting nothing more than to just sit with my parents and hear every detail. But this whole terrible day has made that impossible.

William runs his finger under the flap to break the seal and slides out a single piece of paper. He takes a second to read it before showing it to me.

INNOCENT PEOPLE DIED.
YOU COVERED IT UP.
NOW YOU WILL DIE.

We stare at each other, and my mind spins. *Now you will die.* I turn a slow circle, searching the darkness around us. The car I drove here is a half mile away. Even if they tracked it, they would need more time to scan the area for our exact location.

Unless they planted a bomb in the car. Maybe, but they'd have to know I wouldn't park near William. Which means the bomb—if there is one—is on me.

My stomach tosses with sickness, and I pat my body. What did they put on me? I run my fingers up and down my legs and over my torso, but I don't find anything. I look up at William, and his eyes widen as he realizes what I'm thinking.

The bomb is on me.

I came here ready to convince him to fake his own death. But that's not going to be necessary because we really are going to die.

My ear!

I shove him away and run in the opposite direction.

I dig inside and pull the piece out, and I hurl it as hard as I can into the night at the exact second it explodes and propels me backward.

I land with a hard thud, my body bouncing off the ground, and a ring resonates through my brain. Dots dance across my eyes, and I try to get up, but a wave of heat hits me, pushing me right back down. Flames flick across the dry grass before gradually dying out.

Rolling over onto my hands and knees, I regain my equilibrium. William is just a few yards away, lying in the grass. He ran toward me. He was trying to help. Beside him is one of his men, lying unconscious, too. I look around for the other, but I don't see him.

"William!" I yell, scrambling over.

I press my fingers to his pulse, and there's nothing

there. I press harder, and still nothing. "No," I whisper.

Putting my ear to his nose and mouth, I pray for a breath. But still, nothing.

I tilt his head to clear his airway and begin chest compressions. I push hard and fast, delivering thirty compressions, before pinching his nose and breathing into his mouth.

I go back to his chest, then back to breathing into his mouth. "No," I sob. "Please. Please."

The other secret service officer runs toward me. I breathe a sigh of relief at the exact second it registers that he's running toward me with his gun drawn.

"Stop!" he yells.

Stop what? Chest compressions? But if I do that, he'll surely die, if he isn't dead already.

Stop. My God, he wants the VP to die. The agent is working for the cell, too.

I leap to my feet, and nausea rolls in my stomach when I turn and sprint away from William, leaving him to die. But it's the only way to save Mom.

THE PRESIDENT'S COUNTRY HOME

Northern Virginia
Sunday, 1:00 a.m.

With tears streaming down my cheeks, I dash from the baseball field. I don't go back to the car but head in the other direction, blindly racing down the dark country road. About a half mile in, I crest a hill and catch sight of a twenty-four-hour gas station.

Aside from the attendant, the place sits empty, and I don't hesitate to hurry inside. "Can I use your phone?"

If the twenty-something man behind the counter recognizes me, he doesn't let on, and in fact, barely even registers me as he hands me the cordless landline.

I pace away, quickly dialing the last disposable number Zeke was using, praying he still has it. I nearly crumble with relief when he picks up. "Hi," I breathe.

"Jesus Christ, where the hell are you? We have looked everywhere for you and Callie. Please tell me she's with you."

My heart sinks. "No. Just come get me. Please." Quickly, I give him the address of the station and then

I hang up.

I wait outside, hiding in the shadows, fighting the images of what just happened. *William.*

My focus freezes on an oil spill darkening the concrete. I don't know how much time goes by as I stand in the shadows. The memories of those I've lost in the last twenty-four hours suffocate me.

Giggling, Britta playfully shoves Erik as he goes in for another neck nuzzle…

Crossing his eyes, Danforth sticks out his tongue…

William slaps his leg, snorting he's laughing so hard…

"Rock, paper, scissors," Erik and I say, and as usual he picks scissors…

Mom sneaks up behind Dad. "Boo!" she yells and he screams…

Good people who are now missing, a hostage, or confirmed dead.

Thank God Dad is safe.

Sometime later, Zeke and Jackson pull up in Callie's Volkswagen, and all the tension coiling through my shoulders releases. God, it's good to see them.

Zeke opens the driver's side and climbs out, and with purposeful strides, he comes right toward me, not even stopping as his fingers slide into my curly hair and his strong hands cup the sides of my face. His dark green eyes momentarily meet mine in relief, and then his lips come down firm.

My hands lift to his sides, and my fingers flex into his muscles. Every ounce of love for this boy that I have kept close to my heart comes through as I open my mouth and freefall into the kiss.

He lifts his head, his lips leaving mine, and I expect to see shock in his expression at what we just did, but I don't at all. There's only relief that we're both alive and that we're safe.

The muscles in his jaw tighten as he looks at my eye. "Who did that to you?"

I smile a little to let him know I'm okay. "Danielle Fox."

Jackson clears his throat, and with a tender look, Zeke steps away to give him room to hug me, too. If he thinks it's odd we were just kissing, he doesn't say a word.

"Where's Callie?" I ask, stepping out of my friend's hug.

He shakes his head. "No clue. The last we saw you, you were being led into that house. We doubled back to the camper and found her gone."

With a groan, I close my eyes. "Not her, too."

"Then we picked you up when you were in Max's apartment, via the audio device you planted," Zeke says. "But it came across weak and garbled, as if someone was scrambling it. And by the time we got there, you were gone."

"Taken, actually." I tell them everything that's happened, including the events surrounding the VP.

The guys exchange a pained look.

"I know," I whisper. "The VP, also." The three of us let that sink in, and then I say, "I think they took Mom back to our country home."

Jackson nods. "Then that's where we're headed."

As the camper flies toward our house in Virginia, I focus on how we can save Mom.

If my theory is right about them either auctioning her off or killing her and broadcasting it, our home would be the place. Everyone knows my parents love it. It's been in our family for generations and is the perfect middle-finger, *up yours* message for the terrorists to send.

BAIN could make a shit-ton of money selling the President of the United States. Money that will fund them for a very long time.

"What's the plan?" Jackson asks.

"You should be our eyes and ears outside," I say. "I'm definitely going in."

"And obviously I'm going with you," Zeke says.

I think for a second. It's not like we can walk in the front door. "There's a tunnel that opens a half mile away in an empty field. Back in the day, it was used to smuggle slaves. But when my parents inherited the house, they had the tunnel sealed and protected with laser security. It won't be easy breaking in, but it's doable."

"Lasers," Zeke says thoughtfully. "We'll use refractors."

I nod. "The tunnel opens into the basement. From there we can make our way up to my parents' suite. They keep several master keys in Mom's jewelry box."

"Master key to what?" Jackson asks.

"After I got stuck all those years ago, my parents had the passageways secured and master keys made. If we have those, we'll be able to move around undetected through the hidden corridors. We can get a clearer idea of how many terrorists are in there, how many hostages, and then better devise a plan."

"What about the interior cameras that monitor your home?" Jackson asks. "They've likely placed someone in the control room to monitor all activity."

The control room is located off the kitchen. Jackson's right.

"We could take the person out," Zeke suggests.

It should bother me that we're talking about taking someone's life, but it doesn't. "I know where all the cameras are. It's just as easy to avoid them. Plus if we take a guy out, that'll just alert everyone that we're inside. Better to hold our cards close until we're absolutely ready to play them."

Up ahead is a cutoff in the road. I point. "There, take that. It leads to the tunnel opening."

Zeke cuts the headlights, and we leave the road to bump over the field. I watch the terrain carefully, and a few minutes later, I signal for him to stop.

Jackson checks the flowered laptop, keying a few things. "Yeah, they're definitely in there, because all signals are jammed. So even if someone on the inside wanted to reach out, it would be impossible."

"Then how are they going to broadcast, when the time comes?" Zeke asks.

"They won't chance turning off the scrambler; they'll do some sort of portal," he tells us. "Unless you two can find the scrambler and disable it. That'll really screw with things."

"Our priority is Mom," I remind them, and they nod.

We open the camper and climb out. Using several sets of pliers we found in Callie's supplies, we work together to snip away the vines that cover the tunnel's opening.

Then we clip the wires of the grill.

As the guys finish the last few cuts, I glance through the night toward our house, a half-mile away. A faint glow from interior lights is the only indication there is a building in all of this darkness. Even if they had someone posted on the roof, there is no way anyone could see us, especially with the towering trees that cover the field.

The grill covering the tunnel opening is finally cut free. We take a minute to outfit ourselves with gear: throwing daggers, a vest with tools, rope, infrared headgear, coms that may or may not work with the jammed signals—but we're taking them anyway—and a few other miscellaneous things.

Zeke flicks on a light attached to his head, and a red glow illuminates the narrow, half-mile-long tunnel. From here it appears to go on forever, and I cringe at what is to come.

He turns to me, covering the red light with his hand, and the surrounding shadows cast dark circles around his eyes. "You've got this. Just move and don't think."

I appreciate his encouragement, but that's easier said than done.

"I'll be right with you the whole time," he promises.

"The laser security begins halfway," I tell him. "They're red. You can't miss them."

With a nod, he goes in first, and I follow.

"Good luck," Jackson whispers.

PRESIDENT'S TUNNEL

Country Home
Sunday, 1:30 a.m.

"When I was seven, I was on a soap opera for exactly one episode," Zeke says. "Did I ever tell you that?"

I laugh. "No."

"We lived in New York before we moved here, and Mom took me to an open audition. The casting director wanted me to sing the Oscar Mayer song."

"You aren't serious."

He clears his throat. "My bologna has a first name, it's O-S-C-A-R. My bologna has a second name, it's M-A-Y-E-R. Oh, I love to eat it every day, and if you ask me why I'll say, 'cause Oscar Mayer has a way with B-O-L-O-G-N-A."

"Oh my God." I chuckle. "Please tell me you have that episode recorded."

"I do, and when we get out of all this, I'll let you see it."

I love that he said "when" and not "if."

He comes to a stop. "Red lasers."

"Wow, we got here quicker than I thought we would."

"Get the refractors from my pack."

Inching forward, I unzip the bottom pocket and pull them out. Eyeballing the position, I plant one on the right side of the tunnel, and he does the same to the left. They do their thing, and the red beams shoot straight up onto the ceiling of the tunnel.

"It's just like we practiced a few months ago in that simulation," I say.

"I remember."

"Now just don't hit them," I joke.

He chuckles, and the deep sound echoes around us. "Yeah, no kidding."

We continue crawling on our hands and knees, and time seems to slow. I wish he'd keep talking. Tell me another memory. Sing another song. I'm not picky. Or maybe I should say something—but what? I search my brain for a tiny bit of anything, but it's too crowded with thoughts of this tight space.

I glance past Zeke, and the tunnel in front of him stretches and morphs. Where's the end? Shouldn't we be there by now? Please let us be close.

My heart ping-pongs in my chest, and I recognize the panic pushing in.

Calm down, Sophie.

I breathe in. Out.

Digging around in my brain, I search for anything to distract me, but the air surrounding me thickens. My ping-ponging heart grinds to a halt, then kicks back into a frantic flutter. Sweat pops to my skin. My limbs tremble. Terror swoops in.

I can't breathe. My heart. The curved walls warp. I

stop moving. Nausea claws the back of my throat. My body goes numb. I'm going to die. I press my hand to my chest. I open my mouth. No air comes in. Help. *Help!*

"Let's take a quick break," Zeke suggests. "Lie down. Breathe. Close your eyes. Listen to my voice. You're okay."

I lie down in the tunnel, squeezing my eyes shut. My panting breath takes in dust, and I cough.

He shifts, and his warm hand slides along the back of my neck. Gently, he squeezes, massaging the stress.

"I was just thinking about that time we were on the gun range and they had switched out the clowns for cartoon characters," he says, in a calm and steady voice. "Because Callie was there, you insisted we put the clowns back up. You knew how much they freak her out, and you thought it would help her get over her fear. Boy, did it ever. She loved shooting those clowns. Especially the one with the purple polka-dots."

He laughs. "Do you remember that time we were zip-lining in Maryland? The place with the Spider-Man net? Jackson zipped over and hit the net. He was supposed to climb up to the next platform, but he couldn't do it because his foot got stuck in the rope.

All the zip workers came over, and they were standing on the ground looking up, trying to tell Jackson how to get unstuck. Finally, that really cute girl strapped on gear and came to his rescue. He was so embarrassed, wasn't he?"

I listen to his voice, breathing, so appreciative of what he's doing right now.

His fingers flex, moving from my neck to massage into my hair. "I remember the first time I met you. It was at Langley in that small auditorium. There was a bunch of us agency kids attending a TIA introductory meeting. I think there were probably fifty of us in there.

"You came in the side door with Frank right behind you. You were carrying a white cardboard box. The whole place erupted in whispers. No one could believe that *the* Sophie Washington was there. That you were going to be in the TIA.

I thought you would quietly take a seat and keep to yourself. But you didn't. You stopped walking, and you looked up at all of us who had gathered. With a big smile, you held up the white cardboard box and said, 'Guess what? I made brownies!' Then you proceeded to walk up and down the rows and hand them out."

And when I gave Zeke his, our eyes locked, and it was crush at first sight. I get back up on my hands and knees, breathing now steady, my heart rate normal. "Thank you," I say.

His fingers flex one last time in my hair, and he releases me. "You're welcome."

He talks the rest of the way, moving from memory to memory, and I listen to his voice and his words. Eventually, we come to the end of the tunnel.

Drenched in sweat, I move in front of him. I press my ear to the round metal door, but I hear nothing. It's a thick door, though, and I can't know for sure. Braced for what might come, I flip the rusty latch and swing the door outward, quick. Better to take someone off guard.

But an empty basement greets us.

Blowing out a relieved breath, I scoot out and onto the floor. Zeke follows, securing the door back in place.

"You okay?" he whispers, his face close to mine.

"Yes, but that tunnel sucked. Thank you again."

"No problem." We share a quick smile, and it provides a modicum of calm and stress relief.

We make our way across the basement. This is my home, my turf, and I should have one up on any invaders, but I don't.

I'm not sure what to expect next.

PRESIDENT'S MASTER SUITE

Country Home
Sunday, 2:00 a.m.

We brought a flexible camera with us, and Zeke slips the snakelike device under the basement door.

After he nods the all clear, I open the door and step out into the hall. To the left stretches a passageway that leads up to the dining room, and to the right spans the one that leads to my parents' suite where the master keys are located.

I move right and into the stairwell, taking it one flight up. Once I get those keys, we can hopefully move through the house undetected.

At the top of the stairwell, there's another door, and Zeke uses the camera. With an all clear, we move on. An eerie cautiousness settles through me as we do. I don't know how many terrorists are here in the house, but the place is thirty thousand square feet—there can't be enough of them to cover the entire space.

Which means they've likely rigged key areas with extra monitors. I put my hand on Zeke's bicep. *Motion sensors,* I mouth.

Quickly and softly, we walk forward, anxiously checking for any signs of sensors. One more hallway and a flight of steps to go, then we'll be at my parents' suite.

There's a concealed security camera in this stairwell, and I motion him to drop below its angle. Together we crawl up the steps. The door at the top, hidden and made to look like part of the wall, leads to my parents' bathroom.

Behind me, Zeke guards the stairwell. The seams of the door are too tight for the flexible camera, so I press my ear to listen. Silence greets me.

Not even my parents knew the extent of the passageways when they inherited the home, and they've done an excellent job of keeping the details private. I'm sure there are some that I still don't know about, though my brother has likely explored them all.

Thoughts of Erik has fresh and raw emotion moving in, and I push it down. Not now.

I run my finger along a seam lying between two wood planks and locate the release lever. I give it a little push, and the door opens a sliver. I step through and into the master bath. Zeke inches in behind me, his warmth surrounding me, and the door merges back with the wall to look unmoved and untouched.

Across the tile floor, everything appears dark in my parents' room. Zeke moves forward, using the infrared to navigate by.

We step into and then across the bedroom. His arm comes up in front of me, stopping me in my tracks, and he points across the room to the main door that leads out into the upstairs hall. There's a trip wire running across the floor. Attached to what, I'm not sure. But my gut tells me a bomb.

Bombs are quickly becoming my least favorite thing.

We walk the perimeter of the room, studying the baseboards and glancing behind furniture. I find a small metal box, but in the dark, I can't really see. I crouch down, repositioning my red headlamp, and find a trip wire attached to it.

By the dimensions of it, the green blinking light, and the digital display, I'm pretty sure it contains C-4, just like the one with Erik. Enough, in fact, to blow this entire section of the house off the map.

Something seems off about it, though. There's a trip wire, sure, but there's an extra wire, as well. A short one with a tiny black ball on the end. In all our TIA studies about bombs, I don't recall seeing that before.

I wish the signal wasn't jammed and that we had communication with Jackson. He'd likely be able to tell me.

I can't diffuse the bomb, and there's no time to waste.

I find Mom's jewelry box, and I press the hidden bottom compartment. Out pops a green velvet tray, and inside lie four master keys. I grab them all, and when I turn, I freeze.

I'm not sure how I missed it my first time through, and it takes me a second to fully understand what I'm looking at. But over by Mom's dresser, a large splotch of blood stains the carpet. My temper boils.

So help me God, that had better not belong to my mother.

THIRD FLOOR

Country Home
Sunday, 2:15 a.m.

W ith the trip wire and a bomb rigged to the main entrance of my parents' suite, the only way out and into the upstairs is through a hidden door in the clothes closet. We could go back through the master bath, down past the basement, and navigate up to the dining room. But entering that way would expose us too much.

No, we have to stay hidden until we know better what's going on.

I lead Zeke across the bedroom and into the walk-in closet. Parting my dad's suits, I locate the tiny keyhole down near the baseboard and insert the master key.

This is the first time I've ever done this.

Please work.

I turn it to the left. It clicks, and the wall pops out an inch. Zeke's eyes crinkle with a relieved smile.

A sliver of light illuminates the third-floor hallway, and I take a second to survey with the flexible camera to find it empty. The security camera that monitors this hall is located all the way at the end and braced in the top left corner. It's a sweeping camera, though, and we'll have to count it down before we leave.

I swivel the flexible wand up. The security camera has just reached our angle and rotates in the opposite direction. Once we move across the hall and into the next room, we can then traverse the whole house via the inner passages. We won't have to worry about cameras monitoring us anymore.

I turn to him, handing him his own master key. "We'll go on the next sweep," I whisper.

With a nod, he pockets the key.

Once the camera changes the other way, I don't hesitate a second in moving.

I scoot across the hall. With the flexible snake I check beneath the door, find the room empty, and we slip right inside. As we do, the camera sweeps back. We just made it.

A scream shatters the stillness. I jump back, landing hard against Zeke. His hands come up to steady me.

I don't move as I fight to get my nerves back under control. I turn to face him, and a mixture of dread and anger courses through me.

"Do you think that was Mom?" I whisper.

SECOND FLOOR

Country Home
Sunday, 2:30 a.m.

We make our way through the study, down a back stairwell, and into a guest room beside the one where the scream came from. Where Mom might be. The muffled sounds of a woman crying filter through the wall, followed by a distorted chuckle.

That dark laugh moves through me, cementing my resolve. I'll do what I have to in order to save my mom. I will kill someone if need be.

I head over to the closet where the hidden door is located, with Zeke close behind. I insert the master key and turn it, and the release click reverberates in the air around me.

Several beats go by, filled only by the thumping of my heart and Zeke's careful breathing. Another distorted chuckle, and I'm confident whoever is in there didn't hear the click.

I peer through the crack in the wall and see the back of a person wearing a ski mask. He looms over a seated figure, and my heart lurches. Callie.

Gagged, with her arms tied around the back of the chair, she shakes as the person taunts her, trailing a knife over her neck.

Behind me, Zeke shifts. He pushes the wall open another inch, and I do a visual sweep of the room to find they are the only two people in here. Using his knife, the terrorist flicks our friend's neck, a little bit of blood spurts, and she cries.

He shifts, stepping away, and from the build, I see it's not a man but a woman. She presses her finger to her ear like she's listening to something through an earpiece, then she leaves the room.

As soon as the door closes, I don't waste another second rushing in. My friend's eyes widen. Tears stream down her cheeks and over the gag wrapped tightly around her neck.

"Oh, Callie," I whisper, crouching down to untie her.

When Zeke takes the gag out of her mouth, a loud sob escapes her.

"No," he tells her, putting his hand over her mouth. "Shhh."

She presses her lips together.

"We have to move quickly." I finish with the ties around her wrists.

"But they'll know I'm gone," she whispers, and I'm so glad she's regaining enough control to think ahead.

"Are they all wearing ski masks?" I ask.

"Yes."

So she hasn't seen them. I look around the room, coming up with a plan.

"They wanted my laptop and fingerprint so they could find out everything we knew. I'm sorry," she murmurs.

"Were you able to hack the last piece of data with the identities of the inside people?" Zeke asks, and she shakes her head.

"That's good," I say. "If you don't know who the inside people are, that means they may not care if you 'escape.'"

He cuts me a curious look.

"And how am I going to do that?" she anxiously whispers.

I walk back over to the chair she was just in, and I reposition the rope to make it look more like she worked her hands free than like someone untied her. Then I head to the window and peer out.

"As soon as I lift this, it'll trigger the silent alarm, and they'll know Callie 'escaped.' There's a fire ladder rolled up and secured under the window. She can theoretically make it down this ladder and over to the woods bordering our property in under a minute. They'll likely send one or two people after you. Either way, they'll never suspect you're still in the house."

I glance between them. "What do you think?"

He nods. "Let's do this."

"Okay, here we go." I slide the window up, triggering the silent alarm, throw the fire escape ladder out, and we disappear through the wall and back into the closet on the other side.

Right as I'm sliding the master key out, heavy footsteps thud down the hall. On the other side of the wall, the door to the guest room opens, and feet move in.

"Fuck!" one of them snaps, his voice garbled.

Callie reaches over and grasps my hand, and I ignore her shaking fingers as I focus.

"What the hell?" another one says, his voice distorted as well.

They move around the room as if taking in the scene. The hair on my neck lifts when one of them crosses right by the wall.

"She went out the window."

"Do you want me to go after her?" one of them asks.

"Yes, and take Karen with you."

My eyes widen as I look over to Zeke. *Karen?*

Their footsteps move as they shuffle back across the room and exit the door, closing it behind them. I turn to my friends. *"Karen?"* I whisper, shaking my head in disbelief. "I've known her almost as long as I have Frank, and I cannot see her masterminding all of this."

"Who's to say she's the mastermind?" Zeke says. "She may just be one of the many peons."

"But why her?" No connection to this jumps out at me. Was she a community survivor, like Danielle, and changed her name? Or perhaps she's related to someone from that day.

"We really don't have time to think too hard about it," he says. "We need to move."

Callie's still shaking, and I hug her. "It's going to be okay."

"I know. I'm fine." She sniffs. "Who am I kidding? I am so not."

With a reassuring smile, I squeeze her hand. "It's okay to be scared."

Her bottom lip quivers. "If you hadn't shown up,

there's no telling what else she was going to do to me. Thank you. Thank you both."

"You're welcome." I give her another smile.

Her breath shudders. "You're both so in control, and I'm a blubbering mess."

"You deserve to be," Zeke assures her.

I wait for her to get better control of herself, because I really need to ask her some questions.

"There's a reason why I prefer computers," she jokes.

Despite everything, I still smile. "Where are they keeping my mom?"

"I don't know," she murmurs. "Separate from the housekeeping staff and the agents, though. They shot one of the agents right in the head, and…" Her eyes squeeze shut. "I watched."

"Jesus," Zeke whispers.

A coldness settles through me. "You said the staff is separate from Mom. Where are they?"

"In the dining room," she answers.

"That makes sense. It's in the middle of the house, and there are no windows." Thank God we didn't backtrack past the basement and enter through there. We would've walked right into a trap. "How many of them are there?"

"Ten that I know of. But there could be more."

"Anything else?" he prompts. "Anything they said?"

She hesitates. "They're auctioning off your mom. I'm so sorry. It's my fault. I couldn't take watching them shoot another person in the head." She covers her face with her hands. "I opened up the portal for the bidding."

I pull her in for a hard hug. "None of this is your fault. This falls solely on the shoulders of those extremists who are out in my house right now. Do you hear me?"

She sniffs. "Where's Jackson?"

"Out in the field with your camper."

"What they don't know is that he has the data, too." She wipes her eyes. "If he can crack that one last encrypted chunk, we'll know the names of all the people on the inside."

I want to lead her to the tunnel and safety, but we don't have time. I need to figure out where they're keeping Mom.

Then it hits me. The vault.

It's a secure room contained by four walls, no windows, and a state-of-the-art locking device. It's exactly where I would keep someone.

"I just figured out where Mom is."

THE VAULT

Country Home
Sunday, 3:00 a.m.

With my friends right behind me, I slip inside the room my grandparents use when they visit. I make it to the adjoining bathroom and to the hidden passage that will lead us down to the floor where the vault is located.

The walls press in on me as we traverse the passage, and I take some slow and deep breaths. The absolute last thing any of us needs is for me to have another panic attack.

"Almost there," Zeke whispers, reaching forward to link fingers with me.

I grip his hand hard, taking the last few steps. Talk about being forced to face my fear of small spaces.

"Here," I tell them both, pointing to the hidden door that will lead us down to the vault.

Beside me, he kneels, and as he goes to slip the flexible camera through the bottom, he freezes. It's dark in here and lighter on the other side, and if it weren't for that, I wouldn't see what alarmed him. It's a slight variation in light. A shifting of shadows. But someone is definitely there.

Scooching down beside him, I take the flexible snake. I insert it, tilting it a little, and almost bump right into dark boots. I swivel the camera, sliding it back toward me, and catch sight of a very real and distinct rifle.

I pull the camera back in as the shadow shifts and the feet move on.

"He's patrolling," Callie whispers. "He'll be back. We need to move now."

Quickly, I go through the hidden door and out into the hall, and I reach the spiral stairs leading down to the vault.

Zeke stays up top to keep watch, and with our backs pressed against the wall, Callie and I descend the stairs. When I reach the first switchback, I peer around the corner. Shadows play across the metal stairs.

At the second switchback, I use the flexible snake. The steps and the vault door are clear.

Directly above my head sits a concealed camera pointed straight at the vault. I lift the ceiling panel and pull out the small camera and its back wiring. From my pack, Callie pulls pliers and strippers, and it doesn't take her a second to splice and reconnect, looping the video feed. Whoever is watching the monitor will see a constant loop of a perfectly untouched vault.

With that done, we waste no more time covering the remaining steps to the vault's door. I key in the code, and the door hisses open from the air seal. But it's not my mother who is in here, it's… "Dad?"

His eyes widen. "Sophie!"

"Dad!" I rush over.

"Oh…" He pulls me in for a hard hug. "I thought you were dead."

I squeeze him tight, shaking my head. "No, no, I'm very much alive."

Dad grabs the sides of my head and pushes me back a little bit so he can look me in the eyes. It's then that I really notice his face. It's swollen and bruised, and from the way he's leaning to the right, his ribs must be injured, too.

"What did they do to you?" I ask, already suspecting the answer. They're using him to intimidate Mom.

He shakes his head. "It doesn't matter. They check on me every ten minutes. You can't stay here."

"I'm not leaving you!"

"You have to. If I go with you, they'll know someone's inside the house. You can get me later. It's more important that you save your mother."

My brain tells me he's right, but my heart doesn't want to admit it, so I try to focus on other things I need to know. "The last I heard, Frank had gotten you to safety."

"Yes, but he was taken, too. He's here somewhere with the hostages. I haven't seen him since our transport was jacked. Karen is working for these people."

"We know, and Callie said the other hostages are in the dining room."

She scoots forward. "That's probably where they have Frank. But what about the president? Where else would she be?"

"I don't know." Dad looks sick when he says, "There's something else. They've rigged our entire home to explode."

The bomb in my parents' bedroom and the wire sticking out of it make sense. It's a transceiver, and it's talking to the other bombs, which means there's a chain system. The only way to diffuse a chain is to disarm the main unit.

On a surge of hope, I look between them. "But if we can find the main unit, we can disarm it."

Dad grabs my shoulders. "You may have practiced disarming bombs in the TIA, but this is real. This is not a simulation. They are auctioning your mother as we speak. As soon as she leaves, they are going to blow this place wide and gain international fame on the terrorist market. You have got to find your mother. She is the President of the United States. You do not have time to find and try to diffuse the main bomb."

Nausea claws at my stomach. "You're asking me to choose between her and you, not to mention Frank and the other hostages. I can't do that."

"Which is why I'm doing it for you." He pulls me in for another hug and a kiss, and I cling to him as he pushes me and my friend out the vault's door. "I love you, and I'm so very proud of the young woman you've become. You will continue to do grand and wonderful things in this world. You will make a difference. No matter what happens, always remember those words."

"Dad…" My breath catches on a constrained sob. "There has to be another way."

But he doesn't answer and instead clicks the vault closed, and I'm left staring at the metal door. My dad is right there on the other side. I can key in the code again and open it and make him come with me. My friends can help me drag him out.

But realization seeps in. He won't come, and the longer I argue with him, the more time goes by, and the patrol person will return. Then our cover will most definitely be blown.

Callie puts a gentle hand on my forearm. "We need to go."

I force myself to turn away from the door and Dad, and I follow her up the spiral staircase. With Zeke, we disappear back through the concealed door and into the passage.

Dad wants me to find Mom, but I can find the main unit and disable it and get everyone to safety.

You were born to make a difference.

My friends and I will do this.

This is not a simulation. I force Dad's words aside and focus.

We leave the passage and are now back in my grandparents' bathroom.

"The most logical place for the main unit is also where the hostages are being held. In the dining room, right in the center of the house," I say. "A blast would start there and ricochet out to all the other units."

Zeke blows out a breath. "I really hate bombs."

"Me, too," Callie says.

"We could wind our way back up to my parents' bath, down the stairs past the basement, and up into the dining room that way, but it'll take too long." I think for a second… "There's something closer. A chute of sorts. An air duct that lands at a vent in the upper corner of the dining room.

"If anything, it'll give us a view of the whole room so we can see what we're up against. Plus, there's the secret door that leads to the basement and the tunnel off the property. It's located in the floor, actually. We can get the hostages through it."

Zeke goes to get up. "Sounds like we're traversing a chute then."

"Guys," I softly say, looking earnestly at my two friends. "Do you...do you think I'm making the right decision, focusing on the bomb instead of Mom?"

"Yes," they agree in unison, and I expect that niggle of doubt to dissipate, but it doesn't. Because Dad's right.

This is not a simulation.

But he's there locked in the vault, full of obligation to his family and country, beaten up and yet still sending me back out. His bravery bolsters me.

I can do this.

AIR DUCT

Country Home
Sunday, 3:30 a.m.

We move through the passageways that connect the interior rooms of the house. There are a lot of people depending on us, and a chilling fright settles through me. We'll either stop the terrorist cell or we won't, and if we don't, this whole place will blow and everyone inside will die, including me.

Behind me, Zeke trails his fingers along the back of my neck and squeezes. Reassuring me that he's here, that we're in this together. In all the years I've known him, he's always done that—squeezed the back of my neck when I needed comfort or encouragement. I love that he can read me.

I place my fingers over his and squeeze, silently thanking him.

When I reach the last door, I slip the master key in, and my hands shake a little as I click it left. I crack the door open. After making sure the hallway is clear, I step completely into view with my friends right behind me.

I scamper to the storage room. Once inside, we quietly close the door behind us, and I turn on my red headlamp. In the corner under a shelf sits the opening to the chute, and I crouch to give it a good study.

As I do, my nerves flare. It's a tight space. I can fit, and so can Callie, but Zeke is definitely too big.

"Let's do this," he says, taking a small knife from his vest. Clicking it open, he goes about backing out the screws of the grill, and I take my pack off and slim things down to just what I need.

Callie moves in, eyeing the space. "Are you sure, Sophie?"

"Yes, it's my family." I can traverse a chute. My claustrophobia will not control me.

He lays the grill aside. "We're doing a safety tie."

"Good idea," I agree, and the two of them tie a rope around my ankles.

"Three tugs," he tells me, "and we'll pull you back out. Two and we'll give you slack."

I nod, and with one last deep breath, I slide to my stomach and crawl partially in.

My light reflects off the duct work, and another couple of feet ahead lies the chute that leads straight down to the dining room where the hostages and the main explosive unit probably are. I squeeze and wiggle completely into the tight space, refusing to let my mind register the cramped area.

I place all my concentration on the thin rope tied around my ankles and anchored to my friends on the other end.

Twenty-four hours ago, would this have been me? I

sure as hell wouldn't have willingly gone into this chute. Proactive, not reactive. I've taken control. The outcome is in my hands now.

The rope around my ankles snags, but the space is too tight for me to see what it's hung on. I hold myself planked in place and shift my legs until it slips free and I can continue.

The duct curves, and I shift my body accordingly. A few more feet now. This should bring me some relief. Instead, I'm hyperaware of the restricted and dusty area surrounding me.

Zeke's singing voice trickles through my head. *My bologna has a first name, it's O-S-C-A-R. My bologna has a second name, it's M-A-Y-E-R. Oh, I love to eat it every day, and if you ask me why I'll say, 'cause Oscar Mayer has a way with B-O-L-O-G-N-A.* That was the first time I've heard him sing, and he has a more than decent voice. Who would've guessed?

Just then a voice filters in, and I flick off the light that's attached to my head. I scoot another few inches, and new light filters up from the dining room through the slats of the grate. I take a second to catch my breath, and as I inch forward, I put all my concentration into not making a sound. More light filters in, and I move my head over the slats to peer down.

Two terrorists wearing black ski masks are bent over someone seated. I survey the room. They've moved all of the furniture out of the way, and the chair is dead center.

Off to the left and covered by a throw rug lies the section of the floor that, once opened, will lead to the basement and the tunnel out of here.

My eyes trail up and down the walls and across the ceiling, looking for the main bomb, but I don't see it. There's a signal-jamming device just a foot or so from the grate I'm peering out of. If I can disable it, we can establish communication with Jackson, and he can contact Prax.

I never imagined I'd be thinking of the director as an ally, but at this point, he's the only one left on the outside. Everyone else is either dead or in here with me. Unless he's in here, too…

The terrorists shift, and my heart pinches. Mom's tied to a chair with a bomb strapped across her stomach. I can't know for sure, but it's likely the main unit that, once triggered, will set off all the others.

The explosion surrounding Erik's death ricochets through my brain, and I want to recoil.

But I know what I have to do.

I'm going to call their bluff.

They exit the room, and I put my plan in motion. Rotating in the chute, I slip the tools I need from my vest, and I work them through the wide slats in the grate. The movement draws my mother's attention, and her eyes track up to meet mine. They widen in recognition, and I shake my head, indicating for her not to speak.

Wetness pools in her eyes. She probably thought I was dead. I smile. Her lips tremble as she grins back, and tears drop to her cheeks. I'm filled with determination and focus.

There's blood on her face, and killing the bad guys is my new goal. Right after I save the people I love.

Her worried gaze moves away from me and over to the door where the two just left. Then she gives me a quick go-ahead nod.

The signal-jamming box is just a foot away from me and attached to the ceiling. Using my flexible camera, I study the dials and digital readout. I know this box. We practiced on this exact one in the TIA.

"The key is to cut the pink-and-white striped wire. The signals in and out will no longer be jammed." The instructor demonstrates. "Note the green light on the front is still blinking. It gives the appearance as if the signal jam is still in effect."

Leaving the camera where it is, I slip tiny needle-nose pliers attached to an extension through the slats and work them over to the box.

With steady hands, I maneuver the pliers behind the box and make sure I have the correct pink-and-white wire. I twist the handle end of the extension, and the pliers snip cleanly through. But as I'm doing this, I remember that I forgot to ground the tool, and a shock of electricity zings along the metal extension, right through the slats and up my arm.

I hiss, jerking with the shock and fumbling the tools, and it's all I can do not to lose my grip on everything as I pull it all back in. A quick check of the box shows the green light is still blinking.

I whisper to Mom, "Hostages?"

"Gym," she whispers back.

"Is that the main unit?" I ask, meaning the bomb strapped to her. I already suspect the answer.

She nods.

I hear one of the extremists coming. "I'll be back," I whisper, and then I yank on the rope three firm times, and my friends pull me up.

For my plan to work, we'll need to split up.

"I know I'm asking a lot," I say when I'm out of the chute and back in the closet with them. "I won't think any less if—"

"Absolutely not." Callie shakes her head. "We're either living or dying together. All for one."

Zeke nods. "Agreed."

From the pack, she pulls out the coms, and we all suit up, each wedging a receiver into our ear and wrapping the transmitter around our wrists. Callie takes a second to dial into our private channel, before asking, "Jackson, you copy?"

Static crinkles through the line, followed by his voice. "Callie? Is that you? Are you okay?"

"We're all here," Zeke tells him.

Jackson launches right in. "There's still one more layer of encryption, but I broke through a wall. The director is one of the inside people. He knew he had a target on his back, and so he cut a deal. His life for inside information on the president."

Their startled expressions tell me they're thinking the same thing I am. The Director of the CIA is helping the terrorist cell. Holy shit.

"Wh—" I clear my throat. "Where is Prax right now?"

"I don't know," he quickly says.

"Fucking bastard," Zeke spits.

I agree. But this? This is too much.

"What about the rest?" Callie asks, fiddling with the ends of her hair. "Prax, Karen… who else is on the inside?"

"I'm almost through the last layer," Jackson says. "I'll let you know as soon as I do. But Prax…that's a huge find."

"Okay," I say, gathering my thoughts. "Here's the plan. Callie's going to get Dad. Zeke will go to the gym where the other hostages are located. And I'm going for Mom."

A quick and hot flash of nerves heats my skin. "She's attached to the main unit, and when I take it off her, it'll set the timer in motion and create a diversion that'll flush everyone out."

Logic tells me that Dad will be okay in the vault, even in a bombing, but I'm not taking any chances. For all I know they've rigged the vault, as well. "That leaves you, Jackson. We need people on the outside, ready to move in and take them into custody before they run."

He chuckles and tells me, "Hang on."

More static comes through the com, and then I hear a familiar voice say, "Sophie?"

"William," I gasp. "You're okay? Oh, God, I thought you were dead."

"I'm okay, thanks to your quick-thinking CPR. Don't worry."

"But one of your agents was on their side, wasn't he?"

"Yes, one was, and one wasn't. The good one was unconscious. He ended up waking up as you were running away. He fought with the other one, who is now dead. We used the opportunity to fake my death and yours. Prax thinks both of us are gone, which means the terrorists think so, too."

"Good, it's exactly what I wanted." And it explains, even more, why my parents were shocked to see me. Everyone thinks I'm dead.

"I'm here with Jackson," William says. "I have a whole team. We're ready out here. Just tell us what you need."

COUNTRY HOME

Northern Virginia
Sunday, 4:30 a.m.

We take a moment to map out Zeke's route to the gym and hostages, and Callie's back to the vault and Dad. I, of course, will go down the chute to Mom.

Zeke assures me, "We're good. Time to roll the dice and get this done."

This may be the last time I ever see them.

I promise them, "If—no, *when* we make it out alive, we are going on one hell of an adventure. Just the four of us. We'll go climb a mountain or zip a jungle or sail an ocean. Agreed? Even if we have to ditch my security, we're doing it. Just us."

"Agreed." Callie pulls me in for a quick and firm hug. "I don't have a whole lot of friends, and in the almost eighteen years I've been alive, you three are it for me. I seriously cannot think of a better bunch of dorks."

She grabs Zeke's hand. "We're unstoppable. This isn't the end, and don't let yourself think so." Pulling him in, she plants a hard kiss on his mouth before doing the same to me. "See you on the other side." Then without a glance back, she takes her master key and slips from the storage room.

I've always adored her, but I seriously love her hard after that speech. With a sigh, I shift my body toward Zeke to find him already staring at the side of my face.

"Well," he quietly says.

"Yeah," I respond, just as quietly. "I've, um—" Words tumble around in my head, and I find myself unable to articulate what I want to say.

"No—" He cuts me off, moving in. "This isn't the end, and I don't want either of us talking like it is. Whatever we want to say, we'll say it afterward." Gently he grasps both sides of my face and tenderly presses his lips to mine, breathing me in deep, making me feel both lost and found at the same time. "Okay? Afterward."

No. It's the first word that pops into my mind. I want to say everything to him now. But I don't, and instead, I nod. "Okay."

Our gazes hold and lock for several beats, and he moves away first, taking my hands and placing a kiss in each palm. As he does, I stare at the crown of his dark head, promising myself I will see him again.

Like Callie, he takes his master key and quickly slips from the room. He doesn't glance back, either. I wish he would have, and I'm also glad he didn't. I likely would have pulled him back if he had.

Afterward, I remind myself. I'll see him after.

Shifting down on my hands and knees, I crawl into the chute. Halfway down, Callie speaks in my ear, saying, "I've reached your dad."

Those words alone help me breathe easier, and I keep going, all the way down until the very end. Through the slats in the ceiling vent, I spy Mom still strapped to the chair, and as I remove the vent's cover, Zeke says, "I've reached the hostages."

"And I'm with Mom," I whisper, working the cover free and slipping it inside the chute with me.

"We'll wait for your go-ahead," he says.

Mom looks up at me. I climb out of the vent feet first, dangling from my fingers, and drop the few feet to the floor.

I race across the dining room, going first to the throw rug that covers the concealed door and getting it unlocked and ready. Then I come down in front of Mom, and my eyes track across the bomb strapped to her stomach.

A red light blinks, and I know as soon as I lift the device off of her, the light will turn green and the timer will start. Callie will grab my dad and run. Zeke will grab the hostages and run. I'll take off with Mom. And the extremists will race out into the open where William's team will be waiting.

With one final breath, I look Mom in the eyes. "I'm going to take this off of you. When I do, it will trigger the timer. We are going to disappear through the floor and run like our asses are on fire to the basement and the tunnel off this property. Callie's got Dad. Zeke is in charge of the hostages. William is outside with a team ready."

Mom closes her eyes for a second, and when she reopens them, I detect fear and determination, yes, but also love. And it's the love that washes through me and cleanses me of any last doubt.

"We can do this," Mom says.

"I love you," I whisper.

"Me, too, baby."

"Stand by," I say to my friends.

Slipping the dagger from my ankle holder, I first cut the ties around Mom's ankles and wrists. Then I poise the knife at the strap holding the bomb to her stomach. I look at her one last time, together we take a breath, and then I slice it and carefully set the bomb aside.

Mom stands, and we both stare down at the device, but it doesn't flip from red to green.

She looks at me.

I look at her.

We both look back at the bomb.

Maybe I was wrong.

Click. The sound of it jolts through me. The red light blinks to green, and the digital readout reads 00:04:59

"T-minus five!" I yell.

Mom surges forward and down through the floor, and I'm right behind her, slamming the hatch over us. Unless the terrorists somehow magically got a master key, they can't get through.

Darkness surrounds us as we sprint down the passage, and our heavy breaths echo off the stone walls. I hear feet pounding above us as the extremists race into the dining room where Mom just was. Loud voices follow, people shouting, then more heavy footsteps as they split off into different directions.

We're in the basement now, and Mom slides across a wet spot, losing her footing. I yank her up. Throwing open the hatch that covers the tunnel, I grab her lower body and shove her inside the opening. Good thing she's little.

"Go!" I yell.

I leap up behind her, slamming the hatch closed. When the bomb goes off, there will be fire, and closing that will keep it from entering the tunnel.

At least, I hope.

We scramble down. I don't waste a valuable second looking at my watch because there is no way we're going to make it. This tunnel is too long, and we're on our hands and knees.

A faint whistling fills the air, followed by a deep bass, like in the fragile seconds surrounding Erik's death. Another sound, this one sharp and quick, then one that rolls over me, pressing in, like there's cotton in my ears and hundreds of tiny hands pushing against me.

A wave of warmth follows, and I keep crawling, praying that everyone else got out.

Popping and cracking come next. Then what sounds like hail falling. It must be debris sprinkling the ground above us.

"Zeke!" I yell. "Callie?"

There's nothing but static.

My heart pangs deep and heavy.

We keep moving. Silence descends, filling the space with a deafening quiet. Mom gasps for breath.

"You've got this," I tell her.

On we go, and I focus on Mom's shoes as she shuffles forward.

After what feels like an eternity, the air shifts to carry the scent of motor oil and burning timber. We must be getting near the end.

The sound of voices fills the air, people yelling. Emergency sirens blare.

We emerge from the tunnel and into complete chaos—people running around, shouting, fire, smoke. Static still fills my ears, and I have no clue if my friends made it out with Dad, Frank, and the hostages.

Mom and I stand, neither of us fully grasping that we're alive and that our home has been blown apart. Flames blaze through the early-morning darkness, glowing around the pile of rubble that was once our home.

It's Mom who reaches for me first, wrapping her slender arms around me and hugging me so very hard. I bury my nose in the crook of her neck and simply breathe her in. We're alive.

"I love you," she whispers.

"I love you, too," I whisper back.

The com still lodged in my ear crackles. "Sophie, are you there? It's Jackson."

"Jackson!" I step back from Mom. "Yes, we're here. Mom and I are safe. We're in the field. Where are you?"

"The mastermind behind this day is—"

"Frank!" Mom yells, waving. I turn to see him running right toward us through the trees and a cloud of smoke and dust.

"What did she just say?" Jackson asks.

"Frank!" I yell, waving, too.

But something's different about his face, a distant expression I've never seen before, and it's then that I note he's running with his weapon out of the holster.

"No!" Jackson yells. "He's one of the terrorists! He's the main one! Run!"

I freeze. And like I'm watching a movie in fast rewind, my life with Frank strobes through my mind.

"Let's practice elbow strikes today," he says, tying on my MMA gloves…

He helps me from the mud. "That damn horse bests you every time."…

With a scowl, I check out my new braces. "Ugly," I say. "Pretty," he counters…

"Don't be frustrated. Here." Frank hot glues a felt sun to my science project…

I sneeze. Cough. Moan. Frank hands me soup. "Good for the flu."…

And when he played video games with me…

When he helped me wrap Erik's Christmas gift…

When he said, *If I had a daughter, I'd want her to be just like you.*

"Because of you, my family is dead!" he yells. "I dedicated my life to this."

Behind him and through the smoke emerge several men and women in military fatigues, racing toward us. But it's too late. He points and aims.

"No!" I scream.

He fires several rounds, and as they rip through the dark morning, I do the only thing I can. I dive in front of Mom and pray I save her life.

WALTER REED MEDICAL CENTER

Washington, D. C.
One week later

*C*linging to the rope ladder twenty-five feet below the
cave's entrance, I take one last look around. I belt out
a few lines of the Oscar Mayer song just to hear it echo
around me.

Adjusting my helmet's lamp for a wider beam, I scan
the moist, gleaming walls of the cylindrical-shaped shaft.
The scent of musky, damp earth fills the air. Below me, the
ladder disappears into the blackness of depth.

One hundred feet. That's how far down we went, and
I didn't freak out once.

My friends wait at the top, having already ascended.
Even from my dangling perch, I see Zeke's sunlit silhouette,
fists planted on his hips as he stares down at me.

"I should have never sung that song!" he shouts.

I laugh. "No, you shouldn't have!"

I come from the dream gradually, my lashes fluttering
open, and a smile curves my lips. I'm not sure I ever will
go into a cave, but dreaming about it sure is fun.

There's a light overhead, and though it's dim, I still squint. A loud beeping from the right pulses down my ear, and I wince.

I try to swallow, but everything in my mouth is thick and dry. My head feels weighted and lifting it off the pillow is impossible. I manage to roll it to the side. Mom sits in the corner, curled up in a reclining chair, sleeping and very much alive.

Dad is right here beside me, holding my hand, which is punctured and taped with an IV. His head lies at an awkward angle on my bed, and I soak both of them in. My parents. Alive.

"Dad?" I croak, and his head snaps up so quickly I fear he might get whiplash.

He surges to his feet. "Oh my God." His shaky fingers go to my face as he touches my cheeks, brow, hair, neck, lips, and my ears. "Can you hear me okay? Can you see me? Oh, sweetie, you've been unconscious for a week. We've been beside ourselves."

I try to smile and assure him I'm okay, but my mouth is so dry. "Water," I croak, and he jumps into action, grabbing ice chips and sliding them between my lips one tiny chip at a time.

They melt and slip down my throat, and I groan from the comfort. So good.

Mom is here now on the other side of the bed. "How long has she been awake?"

"Just now," he tells her.

She cries, and I smile. "I'm okay," I assure her.

I take a breath and wince at the intense hot pain in my stomach.

"I'll go get someone," Dad says and hurries from the room.

"You were shot in the stomach," she tells me. "You've been out a week. Surgery, internal bleeding, more surgery." Fresh tears fall down her face. "We've been so worried."

I look up into her familiar, sweet face, and despite the pain in my stomach, I smile as I say again, "I'm okay."

She presses a kiss to my forehead as she soothes my head with her hand.

"My friends?" I ask.

Mom's lips tremble into a smile. "They're fine. They've been here every single day to visit you. William, too."

"Britta?"

Her smile gets bigger. "She's fine. We found her in Rock Creek Park. They left her for dead. She was in bad shape, but she's alive. She's here on the floor below you."

"Oh," I breathe. "Good."

Grabbing the ice chips, Mom offers me a couple more, and I gladly accept them, swallowing, groaning again at how good that feels. "Frank?" I ask.

Her smile slides away. "The inside list went deep. Prax, Frank, Karen, and several other people across all the agencies. All of whom are currently in custody. The only person who still remains at large is Danielle Fox."

Mom takes a breath as she stares into my eyes with so much shame weighing down on her. "Oh, honey, I am so sorry I lied to you and your brother, and to the American people. Danielle, Frank, Karen—they were all from the same community.

"After the drone misfire, the Lone Eagle team made sure everyone had all the help we could give them—that

Max and the other orphaned children had homes and that others had jobs. We truly tried to make amends. We had no idea of the festering anger and contempt that some of the survivors held. Frank lost his daughter that day. She was your age."

That's why he picked my birthday to put his plan into place. Eye for an eye.

"And your brother…"

A heavy and guilty sigh comes from deep within her chest. "He and his friend knew, and they were trying to work things from the inside. They thought they could stop the events set to transpire. I wish they would've come to me. And Danforth…so much collateral damage. It's all my fault. I only hope one day that you can forgive me."

"I already have," I say without a second of hesitation.

She cries quietly. "I hope you know how much I treasure you. And I'm so sorry for all the arguments of late. I've always wanted you to be strong and independent, but when you started to be, it freaked me out a little. I didn't handle it very well."

"It's okay, Mom, I get it. We both didn't handle it well."

The doctor comes in then with Dad right behind. Wiping her eyes, she moves away to give the doctor room. Yes, I've forgiven her, and I can only hope America will, too.

One week later my friends crowd into my hospital room. I lie propped up in bed, still connected to an IV and multiple monitors. Zeke reclines beside me, his legs stretched out and crossed at the ankles, resting alongside mine. His arm stretches above my head, and I relax against him.

Over in the corner, Britta sits in the same chair Mom was in when I first woke up a week ago. With her arm in a sling and bruises dotting her pretty face, she looks battered but alive. Very much alive. She was released from the hospital yesterday. Unfortunately, I still have a week or more to go. I can't wait.

Britta is staring at me and Zeke, sharing the bed, and she must sense my eyes because she looks at me. I smile a little and so does she, sadly. I lost a brother, and she lost her first love. When she came to visit me yesterday, she broke down in tears that tore a fresh hole in my heart. I hope she knows that I'll always think of her as a sister. Just because Erik is now gone doesn't mean she has to leave our lives.

Jackson hangs up the phone call he was just on and plops down in a vacant chair on the other side of my bed. "Mom said to tell you hi and that she's bringing you pizza from Ledo's later."

"Yum." I smile.

"Okay." Callie rubs her hands together. "I have been *dying* to tell you all what I have in mind." She runs an excited gaze around the room. "Ever since Sophie said she wanted one hell of an adventure, I have been digging around. The problem is, there is so much to do! But what do you all think about a rim-to-rim hike in the Grand Canyon with camping at the bottom?"

"I'd do that," Jackson says.

"Me, too," Zeke says.

Callie looks at Britta, and she seems surprised we're

including her. "Yes," she softly says. "I'd go."

Everyone looks at me. But I don't answer. There's no way my parents will agree to anything, especially after the events that have transpired. And though I said I'd ditch security—I won't do that to them. Not now.

"She'll go," Mom says, and we all turn to see her standing in the open door.

My eyes widen. "Really?"

She steps into the room with Dad behind her. "I think you all have more than proved you can take care of not only yourselves, but America, too. It's past time you had a grand adventure. As long as I'm in office, I can't agree to no security, but I'll agree to light."

Wow, that's a first. "Light as in?"

"Two," she says.

With a smile, I look at my friends. "We'll be as off the grid as possible. The Grand Canyon is an option, but what are your thoughts on caving?"

WHITE HOUSE

Washington, D.C.
Two weeks later

Dad, Mom, and William made a united front as they came clean to America about the events and subsequent fallout surrounding Lone Eagle and the drone misfire. It's been a long few weeks, riddled with every news outlet weighing in on the cover-up. Soon Mom and William will begin a Town Hall type tour of America as they truthfully answer all of their constituents' questions.

America seems divided right now—half ready to condemn and the other half commending the way the two of them are handling things.

Prax is going away for a very long time.

I truly believe as the weeks and months move forward, America's division on the topic will close, and my mom will, once again, have the public trust.

I place my palm over the thick bandage that covers the right side of my stomach where Frank's bullet went clean through. I've only been out of the hospital for a few days, and I can say with complete confidence that I never want to see the inside of one again.

"You okay?" Dad asks, bringing me from my thoughts.

I nod. "Just thinking."

"About your big adventure, I hope." He smiles.

My eyes light up. It's still months away, but now that he's brought it up, yes. Big yes. Can't wait.

The door to the Blue Room opens, and Mom's secretary tells us, "They're ready for you."

With Mom on my right and Dad my left, we make our way down the corridor to the East Room where the Medal for Valor ceremony is being held. Two agents open the wide double doors. Cameras flash, and I glance toward the stage to see everyone in place: William, Callie, Jackson, Britta, and Zeke.

Zeke's green eyes crinkle when he sees me. The love of my life. Not so one-sided after all. Dressed in a black suit, he's so very handsome as he comes down off the stage, looking between my parents. "May I?"

Dad smiles. "Sure."

Zeke holds his arm out, and I step forward, curling my hand around his bicep. "Looking good," he whispers.

A weak chuckle escapes my lips. "Thanks."

His gaze travels over my face before coming to land on my eyes. "You ready?"

I nod. "Let's do this."

We climb the stairs, and my eyes lift, grazing over William, Callie, Jackson, and Britta before coming to land on several poster-sized photos—Danforth, Max, and Erik.

The ghost of my brother's laughter floats through my mind and brings a fond smile to my lips. Me getting the Medal for Valor. Neither of us saw that coming; I only wish he were here to share it with me.

I reach the stage, and the crowd cheers. I turn to look out over the sea of people, and all the way in the back I imagine my brother, smiling proudly. *I love you, Erik. I will miss you always.*

A SECLUDED CAVE

New Mexico
Holiday Break

I touch down on the cave's floor with a soft thud. Above me a wide hole lets in bright sunlight. It's so much like the dream I had in the hospital, that it's weird. "How'd you discover this place?"

Callie grins. "I know all the best spots."

Glancing down at my carabiner, Zeke motions for me to unhook, and I do.

Callie takes off her gloves and reaches inside a canvas bag to pull out a map and penlight. While she spreads the map out on the dirt floor, Jackson moves in and kneels beside her. Now, if Britta had come, this would have been perfect. But she's busy with college, and despite my best efforts, she's pulled away from me and my family. I get it, and I try to respect it, but I do miss her.

Callie twists on the penlight to illuminate the map. "To the east, it's mapped to about a half mile, standard formations, nothing too spectacular, muddy terrain, and a dead end." She glances up at us, excitement dancing in her eyes. "But south is another story."

Refocusing on the map, she trails a finger along a black dotted line. "Look at all the segments and caverns joined by narrow passages. I've nicknamed this path the centipede. It's so much fun to explore, and every room is different in size. The biggest one measures five acres."

"Wow," Zeke says. "That is huge."

I lean in, taking a closer look at the map and the penciled notations. The drawings, dimensions, symbols, compass bearings, and angles of slopes. "You did all of that? You are so talented."

She waves that off. "I've been here a few times now. You guys are going to love it." Folding the map back together, she places it and the penlight back inside her canvas bag.

Jackson gets to his feet. "I'm beyond ready. Let's do this."

Callie flips on her helmet light and nearly skips off into the dark. We flick on our headlamps, too, and trail behind her. No more than a minute later, we reach the first of the skinny crawl spaces in the centipede.

I blow out a quick breath. I got this. I wanted to do this. I will do this.

Zeke gently squeezes my neck. "Teamwork. We've got your back."

Callie efficiently scales a rocky, ten-foot wall and disappears into a sliver of blackness. Jackson follows. I'm next. They made it look easier than it is. After trying and slipping back down, I finally fumble my way to the opening. Zeke is just behind me.

Once inside the narrow passage, I crawl forward on

my stomach, keeping Jackson's boots in sight. A few feet into the crawl, the passage turns to mud.

"I thought caves were supposed to be dry," Jackson gripes.

"Not this one," Callie says. "Live caves are semi-liquid."

"Great," he mumbles, and behind me, Zeke chuckles.

A few minutes later, we drop down into one of the rooms of the centipede. Closing my eyes, I inhale the earthy, peaceful scent, and I smile. I did it.

Covered in sludge, Zeke moves in beside me. "Good job."

"Thanks."

Callie says, "This room measures thirty-by-thirty. Check out the stalactites. Aren't they amazing?"

Opening my eyes, I look up at the hundreds of carrot-shaped objects hanging from the ceiling, some inches long, others a foot or longer. "Wow."

She walks across the room. "Wait 'til you see the next segment."

We follow, going down on our stomachs to slither under a large rock. Inch by inch we disappear, head first, back, butt, legs, and finally boots.

Seconds later, the crawlspace opens into another chamber, this one smaller than the first. I inch my way out and look back to see Zeke do the same.

He pushes up to stand beside me. "Man, you sure gotta be agile to do this."

"Be very careful in these rooms," Callie cautions. "Any physical contact will introduce bacteria and cause discoloration or algae growth."

I scan the area, lighting it with my headlamp. A

labyrinth of floor-to-ceiling corkscrew-shaped objects fills the room. They each stand roughly ten feet tall with a foot of space between them. "This is unbelievable. Who would've ever guessed this existed down here?"

"Stay to the outside." Callie edges her way around the outer wall. "I don't want to take any chances with breaking one of those."

Jackson follows her, inching his way along, his eyes fixed on the miracle in front of him. His helmet light plays off the maze, illuminating the pale, translucent blue objects. "How many years does it take to make one of those?"

"Possibly thousands," she says. "Depends on the rate of water drip. Of course, if there's a drought, they won't grow at all."

We make it halfway around the room and come to a stop. "Okay, the next chamber is above us. We have to climb a twenty-foot shaft to get to it. Watch how I do it and follow my example."

She steps into a hollowed out, three-foot-wide portion of the wall. With her back braced against one side and her feet on the other, she inches her way skyward in the chimney-shaped cavity.

Jackson follows. He reaches the top and slides onto the landing, signaling me to begin my ascent. I do exactly what they did. "The dryness of the rock walls makes it easy."

As I near the top, I scoot over to make room for Zeke on the small landing, and seconds later, he pushes himself up beside me.

The four of us crowd onto the tiny landing, and Callie turns on a Maglite to brighten the next cavern.

"Holy…" Jackson breathes.

A sigh of contentment flows from her. "I know."

Our small perch juts from a rock wall close to the ceiling. Roughly thirty feet below us spans a chamber an acre in size. A magnificent flow of delicate, milky-aqua, translucent curtains covers three of the four sloping walls. They merge at the bottom of the room into a still pool.

Zeke nudges in closer and peers over my shoulder. "Is it alive? I mean is it flowing? Is it liquid or solid? I can't tell."

I turn my head, and our helmets bump, blinding us both with each other's lights.

"Sorry." He laughs, and it echoes through the chamber.

Callie says, "Flowstone is solid. But it takes running water to make it, so the outside will be slick from the wall and ceiling leakage. See?" She directs her light to the ceiling, glistening with damp. "This cave is very much active."

"This is a chemical reaction between limestone and rain?" Jackson asks.

"You got it." She shifts onto her knees. "This is a dead end. We have to go back down the shaft and through another crawlspace to get to the final room."

"The centipede's deformed," I say, turning to follow Zeke back down.

But he doesn't move and, instead, just looks at me.

"What?" I ask.

Zeke shakes his head. "Nothing. You're kind of adorable all dirty-faced and white-teethed."

My cheeks flush, and I roll my eyes.

Jackson gags, and Callie giggles.

Reaching up, Zeke straightens my helmet, and it

makes my stomach do all kinds of fluttery things. Then he disappears back down the shaft into the corkscrew chamber.

I come down after him, still flushed, and grinning, he pulls me in for a quick kiss.

"The final crawlspace is sloped and slimy," Callie says. "If you're not careful you'll slide right down it like a laundry chute. But the end result? Just wait."

"More mud," Jackson mumbles. "Sounds *so* fun."

"When did you become this high maintenance?" I joke, and he makes a face.

Callie leads us a quarter of the way around the room and then spider-climbs up twelve feet to the next passage. "Put at least six feet of space between each of you in case someone slides. You'll see what I mean."

We follow, slipping in the gunk coating the top, bottom, and sides of the tubular passage.

Jackson moans. "I get to pick the next adventure."

He squish-crawls his way forward, and when he's six feet ahead, I follow.

"How long is this?" Zeke asks.

"The longest one yet," Callie says. "Fifty feet."

Up ahead Jackson stops to fling goo from his gloved fingers. "There's nothing living in this ooze is there?"

"What's wrong?" I tease. "Afraid of a little salamander?"

"Ha-ha-ha."

"You all better pay attention," Callie warns. "Don't lose—"

"Ssshhhiiittt…" Zeke loses hold and gravity pulls him down the sloped chute straight toward me.

I register his body right before he slides on top of me and comes to an abrupt stop. Neither of us says anything as we lie, slicked in mud, his front to my back, lodged in the narrow, body-hugging chute.

Slowly, I shake my helmeted head. "Zeke, Zeke, Zeke."

"Oh, zip it," he grumbles.

I laugh. "Put your hands beside me and lift up, and I'll try and scoot out."

He plants his hands in the slime and does as I ask. I move forward a few inches, and our harnesses snag.

I wiggle. "What happened?"

"We're caught."

I wiggle again. "Are you sure?"

"Yes, I'm sure."

I wiggle harder. "Where're we caught?"

"Our harnesses."

I give a hard jerk. "Can you reach it?"

"Stop moving. Good God, you're making it worse."

I still.

He inhales slowly. "Stay still and let me unhook us."

He wedges his hand between our bodies and nudges it along my lower back, trying to find where we're hooked. He inches his fingers lower and brushes my butt.

"Enjoying yourself?"

"Very much, thank you. Ah." His finger hooks in the strap circling the bend of my leg. "Here we go." He flicks it free from the metal clasp on his harness. "You're free to go."

"Was it as good for you as it was for me?"

"Funny." He gives me a little push, and I go sliding off ahead of him.

When we near the end, I curl my legs up next to my

chest, scooching in beside Callie and Jackson.

Callie says, "Whoever charted this cave rigged a series of pulleys to the walls and ceiling and attached a line. It's at a forty-five-degree angle. You're going to clip your harness to the line and slide over the lake to the other side."

Beside her, she places the canvas sack. Reaching inside, she rustles around and pulls out a foot-long, thin, tubular object. She cracks it against her knee, making it glow green, and throws it into the room. Then, clipping her carabiner to the wire, she slides from the crawlspace.

Dangling there, she glances back at us. "At five acres this is the largest room. It also has the best acoustics. Fifty feet below us, the lake fills the entire area, minus that small path on the other side where we're headed."

Her flare already hit our destination and casts an eerie green glow over the walls, ceiling, floor, and lake.

I crane my neck to study the pulley system.

Someone drove a piton into the wall a foot above the passage opening that we're crowded in. A cable attaches to its eye and slopes downward to the other side of the lake, where another piton has already been secured in a rock.

"You sure this thing's gonna hold me?" Jackson asks.

"It's thousand-pound test. I think it'll hold you." With a grin, she zips off, yelling like Tarzan, and it echoes all around us. She's right—great acoustics.

Seconds later, she touches down fifty feet below on the other side of the lake.

Jackson scrutinizes the cable again and the lake below. "If I fall in that lake, someone better rescue me."

"We'll think about it," Callie calls back as she unclips her harness. "Your turn."

Jackson pushes his upper body from the crawlspace and clips his safety carabiner to the cable. With feet dangling in the air, he slides down to where she stands. He glances back across the lake and up to Zeke and me and, unclipping his harness, signals us to go.

I look down, idly watching the water lap against the tiny shore they're both on. Something moves beneath the clear, green surface, and I refocus.

Zeke moves in. "What is it?"

"Watch." I point, and a few seconds later, a couple of large white fish, each about three feet long, surface.

"They don't have any eyes," Callie calls up to us. "Pretty cool, huh?"

Zeke and I exchange a grin. "This is amazing, isn't it?" I ask.

"It truly is." He leans in, kissing me. "Proud of you."

"Thank you."

He points to the wire. "Do you mind if I go first? Since this is our last room, I want to get a picture of you zipping down."

"Sure."

It doesn't take him but a minute to clip on and zip across the lake to where our friends wait. Then it's my turn. But as I clip on and get ready, an ornery thought sneaks in. *It also has the best acoustics.*

I zip across, singing at the top of my lungs, "My bologna has a first name, it's O-S-C-A-R…"

"I should have never told you that story!" Zeke yells, and we all laugh.

Read on for fun bonus content with character profiles, case studies, a Q&A with the author, and more to keep the thrill ride going!

Personality Profiles
(Completed After Terrorist Attack)

SOPHIE WASHINGTON
1. Openness to New Experience (22nd percentile): Subject scored as a traditionalist, down to earth, practical, and conservative.
2. Work Ethic (95th percentile): Subject scored as strongly inclined to be conscientious, disciplined, efficient, and well organized.
3. Extraversion (67th percentile): Subject scored as reserved yet friendly and assertive.
4. Agreeableness (86th percentile): Subject scored as compassionate, eager, and good natured.
5. Emotional Stability (6th percentile): Subject scored as relaxed and not easily upset in stressful situations.
6. Conclusion: The personality trait likely to have the greatest influence on Sophie's overall behavior, motivation, values, and reactions in further situations is Work Ethic.

ZEKE CANCIO
1. Openness to New Experience (1st percentile): Subject scored as a traditionalist, down to earth, practical, and conservative.
2. Work Ethic (98th percentile): Subject scored as highly conscientious, disciplined, efficient, and well organized.
3. Extraversion (26th percentile): Subject scored as reserved, formal, serious, and quiet.

4. Agreeableness (67th percentile): Subject scored as hardheaded, skeptical, competitive, and proud, yet compassionate, eager, and good natured.
5. Emotional Stability (13th percentile): Subject scored low as relaxed and not easily upset in stressful situations.
6. Conclusion: The personality trait likely to have the greatest influence on Zeke's overall behavior, motivation, values, and reactions in further situations is Openness to New Experience.

CALLIE HANSEN
1. Openness to New Experience (81st percentile): Subject scored as imaginative, open minded, and experimental.
2. Work Ethic (46th percentile): Subject scored as conscientious, disciplined, and efficient yet spontaneous, disorganized, and with a preference for flexibility.
3. Extraversion (76th percentile): Subject scored as outgoing, friendly, assertive, and enjoys working with others.
4. Agreeableness (67th percentile): Subject scored as hard headed, skeptical, competitive, and proud yet compassionate, eager, and good natured.
5. Emotional Stability (90th percentile): Subject scored as prone to worry and feelings of anxiety. (Note: before the attack subject scored low in this area)
6. Conclusion: The personality trait likely to have the greatest influence on Callie's overall behavior, motivation, values, and reactions in further situations is Emotional Stability.

JACKSON FISCHER

1. Openness to New Experience (30th percentile): Subject scored as a traditionalist, down to earth, practical, and conservative.

2. Work Ethic (90th percentile): Subject scored as conscientious, disciplined, efficient, and well organized.

3. Extraversion (6th percentile): Subject scored as reserved, preferring the company of close friends.

4. Agreeableness (49th percentile): Subject scored as compassionate, eager, and good natured yet skeptical, competitive, and proud.

5. Emotional Stability (23th percentile): Subject scored as relaxed and not easily upset in stressful situations.

6. Conclusion: The personality trait likely to have the greatest influence on Jackson's overall behavior, motivation, values, and reactions in further situations is Extraversion.

TOP SECRET CASE FILE

NAME: Sophie Washington
AGE: 17
HEIGHT: 5 foot 5 inches
WEIGHT: 130 pounds
HAIR: Dark brown
EYES: Light brown
ETHNICITY: Cuban American
LANGUAGES: English, Spanish

SKILLS: Identifying individuals, contacts, and organizations with access to critical intelligence. Detecting opportunities to disrupt terrorist attacks, illegal trade, and counterintelligence threats. Planning and implementation of intelligence collection, counterintelligence, and covert action operations. Integrating specialized training, advanced analytic skills, and in-depth knowledge and experience in operational tradecraft.

FORECAST: Continues training to expectation of work in unified team. Builds foundation of knowledge of clandestine operational tradecraft via classroom training, practical exercises, and applied life experience. Transitions into advanced training in preparation for service in area of respective specialty.

ASSETS: Personal integrity. Strong interpersonal and communication skills. Action and results oriented. Effective performance both independently and as part of a team. Flexible, adaptable, inquisitive and investigative. Determined, focused, and mission driven. Drawn to complex tasks and finding innovative solutions to overcome obstacles. Articulate verbally and in written communication. Ability to shift focus quickly, work on multiple tasks concurrently, and excel in high-pressure/high-impact situations.

AREA FOR IMPROVEMENT: Networks, cyber threats, complex analysis of latest technologies.

SUGGESTION: Maintain relationship with teammates Callie Hansen, Zeke Cancio, and Jackson Fischer.

TOP SECRET CASE FILE

NAME: Zeke Cancio
AGE: 19
HEIGHT: 5 foot 11 inches
WEIGHT: 170 pounds
HAIR: Black
EYES: Green
ETHNICITY: Italian American
LANGUAGES: English, Italian

SKILLS: Providing unique capabilities in support of conventional and unconventional operations. Operating and maintaining infrastructure necessary to facilitate and support missions conducted under unique authorities.

FORECAST: Continues training to expectation of work in unified team. Builds foundation of knowledge of clandestine operational tradecraft via classroom training, practical exercises, and applied life experience. Transitions into advanced training in preparation for service in area of respective specialty. Additionally, is required to successfully complete specialized training for service in hazardous and austere environments overseas.

ASSETS: Personal integrity. Strong interpersonal and communication skills. Action and results oriented. Ability to work effectively as part of a team or independently. Accepts significant, demanding responsibilities and accountability for results. Ability to make decisions to meet existing conditions and mission requirements rather than relying on preset assumptions and goal. Tactical experience. Leadership qualities.

AREA FOR IMPROVEMENT: Fluency in Italian. Social media, technology development, and math. Development of psychological understanding. Counterintelligence.

SUGGESTION: Maintain relationship with teammates Callie Hansen, Sophie Washington, and Jackson Fischer.

TOP SECRET CASE FILE

NAME: Callie Hansen
AGE: 17
HEIGHT: 5 foot 3 inches
WEIGHT: 125 pounds
HAIR: Blonde
EYES: Blue
ETHNICITY: Norwegian American
LANGUAGES: English

SKILLS: Cyber exploitation by using holistic understanding of digital capabilities to evaluate and analyze digital and all source intelligence information. Identifying key adversaries and assessing how they operate and interact. Employing strong critical thinking skills and a variety of digital analytic tools and methods to extract valuable information from data.

FORECAST: Identifies, triages, and reviews items of intelligence and operational interest from technical collections. Leverages advanced methods to analyze data. Creates and refines capabilities to exploit large statistics quickly and accurately. Identifies and prioritizes intelligence gaps, determines the appropriate collection actions needed, and drives the collection process.

ASSETS: Lead position in defining the future of digital expertise. Focus on developing cutting-edge skills, infrastructure, and modernizing the way the CIA does business. Ability to integrate innovative methods and tools to enhance the cyber and digital capabilities on a global scale and ultimately help safeguard the nation.

AREA OF IMPROVEMENT: Continued studies in computer science. Foreign language skill desired. Ability to code to spec and meet analytical time requirements.

SUGGESTION: Maintain relationship with teammates Sophie Washington, Zeke Cancio, and Jackson Fischer.

TOP SECRET CASE FILE

NAME: Jackson Fischer
AGE: 18
HEIGHT: 6 foot 2 inches
WEIGHT: 175 pounds
HAIR: Light brown
EYES: Hazel
ETHNICITY: German American
LANGUAGES: English, ASL

SKILLS: All-source digital forensics. Identify, monitor, assess, and counter the threat posed by cyber actors against U.S. information systems, critical infrastructure, and cyber-related interests. Assessing and providing tactical analysis and advice for operations.

FORECAST: Applies scientific and technical knowledge to solve complex intelligence problems. Produces short-term and long-term briefings to policymakers and the cyber defense community. Maintains and broadens professional ties through academic study, collaboration with peers, and attendance of professional meetings.

ASSETS: Computer science expertise with a specialty in digital forensics. Analytic tradecraft and management, to include critical thinking and problem-solving skills. Initiative to deepen expertise independently. Transformation of incomplete and contradictory information into unique insights that inform decisions. Performance of timely, accurate, and objective intelligence analysis on security and other related issues.

AREA OF IMPROVEMENT: Continued studies in cyber security and information assurance. Ability to work under tight deadlines. Improvement in creative thinking and international affairs.

SUGGESTION: Maintain relationship with teammates Callie Hansen, Zeke Cancio, and Sophie Washington.

READING T-MINUS AT YOUR BOOK GROUP?

Well, the first thing you'll need is Coke or Mountain Dew, and an assortment of junk food as Sophie prefers that to the healthy alternatives. (Then again, you'd better have green tea and hummus on hand in case Jackson strolls through the door.) A great soundtrack helps, too, playing softly in the background. Here are some suggestions:

The Dirtmitts — "Fix and Destroy"
Gustavo Santaolalla — "Iguazu"
Christian Sands — "Tricky"

NEXT YOU'LL NEED DISCUSSION QUESTIONS:

1. What did you like most about T-MINUS? What did you like the least?

2. What do you think would have happened if POTUS came clean about the drone misfire? Do you think she still would have been elected?

3. Which character in this book did you like best? Least?

4. If you were making a movie of this book, who would you cast as the main characters?

5. Share a favorite scene from the book. Why did this scene stand out?

6. What lengths would you go to in order to save your family and friends?

7. Which character in the book would you most like to meet?

8. What do you think of the book's cover? How well does it convey what the book is about?

9. How original and unique was this book?

10. If you could hear this same story from another person's point of view, who would you choose—Zeke, Callie, or Jackson?

11. Did this book seem realistic?

12. How well do you think Shannon Greenland built the world in the book?

13. Did the characters seem believable to you? Did they remind you of anyone?

14. Did the book's pace seem too fast/too slow/just right?

15. Were you surprised to discover who the ultimate mastermind was?

Q&A WITH THE AUTHOR

1. WHAT INSPIRED THIS STORY?

   I have a good friend who works for the CIA in a cover status. This friend has shared a few things with me over the years (non-confidential, of course). It's truly fascinating to me what goes on behind the scenes to ensure our nation is safe. I'm also a big fan of fast-paced thrillers and wanted to challenge myself with a book that takes place within a single day.

2. IS THERE A REAL TRAINING SCHOOL FOR TEENS THAT DOES THIS? (WE THINK THERE SHOULD BE!)

   I think there should be, too! The CIA does offer an internship program as a gateway to employment with the federal government or as a contract employee, but no, they do not offer a training school for teens.

3. DID YOU DO A LOT OF RESEARCH FOR THIS BOOK ON THE INS AND OUTS OF WHAT HAPPENS IN D.C.?

   Yes, I used to live in the D.C. area, and so I'm very familiar with the geography. Some of the logistics in this book are accurate, some are fictitious. As I was writing this novel, I found that I had to tap into artistic freedom to allow the story to take its own path.

4. DID YOU HAVE ANY ADVISORS AND WHAT DID THEY ADD TO YOUR STORY?

My friend who works for the CIA advised me on much of the story. For example I originally used the word "undercover" and they suggested "covert" would be more authentic, just like "motion detectors" would be "motion sensors" and "informant" would be "asset." They were also able to broaden my understanding of what kind of technology the intelligence agencies would use in certain situations and what security measures they would take when a national crisis occurs.

5. WE LOVE THESE CHARACTERS. ARE THEY LOOSELY BASED ON ANYONE YOU KNOW? (YOU DON'T HAVE TO GET SPECIFIC; WE'RE JUST CURIOUS!)

For years now I have kept a journal of character traits. Every time I meet someone who does or says something unique, I jot it down. Then when I'm forming a character, I'll open up that journal and pick traits. That is what I did as I created the various roles in T-MINUS.

6. IT'S PROBABLY LIKE PICKING A FAVORITE CHILD, BUT DO YOU HAVE A FAVORITE CHARACTER, BESIDES THE HEROINE, IN THIS?

I adore both Jackson and Callie. I relate most to Callie, as I am quite the adventurer, like her. I'll climb a mountain or raft a river. I'll zip-line a jungle or sail an ocean. I'll explore a cave or rappel down a ravine. The only thing I will not do is bungee. The thought of plummeting toward earth only to be rubber-banded back up totally freaks me out.

7. WHAT'S YOUR FAVORITE THING ABOUT WRITING?

I was a reluctant reader as a child and a teen. I loved math, and still do! I'm not entirely sure what happened, but one day I picked up a pencil and started scribbling ideas. Those ideas turned into paragraphs then turned into chapters and eventually became an entire novel. I couldn't believe it, and what's more—I loved it! I felt so creative. I loved getting lost in another world. I loved challenging the characters and deciding what would happen to them next. That was years ago now, and that feeling of creativity and disappearing into another world is still what drives me today.

8. WHAT BOOK OR AUTHOR INSPIRED YOU TO WANT TO START WRITING?

As I mentioned, I was a reluctant reader—even into my twenties. I had a good friend who gave me a stack of historical romance novels. I appreciated the gesture, but really, reading wasn't my thing. Then one day out of sheer boredom I picked up one of those novels. I read a page, and then another, then another. Before I knew it, I had read the entire novel! I began devouring genres. I started on one end of our small public library and moved my way across, discovering that suspense and thrillers held my avid interest. Not long after that, I picked up a pencil and started jotting ideas for my first novel.

9. WHAT DOES YOUR WRITING DAY LOOK LIKE?

I love the mornings. I am an early riser and wake up naturally around five. I work at a stand-up desk as I hate to sit. Like many writers, I do love my morning coffee. But after that, I drink a ton of lemon water as I write. It's my thinking process—I'll sip water and think. Come noon, I'm fried and need a much-earned break. It's at that point I work out and switch to other things—social media, answering emails, errands, etcetera. I also work for an online school teaching Creative Writing and various high school math classes like Geometry and Algebra. Most people think it's odd I have a degree in math and yet I'm a writer, but it makes sense to me. I think of novels as complex equations that need solving.

10. WILL YOU BE WRITING MORE ADVENTURES FOR YOUR HEROINE, OR WILL WE SEE SOME OF THE OTHER FOLKS IN HER GANG WITH THEIR STORIES?

Oh, I would love to write another story with Sophie, Zeke, Jackson, and Callie. I would call it OFF THE GRID. They would be on a grand adventure when (of course) something monumental happens that only they can solve. Yes, just typing these words gets me excited about the possibilities!

ACKNOWLEDGMENTS

Many thanks to my top-secret friend who lives in the D.C. area and was able to guide me with the logistics of this book. I'd mention the person by name, but then I'd have to kill you :)

As always to my hard-working and lovely agents, Jenny Bent and Gemma Cooper. We've worked together for years, and I'm still star struck that you signed me!

Lastly (but certainly not least) to the fabulous Liz Pelletier, whip-smart Candace Havens, and the rest of my lovely team at Entangled. Thank you for championing my books!

TURN THE PAGE TO DISCOVER THE LATEST
SERIES THAT READERS ARE CALLING "AN
INCREDIBLY TENSE, TIGHT WHODUNIT"

*Available wherever books
and ebooks are sold!*

CHASING TRUTH

by *NYT* bestselling author Julie Cross

When former con artist Eleanor Ames's homecoming date commits suicide, she's positive there's something more going on. The more questions she asks, though, the more she crosses paths with Miles Beckett. He's sexy, mysterious, arrogant...and he's asking all the same questions.

Eleanor might not trust him - she doesn't even like him - but they can't keep their hands off of each other. Fighting the infuriating attraction is almost as hard as ignoring the fact that Miles isn't telling her the truth...and that there's a good chance he could be the killer.

1

It's not like I haven't seen a topless girl before. I mean, I am one. Not topless. Not now, anyway. But I *am* a girl.

Seeing a topless girl standing on the neighbor's balcony at six a.m., yelling and tossing clothes from the second floor, is definitely not the norm around here.

From my position on my own apartment balcony, I watch the handful of gray and navy clothing land in the pool, right in front of Mrs. Olsen, mid–side stroke. The old lady stops, looks up, sees the topless blonde. A horrified expression takes over her face. She's out of the pool as fast as a seventy-something-year-old woman can be.

"Got anything else you want me to put on?" topless blonde snaps at whoever is pissing her off next door. New neighbors moved in yesterday while I was having a root canal and sleeping it off with pain meds most of the day. "That's right. Stay in there. Like I care. Have a nice life!"

The girl steps back into the apartment and, seconds later, I hear the front door slam and she's thundering down the steps, a blue sundress now hastily thrown on. I stay hidden until she's peeling out of the parking lot, then I tiptoe through the apartment—careful not to wake my sister and her boyfriend who only get to sleep past six on Saturdays—and head down to the pool. If the topless girl hadn't taken off so quickly, I would have thanked her. I'd been waiting twenty minutes for Mrs. Olsen to get out of the pool. Now it's all mine.

I lean over the side, fishing out the clothes floating

near the five-foot end. One gray T-shirt—men's medium. One navy T-shirt—men's medium. Two pairs of navy shorts.

"Uh…sorry about that."

The soggy shorts fall from my fingers and I look up, squinting into the sun at the tall, shadowed figure in front of me. I stare at the tan bare feet then allow my gaze to shift north. His washboard abs distract me for a second, but I reach for the wet shorts again and drop them onto his toes with a plunk before standing up. "Got something against colors?"

Now that I'm standing, I finally get a good look at my new neighbor. I'd expected someone older, but Mr. I-only-wear-gym-shorts-because-I-have-abs-of-steel is definitely more guy than man. Especially with the messy, dark-haired bedhead thing he's got going on.

He frowns at me. "Colors?"

"Yes," I say. "Like red, green, orange. Pink, if you're into that."

"Ah." He shrugs. "Never really thought about it."

The guy swoops down to scoop up the dripping clothes at his feet, and then he flashes me a grin that shows off two perfect dimples. I fold my arms across my chest—I never trust anyone with dimples—and wait for him to offer some kind of explanation. When he doesn't, I prompt him. "Think this will be a regular thing? Should I bring my fishing net tomorrow morning? Or I could ask management to install a pole. If your friend is gonna be here again, in *costume*, she might as well provide some entertainment."

The guy shakes his head and then, to my utter surprise—believe me when I say that I am not easily surprised—he blushes, his gaze bouncing to the parking lot from where Topless Blonde bolted, then back to me. "I'm not— I mean she's not—" He sighs. Defeated.

"What's wrong?" I press. "Not into topless girls?"

"Is it a crime if I'm not?" he says. "Besides, I don't even know her."

"I hear that happens sometimes." I pretend to look deep in thought. "Is it possible that a chemical substance could have been in your bloodstream when you met her? That might explain the memory loss."

Normally I'd roll my eyes and call the guy an asshole inside my head, but there's something almost boyish and innocent about my new neighbor—it wasn't when he first planted his feet beside me, or when he swooped down to pick up his wet clothes, or in his response to my question about his aversion to colorful fashion choices. But when I mentioned Topless Girl—that has me pausing. Curious. It'd been a little bit interesting when the girl was scaring off Mrs. Olsen, but then it was boring. Drunken one-night stand misinterpreted as more.

Now I'm dying to know what their relationships is/ was. But as my wise and foolish—yes, you can be both— father taught me long ago, never show your cards. Not in your hand, not on your face. Not even in the way you breathe.

So instead of getting my answer from Hot Neighbor Boy, I toss my cover-up onto a nearby chair and dive into the pool. When I surface, I catch the tiniest glimpse of him still standing there, holding his dripping-wet clothes, his mouth half open. I force myself into a choppy freestyle, kicking and pulling way too hard for this early in the morning. A minute later, my new neighbor is trudging back up the steps.

I stop to rest at the shallow end, laughing to myself. But then I look up at the empty staircase, the completely desolate apartment complex, and I can't help wondering if maybe this is why I haven't made a lot of friends at my new school.

Except Simon.

My only friend at Holden Prep. Maybe my only real friend in my entire life.

"Hey, kiddo."

I pull my head out of my ass and look up at the tall, dark-skinned person standing on the pool deck. "Hey, Ace."

Aidan, my sister's boyfriend, ignores my use of his code name and tosses his towel onto an empty chair, then dives into the deep end. I watch with a hint of envy as he manages to swim the entire length of the pool without a breath and magically appears beside me on the steps. Over the last six or eight months, I've gotten worse and worse at my poker face with Aidan. To prove this, he gives me a look, obviously reading my thoughts, and says, "Ellie, a few months ago, you couldn't even swim."

A few months ago, I fell into this pool and nearly drowned. I shake off the memory and narrow my eyes at him. "I know that."

He flashes me a grin, which is nothing like the fake, dimple-filled grin of New Neighbor Guy. "Have patience, young Grasshopper. We have much to learn." He slaps the water, causing a tidal wave to hit me right in the face. "But you won't get anywhere sitting your lazy ass on those steps. Four laps is not a workout. Don't tell me you've turned all L.A. and taken up sunbathing."

"Virginia is not L.A., last I checked. Plus, I had a freakin' root canal yesterday! And you're taking this spy thing to a whole new level, Ace."

"Secret Service aren't spies," he corrects, though I know this already. "And yes, I saw your entire workout." He hits more water in my direction, probably trying to get me fired up. "Saw you scaring off our new neighbor, too. Well done. One less boy for me to chase away, Eleanor."

My jaw clenches at the use of my full name. It's payback for my calling him by his Secret Service earpiece name. "Think I should have gone easier on him?"

"Nah." Aidan glances at the balcony beside ours. "Miles can handle it."

"Miles?" I lift an eyebrow. "You've met him already? Does he have a keeper?"

Aidan gives his best "I'm a grown-up and thus privy to more information than you" look. "Don't you think I'd check out anyone new moving in?"

By "check out," he means background check. Criminal record. The irony of this statement is too much to not point out. Though if my sister, Harper, were here, I'd keep it to myself. Aidan is surprisingly tolerant of these mentions. "Clearly you possess the ability to bend the rules if you allow yourself to be associated with Harper and me."

"That's another lesson you haven't learned," Aidan says. "You and I aren't that different, kid. We've both made a living out of noticing things, and we're both experts at keeping secrets."

"Is that why they call it the Secret Service?" I joke, not sure what to do with this idea of Aidan being anything like Harper and me. He's the epitome of good. My family is the opposite of good. "I've always wondered where the name came from."

He rolls his eyes. "We both know you could have charmed Miles Beckett in your sleep. But you didn't. You resisted that instinct."

He says it like it's so easy, pushing away everything I've been taught my whole life and adopting this new mantra. I mean, I'm glad that I don't have to con people anymore. I'm here because, like my older sister, I don't want that life. But sometimes…every once in a while… like when I'm at Best Buy and the guy "diagnosing" the problem with my laptop has clearly labeled me as a clueless girl he can rip off, I'm so tempted to show him otherwise, to turn on that part of me I've left behind along with my old last name.

Aidan is more military than he's willing to admit, and our chat ends right then because he says I need to get my lazy ass moving. It's September already, and soon the pool will close. So I swim and swim and swim. Until my father's words are nothing but a phantom memory. Like when he told me swim lessons were for kids with social security numbers. For kids who stayed in the same place longer than six months.

I lose count of how many laps I swim—probably more than I've ever done in one session—but when I finally stop, it isn't just Aidan in the pool with me. Miles Beckett has apparently unpacked enough to find his swim trunks and is coming at me with perfect butterfly strokes. He stops at the wall beside me, barely out of breath, and looks at me like I hadn't made him blush less than an hour ago. "Your freestyle needs work."

I snort back a laugh. "Your one-night stand needs work." I miss his reaction because I hear Aidan laugh. I forgot he was out here.

"Come on, Miss Sunshine." Aidan nods toward our apartment. "Your sister's making waffles."

"And you let her?" I push myself out of the pool. "I can't believe they hire you to save lives."

"You're welcome to join us," Aidan says to Miles.

"Don't. Trust me." I wrap my towel around my waist and pat myself on the back. *Daily civic duty? Check.* I give Aidan a nod. "And that's how you save lives."

I'm halfway up the stairs when I hear, "Nice meeting you, Eleanor Ames."

What the— I stop. Turn slowly and look down at my new neighbor. "I don't remember introducing myself."

The grin he gives me is one I'm all too familiar with: guy trying to charm me (aka—guy trying to get in my pants). "Turns out you're infamous around here."

"Is that right?" I laugh to myself. He's being cute. He has no clue how infamous I am. Or my family, at least. "I'm sure everything you heard is completely true."

Aidan catches up to me and tries to hide his amusement. "This should be a blast."

"Whatever. It's not like I see our neighbors all that much, especially since school started up again last week." I shrug. Aidan looks like he wants to say something else but decides against it. "What?"

"He's going to Holden." Aidan turns more serious, his

hand now on the doorknob to our apartment. "Miles is a good kid."

"Good? You sure about that?" Clearly he missed Topless Girl. "I think you're losing your touch."

He ignores my jab and says, "Might be nice to have another friend at school."

"Right." I nod. "Because the one friend I had went and offed himself. Good luck, Miles."

Aidan pauses on the stairs and turns to face me. "Ellie, Simon's death had nothing to do with you."

I roll my eyes, but inside I'm shaking. "I know that. God, turn off the therapist voice, will you?" And yeah, I do know all this. It's been three months since Simon—a senator's son and my only friend within the ritzy halls of Holden Prep—well, since he…you know, *went to a better place*. The sting of saying his name out loud is slowly wearing off. But I still have questions. And it's taking every ounce of self-control I have to not seek out those answers.

"Plus, you were the new kid last spring," Aidan reminds me. "You should know better than anyone how hard that can be."

Luckily I don't have to spend too much time feeling sorry for Miles Beckett, new kid at school, because when Aidan opens the door, the smoke alarm is blaring and the entire kitchen is in a fog.

IF YOU ENJOYED THIS EXCERPT, GRAB

CHASING TRUTH

WHEREVER BOOKS ARE SOLD

A chilling, intricate mystery perfect for fans of We Were Liars.

we told six lies

by Victoria Scott

Remember how many lies we told, Molly? It's enough to make my head spin. You were wild when I met you, and I was mad for you. But then something happened. And now you're gone.

But don't worry. I'll find you. I just need to sift through the story of us to get to where you might be. I've got places to look, and a list of names.

The police have a list of names, too. See now? There's another lie. There is only one person they're really looking at, Molly.

And that's yours truly.

From New York Times *bestselling author Monica Murphy comes a chilling, intricate mystery perfect for fans of the Pretty Little Liars series.*

PRETTY DEAD GIRLs

by *NYT* bestselling author Monica Murphy

Beautiful. Perfect. Dead.

In the peaceful seaside town of Cape Bonita, wicked secrets and lies are hidden just beneath the surface. But all it takes is one tragedy for them to be exposed.

The most popular girls in school are turning up dead, and Penelope Malone is terrified she's next. All the victims so far have been linked to Penelope—and to a boy from her physics class. The one she's never really noticed before, with the rumored dark past and a brooding stare that cuts right through her.

There's something he isn't telling her. But there's something she's not telling him, either.

Everyone has secrets, and theirs might get them killed.

The Bourne Identity *meets* Boy Nobody
in this YA assassin thriller.

PROJECT PANDORA

by Aden Polydoros

Tyler Bennett trusts no one. Just another foster kid bounced from home to home, he's learned that lesson the hard way. Cue world's tiniest violin. But when strange things start happening— waking up with bloody knuckles and no memory of the night before or the burner phone he can't let out of his sight—Tyler starts to wonder if he can even trust himself.

Even stranger, the girl he's falling for has a burner phone just like his. Finding out what's really happening only leads to more questions…questions that could get them both killed. It's not like someone's kidnapping teens lost in the system and brainwashing them to be assassins or anything, right? And what happens to rogue assets who defy control?

In a race against the clock, they'll have to uncover the truth behind Project Pandora and take it down—before they're reactivated. Good thing the program spent millions training them to kick ass…

Let's be friends!

🐦 @EntangledTeen

📷 @EntangledTeen

📘 @EntangledTeen

📰 bit.ly/TeenNewsletter